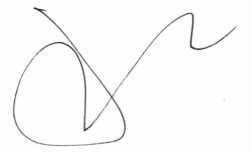

Mother & Child

{ A NOVEL }

CAROLE MASO

COUNTERPOINT
BERKELEY

Library of Congress Cataloging-in-Publication Data is available.

ISBN: 978-1-58243-818-4

Cover design by Natalya Balnova
Interior design by meganjonesdesign.com

Printed in the United States of America

COUNTERPOINT
1919 Fifth Street
Berkeley, CA 94710
www.counterpointpress.com

Distributed by Publishers Group West

10 9 8 7 6 5 4 3 2 1

As we fall through the
Terrible Beauty of Time

Light floods the Children's Garden—
for Nana and Rose

And Music moves through the Heart's Dark Atrium—
for Papa

And for Tata, at the Vortex

Hansel, in the Dark Wood

And in the Soulstorm, Paul.

In memory of the disappearing men,
who were my friends:

Liam Rector
Jason Shinder
David Foster Wallace
Romulus Linney
Peter Jennings
Daniel Simko
David Markson

wind

T HE GREAT WIND came and the maple tree that had stood near the house for two hundred years split in half, and from its center poured a torrent of bats. Inside, the child was stepping from her bath and the mother swaddled her in a towel. Night was all around them. The child thought she could feel the wind moving through her and the places where her wings were beginning to come through. Soon it would be the time of the transformation, the mother said. The child said she was almost ready, but she was not ready yet.

Before bed the mother told the child a story. When your body begins to transform, you will bleed in a new way each month for several days. The child pictured herself as a fountain: a mermaid or a dolphin or a fish spouting blood and magnificence. She closed her eyes. In the Children's Garden, the first rose was about to open. The child's tooth was loose. She tinkered with it and listened to the mother and smelled her hard like an animal and loved her with all her heart. She felt happy to be alive in the blood conversation and in the night and the world that grew deeper and stranger and somehow brighter with her mother's words. She held her arms open to the night, but her eyes closed; she could not hold on to waking life any longer.

The mother looked at the sleeping child before her and indulged herself for a moment in the illusion of stasis. For a full minute nothing changed.

That evening, in the hours still left to her, after the child was asleep, the mother felt at the mercy of all things: the wind, the tree, the story, the child's beautiful and curious face, the rate at which the rose opened. Out the window, pure light flooded from the tree. She tried to look away, and though it filled her with a certain dread, she could not. Whether she was turned toward the tree or away from it, it did not matter now. The world possessed the mother and not the other way around: she did not possess the world. She closed her eyes but something in the empty space above her head was emphatic and hovered and would not let her rest.

Like so many others, she had fled the burning city and returned to this dark wood, but she wondered now if by choosing to come back here to the place of her childhood, she was putting them at risk in some way. No one else would think that: the Valley was a paradise, and in summer it attracted many vacationers and people from the city. The Valley was verdant and the silver river glistened and on the river there were bright boats. With this the mother must have drifted off, for when she opened her eyes, the child was standing over her, holding something glittery in her open hand.

Look, she whispered. The mother sat up. What have you got there? The child opened her hand. Oh, she said, a tooth! It was smooth and shiny and they both admired it. Open your mouth the mother said, and she saw the gap where the tooth had been. Then she turned to the darkened window and looking out she sighed, soon you will be all grown.

She remembered when the child was just a baby and was placed in the silver basin and raised up into the air, her arms and legs open like a star. Tell me that story again of the silver basin and the water and the star, the child said, and the child placed her stuffed lamb and her last baby tooth on the ledge. All blew in the wind, and the mother's story came in and out of audibility, but the star was constant, and the child listened. The night world pressed up against them. There was no way of partitioning it. The mother knew there was no safe place inside, though she did not like to think of it. You never knew what might be happening next: the cat, Bunny Boy, rushing by with a chipmunk in his jowls or a snake or worse. Even her garden, without her, in only a short time would go completely back to wilderness—to loosestrife and milkweed and nettles. A tangle of wild grasses and reeds and dark brambles would take over, and in the deepening furrows, rodents, winged and not, would come in great drifts, and moths and beetles in abundance.

Yes, she said, pulling herself back from the welter, when you were a baby and had been placed in the silver basin and then raised up into the air by the feeble priest, you had opened (it was December) like a Christmas star and sin was washed away.

After the story was finished, the child retrieved her lamb from the sill and placed the tooth under her pillow, and the world, unfastened, blew by. There was much swirling and world being blown in backwards through the chimney to them, but at that moment all that mattered was the child, the tooth, and the lamb. In the distance they heard the sound of sirens. It was one of those nights, rare even in the life of a person who has lived a long time, when clarity comes. The mother looked out the window, as if something long concealed could now be seen in stark relief.

Even though it was night, bright light poured from the center of the felled tree. She had experienced such a fall into brightness only once. So much illuminated in an instant, so little time. Though the moment had not yet arrived, it was fast upon them. The child closed her eyes, and soon enough, she was asleep once more. And though the lamb and the tooth had been removed from the sill, their traces remained, insinuating their way into the mother's consciousness.

The mother would like to keep them in this moment, to stop the process now, to hold them like this a while longer, but no one was interested in what the mother wanted. Was there nothing but indifference, she wondered? She remembered last Sunday's Mass. At the service, they announced that the God was not there, and His presence in the sacred species had been relegated to a static state, and the congregants reduced to a passive presence. They would have to sit with the absence. No priest available to animate the dormant God. The child had not understood.

Now all was darkness. Sometime in the night, the power had gone out. The wind had not let up. In the early morning when she opened her eyes, the empty space above her head had been filled. The night before, a flame had descended on her head in a dream. She was sure of it, and she was afraid. There was not a soul who could help her now. She heard babbling and chatter, and the child in turn began chattering in her sleep.

Something had entered the house.

LEAVES BLEW BY and branches and brambles covered the floor. The child did not know how the tree had gotten inside. She could barely move around the wreckage. As exciting as it was, she knew that a tree did not belong in the house. Suddenly she remembered the tooth and she found her way to her pillow. The tooth was gone and in its

place was a sparkling Sacajawea dollar. She held the radiant head of
the Indian girl and walked through an eternity of green in search of
her mother. As she made her way to the kitchen with the coin and the
lamb, her feet made a whispering and crisping sound that grew louder
and louder until the sounds, at first so natural, became deafening: the
boughs scratching and keening, and pinecones and nuts bouncing off
the windows. In the violence, the child had to shout to be heard.

She decided to sing, and all other sound was absorbed by the song:
Now I Walk in Beauty—
More than a voice it seemed an act of radical purification.
Beauty is Before Me—
Beauty is Behind Me—
Above and Below Me . . .
There, at the end of the hall, in the predawn, the mother stood. She
was making a fire.

If in the frenzy of embers the child turned her head, the flames
appeared to consume the mother entirely. She stared at the mother
encased in light. The mother smiled now when she saw the child, wiping cinders from her brow.

She remembered the light that day was mesmerizing and though
it was necessary to look away in order to survive, her entire being was
drawn back to that place and there was nothing she could do—thousands of bright souls rushed from the wounded site.

An enormous heat was being generated by the fire and the child
knew not to step too close to the flames. It was not yet time for her
to become a child of glass, or a child of wax; she had barely begun
her life.

The child struggled to speak above the wind and the branches
breaking on their heads. Mother, I have a question, the child implored.

The mother looked up. Yes, she called from across the abyss. She handed the child a small flame in a cup.

How old were you, the child asked, when you transformed?

OVERNIGHT THE HOUSE had changed shape. It was now a marvel of transparency. The walls seemed to disappear, and all around them the green world pulsed. Light spilled onto their nightgowns and sap poured down on them. The child knelt and put her head to it. The mother lay next to her, and together they marveled at the dappled light, and the boughs of the tree, and the way it cradled them.

In the night the Great Wind had pollinated the tree's small, inconspicuous flowers, and they knew that soon the flowers would turn into small fruit that would in turn change into seeds with wings. Wings abounded now, in the tree, in the birds, in the small of the girl's back. The world is resonant with patterns and repetition. In the mother's dream, the descending flame reminded her of another flame, and that flame, another, and if she followed the flames back far enough, she might get back to the first flame, she thought, the one that haunted her—but always she lost her way, or got sleepy or distracted and was left in the end only with an inkling, an intimation, and she walked through the world bearing something inside she could not entirely remember or entirely forget, and she was always pulled in two directions.

She sunk for a moment into the lull of moss and loam—the house had become a lair, and it brought her rest. In a way, the mother loved this new house of leaves. She wanted to stay as inconspicuous as possible, as near to invisible as possible, so she might not be sought out, so that she and the child might be forgotten. She wished to be assumed, taken into its shade and be made a shadow for a while. She wished for an aloof god, a distracted one, not a god that sent wind and animated the night. A serene and patient one—one that did not summon or issue edicts. She wanted only peace. A crib or a husk.

As leaf subsides to leaf . . . She remembered the old poem, *and Eden sinks to grief* . . . Yes, that was it. There was a part of her that wanted to crawl into the hollow of the tree, into its wound, and sleep. She might succumb here in this leafy sepulcher. She might find herself lost in leafstorm or swarm.

The mother clung to the darkly lit hallway where the child once had sung.

The soul seeks solace. The child, who did not care about the soul, pulled at the mother's gown. The mother was large and beautiful even with the tree in the room. That is what struck the child.

WHAT IF THEY fell deep into a tree trance and forgot to leave? How long had they been there anyway? The child grew frightened—she longed to see the world again, and the mother too longed for the spaciousness of day: the sun as it began, the field where corn would one day grow, the animals blooming beautiful and slow, and of course, the bells. They loved the way the bells held the day and marked time and kept things in place, but when the mother and child at last left the house, it was still dark and no bells could be heard.

Now they walk. The wind had awakened a place that had remained remote and nearly dormant in the mother and suddenly awakened to it, she felt dizzy. She looked at the recumbent figures in the distance, the men asleep in the slopes, the city far off in flames. The child ran ahead—how lovely is the laughing and singing child! The wind, which had diminished, picked up a little, and in the distance the mountains seemed to smoke.

She thought of the tree of light, without top or bottom, without beginning or end, endlessly falling in them. In a few days when the tree men come and hoist the great pillar away from the house, something will exit their bodies and a dark shape—a permanence—will take its place.

INFINITE GRACE WAS available to them, that is what the mother wanted the child to know. On a milkweed pod in the meadow, a crowned chrysalis hung serenely in wait.

The morning creatures were at last awakening in the Valley. Even though the mother had lived in nearness to the animals her whole childhood, every time she was surprised and filled with awe at their appearance. They were as astonishing to her now as when she was a small girl. Just the other day she had woken to a deer wading knee-deep in the pond through the water lilies, its haunches blazing red.

She could see still the white of its tail, its leap away inducing a hazy afterimage. Next to it, a slate blue heron.

The gigantic heads of the horses leaned over the fence. In the pasture, a cadence of sheep. A large, long-legged cat without a tail in shadow, hung back. Somewhere, the wolves traveling in silver packs . . .

IT HAD COME with the Great Wind, under the cover of night, while the Valley had been anesthetized, and now that morning had arrived, and the mist was beginning to lift, and the wind had at last departed, it could be seen quite clearly in the distance. *Look!* White sails could be discerned in the distance and a faint music—an accordion, cowbells, a most charming sound, and so inviting, as if conjured not played, could be heard wafting across the meadow.

There it stood, shimmering, next to the river. The mother and child walked toward it and stared, intent on memorizing it, for who knew how long this vision would hold? After all it was the Time of Disappearance, and all across the Valley the men had begun to vanish. As much as it was possible, the mother had grown accustomed to the subtractions and the diminishments, but with the appearance of this extraordinary shape before them—so unexpected, so compelling in the ever-emptying landscape—they were filled with longing.

People had begun to gather. Where had it come from? What was its country of origin? Some conjectured, Belgium. The mother did not know. Estonia.

Germany.

The Caspian Sea.

Arabia.

The Black Forest.

Perhaps Armenia . . .

Or Finland!

Now the child spoke. It says something! As they watched, red letters were hoisted one by one into the air on poles with streamers. It said—but it was hard to decipher. One of the elders took out her binoculars: S-P-I-E-G-E-

Spiegel, it says Spiegel! I told you it was from Germany, one of the Palatines of the Valley said. Spiegel is mirror in German. Spiegel— P-A-L . . . What is a Spiegelpal?

Spiegelpalais, it says Spiegelpalais. It's some sort of tent, someone said finally, and the Spiegelpalais made the meadow new and strange to them.

With spiegels, someone sighed, and at night, white lights.

And a tightrope!

Perhaps it's a kind of circus from Germany.

The sun made its slow passage across the sky. The onlookers increased. It was the Age of Wonders. No one moved.

2

T HAT NIGHT WHEN they were back at home at last, it appeared
to them like an apparition, separating the dark, parting it long
enough to make itself visible and say, I am here. It had come in with
the tree, but in the day it had folded itself up and waited.

Chittering came from the winged one's mouth, and the child cow-
ered and the mother ran to get the broom and the umbrella. It was an
Annunciation clearly, but of what the mother had no idea.

Behold, the creature said, swooping down on them, and then all
was gibberish. Its wingspan in the small room, enormous.

What do you want of us? the mother asked. Her ears grew long
and pointed, best for sound detection, and her eyes grew shining and
focused as she tried to detect what shapes its mouth took. In an instant
her teeth grew sharp in case she needed to chew the child away from it.

Now it was definitive: she was sutured to the wild world and the
wild world to her.

What do you want, the mother asked, and it screeched as if to say,
I was there with you last night in the wind and the dark. I was with you
there. The mother tried to decipher the chitter but could not. I was here
and I did sup a bit from one of you.

How vulnerable are the dwellings we humans make for ourselves
to inhabit, the mother thought later. When the child dwelled in the

mother, the mother had passed oxygen and nutrients to the child through the placenta. She thought of the permeable world and all that was porous and of the insistence of the fetus that had knitted itself within her womb.

It's a bat, the child said. *A bat!*

The mother trembled, fearful of the ferocity of the world and all the things she was at the mercy of—and for the child, who had been fearfully made—and she opened all the windows so that the creature might find its way back to the night.

THE MOTHER REMEMBERED when the time of the Pentecost was fulfilled, they were in one place together, and suddenly there came from the sky a noise like a strong driving wind, and it filled the entire house in which they were.

In the Book of Wisdom it is asked, who can know the bat's counsel or conceive what the bat intends? For the deliberations of mortals are timid, and unsure are their plans. The corruptible body burdens the soul, and the earthen shelter weighs down the mind that has many concerns. And scarcely do we guess the things on earth, and what is within our grasp, we find with great difficulty.

THE MOTHER KNEW the vampire bat extracted blood from large, slumbering, terrestrial mammals. There were bats that aimed for the warm breastplates of birds. She knew there were those who stalked blood bearers on land.

A white-winged vampire bat moves so softly and lovingly, toward the hen, that the hen allows it into its fold. The cozy bat administers, along with its bite, a natural blood clot buster to ensure a steady flow.

Some bats consume half their body weight in blood each night. Woe, the mother thought, to the Blue-Footed Booby, a bat's delicacy.

Sometimes the child felt that the mother knew too many things. Still, the mother and child, despite the night and the bat and the Blue-Footed Booby, grew sleepy and before too long were asleep.

WITH LANTERNS THEY approached the Spiegelpalais. A red velvet curtain rose before them on the forest path, and the audience began to applaud. There was a cacophony of wings—yes, some sort of rubied rabble, there could be no doubt.

Against a white scrim, a shadow figure on a trapeze could be seen swinging and singing in a high voice. *Flittermouse, Flittermouse, what are you doing in the child's house?*

WHEN THE BAT appeared flying low above her head, the mother realized that they had been exposed to something that could not be reversed. The bat had appeared as a messenger, and she was afraid. The child put her hands up against it in protection. A bat, the mother knew, could rest lightly on the neck without you even knowing it and make a puncture with its hatpin teeth in your skin no larger than an insect's—its wings spread like a paper fan, with the weight of a bird, and no one would know. She looked at the child. What did it want? Take these words, it screeched. But what were the words? And bind them to your wrist as a sign. Observe, it screeched, all the statues and decrees that are set before you.

The mother woke with a start. Before the child was born, the mother had been a nurse. She used to love the clean, blinding surfaces—and the white hat.

At night, the mother explained to the child, a bat can land on the face like a fan, then close up, taking your life.

The mother reassured the child that the vaccines against the bat would not be so bad, but that they would need to go to the hospital.

The child could not remember ever having been in a hospital before. The child asked if she could bring her lamb.

WHILE THE MOTHER and the child waited in the Emergency Room for the serum—thick, cloudy, viscous—the child asked if they might play a game of Hangman and the mother complied. Now carrying the recollection of the bat's gibberish in them, the mother and child embraced the babble. A jumbled alphabet poured from them, as the mother tried to decipher the word concealed before her. It's three words actually, the child said. Look. And the mother began to guess the letters of the phrase the child had chosen while slowly the little hanging man materialized.

CALAMITOUS IS THE day. The halls of the Emergency Room fill. The sleeping American tenor is wheeled in while the mother and child wait. The American tenor, destitute, has taken a box of tablets and now slumbers. Here he lies, whooshing past, sedate, supine; no one can revive him.

He is slumbering in the green hills near death; he will not wake again. How difficult suddenly it is to think of him once singing the role of the melancholy lovelorn poet Werther, someone says.

Werther is borrowing a pair of pistols from the husband of the woman he loves, only to shoot himself with them, in the last act, on Christmas Eve.

Angel face with flaxen hair, did you ever care?

The mother felt unsettled by the thought of all the men in the Valley who were disappearing, some destined to perish by their own hands, leaving behind the strangest and saddest relics: a Christmas cup, a piano, a treatise on whales, a vortex, a glove.

THE MOTHERS OF Sorrow traipse through the Emergency Room in anguish, following their faltering sons.

A boy who had fallen from a tree comes in. Three days earlier, the boy, who is five, got up and brushed himself off, and talked and walked, only now to fall into an irretrievable sleep. The doctors say the five-year-old had been afflicted with the malady they call Talk and Die.

Another boy dressed head-to-toe in camouflage spots has been wounded. An unspotted Mother of Sorrow follows the body.

A third boy, small and blue and filled with smoke, rescued from the top floor of a house, rushes by.

The mothers cry and beat their breasts and ask why, but no sound comes out, and it does not matter; no answer is forthcoming. The Mothers of Sorrow are getting sleepy, and as they walk they seem to close their eyes, and the Virgin in her grotto is falling asleep as well. Before she drifts off she is seen holding in one arm an infant, and in her other hand, a nail. The sleepiness in the Virgin is called the Virgin Dormition, and the sleepiness in the Mothers of Sorrow is called the Maiden Dormition. The fear is so great for some of the mothers in the Emergency Room that they fall into a kind of stupor and go back to the time before they had children and were maidens and could rest.

The world is so filled with sleep and silence. Once Mother Teresa began her work with the poor and dying in Calcutta, she never heard God's voice again. For fifty years she continued without a word. It takes a special person to forge on anyway. An up-to-date candidate for sainthood would need to be able to bear that much silence and doubt, the mother thinks.

Any vulnerability, the mother reasoned, might drive a bat to one's side.

False gods flew above their heads and were everywhere before them. The mother had dreamt her whole life of becoming something winged, but she didn't know how. That night, medical workers seen from above, drenched in light, waited for casualties, but no casualties came. The mother remembers the hover, a state of suspension that she carries inside her to this day.

At the moment of the American tenor's death, the room flooded with song, and the mother and the child looked up.

THE VIRGIN HAS awoken. The child pulls at the mother's sleeve and directs her attention back to their game of Hangman, and at last from the jumble of alphabet, the mother can read the child's message. I AM SCARED.

I AM SCARED. Her body is changing. They notice it there on the hospital bed as they wait for the vaccination.

You can see now, the mother says, where the wings will fit.

The Virgin beckons for them to come forward.

What do you want of us? the mother asks.

3

THE FOX HAS its den and the Ovenbird its nest, but the mother and the child have no place to rest their heads. Come with me, the Virgin says.

Revelers, mourners, pilgrims, and seekers were on their way to the Spiegelpalais. From the smallest of embers, the Great Wind had ignited fires that burned on the horizon and fell on the heads of the sojourners, granting them wisdom and direction, and though they did not speak the same language, when they at last arrived at the place, each miraculously was able to understand the other.

Many in the Valley stood outside the Spiegelpalais and wondered why pilgrims were arriving from all points on earth, but after the initial flurry of inquiries, such questions passed and did not return again. A mass hypnosis seemed to settle over the Valley, and soon no one remembered a time the Spiegelpalais had not been there, or could imagine a future in which it was not included. Many stood outside and waited, but few gained admittance, so when the mother and child were issued in easily, under the Virgin's auspices, the mother felt vaguely worried, as if it were some sort of trick.

FROM THE OUTSIDE it had seemed a dream arena: ephemeral, unmoored, a ghost ship festooned with banners and flags; but inside, the Spiegelpalais felt more solid, immovable, real. An endless series of rooms and vaults seemed to open in every direction. Some rooms were linked by corridors, some by canals, some by woodland paths, and there was a central atrium where there burned a small live fire.

Soul cakes, someone sang around the fire where a mourning party huddled. Soul cakes were being roasted and a glass orchestra played.

Darkened passages, leading to rabbits and rabbit holes or wood-chucks in their dens and collapsible floors were everywhere. Rooms as if in a dream, inviting, irresistible, moss-laden, called to them.

Off stage right, cordoned off, flowed the Rhine. People gathered at its banks and wept. The mother and child felt their own river, just outside the door, like a silk swathe move through them. Boxes of fog were opened.

All was in motion. There were elevators that rose and fell, trap-doors, ropes and pulleys, dumbwaiters, escape hatches. There were sliding stages. The sky became a canyon, the canyon filled with water and became an Italian lake draped in crepe de chine, the lake froze and a tundra opened before them. They walked through a snow garden, a garden of concrete deities, a children's garden, a fox's garden, a cinder garden where children played, and the glen. In the glen a boy played an irresistible tune on a panpipe. A deer appeared in a clearing—but before the child could reach it, it was gone, vanished in the dark wood.

AN ENORMOUS TURNTABLE filled an airplane hangar at the back of the Spiegelpalais upon which elaborate tableaux were in the process of being constructed. A maple tree was being assembled, a mute man made of straw, a Flagship, a child's truck enlarged to life size, a seed crib. Freed from their burden of narrative, these objects seemed all the more mysterious, and everyone marveled at their inscrutable beauty. A pupa, a papyrus raft, a rose-laden boat.

Out of nothing an entire world had begun to materialize before the mother and child. An array of scene painters and seamstresses and carpenters and artisans of all sorts were busy at work constructing skyscrapers and churches and clock towers and other facades. Pastoral scenes had been rendered with great feeling, a beautiful grotto had been made one rock at a time, and cityscapes were depicted under heartbreakingly blue skies.

Look! the child said. There, and she tugged at her mother's sleeve; on a painted ocean was Uncle Sven—whimsically portrayed.

PARADED BEFORE THEM was all of life. Enigmatic emblems streamed past as the mother and child walked, but they were not afraid. In the place called the Night Archive, inventory of some kind was being taken, and things were being summed up, accounted for, tallied. Piled to the ceilings were logbooks and ledgers and bibles: the Hair Bible, the Bird Atlas, the Red Book of Existence.

When they came to the place called the Aging Stage, the mother and child were stopped. On the Aging Stage, a voice explained, a few steps forward and you are a baby again, a few steps back—an old woman. The mother watched her siblings. What were they doing here?

Five giant steps were taken forward, and suddenly Lars, Ingmar, Anders, Sven, and baby Inga have not yet been born. It frightened the mother. Only the empty black perambulator, funereal, waited stage left for the babies to come.

Back in place and four steps in the other direction, and they were no more.

AN OPEN CALL for extras sounded throughout the Spiegelpalais. We need Human Pollinators, we need totem animals of every sort, we need a steady stream of beekeepers, we need pilgrims for the Concrete Rabbit. Had anyone seen Oscar the Death Cat? Had anyone heard from The Headless Horseman Fife and Drum Corps? An amplified voice spoke with urgency. Soldiers were needed, and before you knew it, they came in endless corridors walking in a continuous column toward the mother and the child, and then away, where they disappeared into the fog. Lost to the Phosphorous, the director murmured. Then more would come, and then go, and always more and more were called.

SOON ENOUGH THE pageant would commence. Various players were being fitted for costumes: Operation Rescue was being measured for bird suits, the President for his evening coat. Pierrot lugged out the Costume Bible. Junot thumbed through the Hair Bible to find where the hair for the Grandmother Wig had been purchased—ah yes—at auction in Sweden for ninety-five dollars an ounce in 1933. There were prop rooms filled with wigs, and wolf suits, and beekeeping paraphernalia.

Out tumbled a hat with antlers, a fish with a face, an ermine head, a mesh dress, a wig of matted hair.

Standing far up on a scaffold, men were assembling what appeared to be a human child, several stories high. Three schoolchildren with backpacks standing under a Scholar Tree looked on. When they saw the mother and child, they ran to them and laughed and pulled at them and asked if they might stay and play and read to them awhile, but the mother demurred and stepped away.

EVERYWHERE REHEARSALS WERE going on in the wings. Actors were running their lines: *Flittermouse, Flittermouse* . . . a haunting falsetto could be heard. The little pope practiced carrying his glass globe. The glass pyramid was rolled out. Now and then you could pick out a word: *wind* or *tooth* or *chrysalis* or *flame*, and the mother thought, how strange.

In the Night Archive the darkness was immense, but there was an abundance of light sources—fireflies, embers encased in jars, and from the vast, arched ceilings, shooting stars.

Velvet and rhinestones were attached to the ceiling to embellish the evening. In the dressing room, grease paint was being applied to the Night Oil Man's fearful visage.

The darkness became such that there was a public plea for daylight. Day in the underground vault was being manufactured with incandescent light and bird effects and sweet breezes and swings.

Charming scenes of country life were being blocked: barn dances and threshings and fall celebrations. Harvest costumes were tweaked and cornstalks arranged.

Cecil Peter and Wise Jean and their Piggle passed by on a float. From his windy perch, Cecil Peter rehearsed his lines, calling through a megaphone that the Age of Funnels was upon them. Heed this warning, he said. The Age of Funnels always brings madness when it returns, and this time would be no exception. Their first Piggle had been born aloft on the whirling and carried away. Nail down your loved ones, Wise Jean could be heard saying, before it's too late. And the blue veil of madness, gossamer, beautifully made, unfurled right on cue. Everywhere there were intimations of the Vortex. Stage crews were adjusting the wind machines to accommodate the endless directives of the script.

Farmers and their wives practiced their reels. Small children tugged at the women, and the women directed their attention to something in the middle distance, and it seemed as if something were about to happen, but then just as suddenly, the scene began to recede. Already? the mother said. It had scarcely seemed to have taken shape and it was already dissolving in the haze. The fiddle faded and moved to mirage, and the farmers and their wives and a whole way of life eerily and without music danced away—quaint, iconic, into the ever-increasing distance. A last do-si-do then. Small figures, hauling bales of hay, waved.

THE THEATER UTOPIA had arrived and had taken up residence on the outdoor stage. *En plein air*—the birds, the wind, the stars, all would be part of the play. Enter warbler, warbling. Tortoise. Whooping Crane. Aunt Eloise and a single bee. On deck was the Bindlestaff Family Circus. And the Arm of the Sea. And the Beloved Bread and Puppets. On the outdoor stage anything might happen.

At the Spiegelpalais the child opened her mouth. Her baby teeth were gone. New teeth were coming in.

At the edge of the meadow, the sleek wolf padding in on rose feet.

BACK INSIDE AT the Court of Miracles, all marveled at the discovery of Dark Matter, and someone lectured about Quintessence and Phantom Energy. At the summit stood the Vortex Man, and all knelt to his power and bowed their heads in reverence. Behold, he said, the planet on the table! It was a blue planet, perfectly round, very beautiful. Is that us? someone dared at last to ask. Yes, the Vortex Man said, a little sadly.

Next to the planet was a human eye, a floating miracle of design. Light enters the pupil, is focused and inverted by the cornea and lens, and is projected at the back of the eye where the retina lies—seven layers of alternating cells, which can convert a light signal into a neural sign. The mother, who had once been a nurse, sighs.

And in the atrium the great orb, which had somehow survived, presided in silence.

A great winged thing was projected now onto a large screen. Behold, the Vortex Man bellowed, the Luna Moth—from the wild silk moth family—and its enormous wings filled the screen. Many gathered, drawn to its light. Behold its diaphanous and fragile beauty, its wings pale green, its transparent eyespots, its long curving tail. Ladies and gentlemen, they love the Persimmon, the Sweet Gum, the Winged Sumac.

In the Miracle Theater a boy's chest was being opened, and from it a flock of birds flew. It was the time of the Bird Count, and the child was handed a tally book and a pencil. But just as she began counting, a commotion arose, and the birds scattered.

Step away, step away, the Vortex Man implored as a large aquarium draped with a sheath was rolled into the Court. In one elegant gesture, he removed the velvet shroud that draped it.

Behold the creature dreaming in its amniotic sac, the place it will reside these next nine months. Elaborate memory tracks are being laid down there, my friends, from the dappled, shadowed world. Associations and sensations are flooding in and being held by the fluid. See for the first time what it sees. On the overhead projector, the close-ups shot from the fetus's point of view resembled flora and lacy ferns and fauna.

The dreamy fetus floats remembering nothing, or so we suppose. Ladies and gentlemen, the fetus is remembering right now. And the fluid retains the memory for a thousand years. Note the beautiful greeny-blue umbilicus attached to the world—like a luminous garden hose.

COME ONE, COME all, and I will show you a species of dreamers
unrivaled in the history of the world. Lost to us for millennia. The
more you learn about them, the more you will love them, these beautiful dreamers, and the more you will miss them. From a distant mil-
lennium—now retrieved for the first time ever and coming soon here
to the Spiegelpalais. The mystery at the heart of the cosmos remains
intact—insoluble to us with our limited consciousness—but not to the
Large-Headed Hominid. Come see its majestic brain—with an internal
life we cannot begin to fathom. Come have life's mysteries at last illuminated. At last—all that lies outside our grasp. Find yourself—

On a foundering ship no more.

Hostage to the Concrete Rabbit no more.

WHO ARE YOU? the child inquired of the Vortex Man.

You may be wondering, the Vortex Man bellowed, indeed who I
am and why we have all gathered here. For a moment everyone stopped
what they were doing and there was absolute silence. At the still point
of the turning world, the Vortex Man spoke:

You have come from near and far. You have worked tirelessly, you
have been faithful and true. A drama of cosmic proportions is about to
be staged. Life and Death before our eyes shall vie for the Mother and
Child. And a spotlight illuminates them. Both Heaven and Earth. See
how they hover in a hanging liminal place, not quite here, but not quite
there either. Death vies for them, but so does Life. Each side possesses
its seductions, oh yes, its considerable charms, oh yes. Both sides. It is
twilight. Or is it dawn? Who is to say? The body collects both sleep
and song.

Who shall be victorious in the end? Even the Vortex Man does not
know.

These and other enigmas shall be contemplated. Behold the Luna Moth. And the Wolf. And the Death Cat. And the mossy path. And the snow. And the lavish green dreaming of the fallen tree.

Staged will be the Eternal Questions for all to ponder:

Why is the man drawn irresistibly to the whale, only to murder it?

Why is it that when we might have gone forward, we stepped back?

If the child severs the silk tether prematurely, what does it mean for her?

Why did we hesitate? And when in our hesitations did we become part of the Too Late.

And where is Uncle Ingmar going now in winter with the grandfather clock strapped to his back? These and other existential conundrums shall be pondered . . .

And with this, the Vortex Man made his exit.

IN THE WINGS, the Cocoon Theater troupe and the wolf-escorts waited. Dapper, stage right, magnified, Mr. Min stood in blue light pulling swollen bats from a hat.

The Virgin in blue, accompanied by a little deer, and holding a lantern, moved majestically to the center. She's looking for the child, but the child has hidden behind the mother's skirt and for now is out of view. The Virgin says she'd like to take the child. She's come, she says, for the child.

The Virgin assumes rightly that if she can only cajole the child to come with her, the mother will come too.

LADIES AND GENTLEMEN, children of all ages—and before them out of nowhere, the blue stars of the Cone Nebula, and the dazzling Horsehead Nebula.

All was beauty and brightness. There was a preponderance of antlers and whiskers and shining coats.

Irrefutable is the night, but the light show is unrivaled and the mother and child stand in awe at the mouth of the nebula. And suddenly the astounding figure of the Grandmother from the North Pole in the lights of the aurora borealis appears in the heavens.

She points and directs the mother's gaze to the room where Aunt Inga lay.

Bathed in light, the mother takes the child's hand and climbs over the large slumbering body of Aunt Inga. The room her younger sister sleeps in is shaped, it seems, like a curving shell. There is a whirling feeling and a whooshing sound. The child asks if they might rest here awhile.

No they may not, the mother says.

The Virgin whispers, it's nearly time. The play is about to begin. Everything is ready now.

As if the strange mix of anticipation and dread were finally too great, the mother falls into a dream, and in her dream she sees quite clearly that the small eternal flame has been left unattended, and the Spiegelpalais has caught fire. Smoke fills the atrium. It becomes so heavy that she can see nothing at all. Where has everybody gone? she wonders. She cuts a drowsy swathe through the smoke. Never has she seen so many sleepers piled one on top of the other, on top of the other, or such thickness, or experienced such peace. There is a thicket of sleep; there is a mountain of sleep.

Lined against the walls were the Seven Sleepers—the polar bear, the snow goose, the arctic fox, the wolverine, the ermine, the vole, the snow leopard—awaiting reanimation. Every stage of sleep could be seen. Before the mother, a caribou was in the process of going still—a foreleg stiffened, the eyes went glassy, and it began to list to one side. It is promised one day, the Vortex Man said, that each shall be retrieved.

She has to pull herself out of the dream now as if a figure out of marble. She knows, above all else, she must keep her eyes open. She rouses the slumbering child and puts her on her back, and in the last moment before it is too late forever, they make their way over the hordes of beautiful sleepers through flames and the irresistible pull of smoke toward home.

That was a close call, the child says.

The mother smiles. It certainly was.

THE MOTHER OPENED her eyes and recalled nothing of the dream, only that she was refreshed and free of worry and care. She had not missed a thing. She looked to the stage. Everyone had taken their seats. The glass orchestra had been joined by the children's choir, and now a hurdy-gurdy could be heard, and a bone piano, a panpipe, and a herald horn. Never, the mother remarked, had music ever sounded so beautiful. Final announcements were being made signaling the play was about to begin. When she looked in the wings, the mother saw all the players were now lined up loosely in order of appearance.

A narrative of great mystery and beauty was about to unfold. A struggle, as they had been told, of epic proportions, if that peculiar fellow was to be believed. It was an odd position to be in, the mother thought—to be at once both part of the audience and part of the performance, and even though they would be entirely at the mercy of the script, something about that comforted her.

Minutes passed. There was some snafu, she was sure of it, and the pageant was delayed, and she felt suddenly relieved to think there might still be a little more time left. The music, however, seemed to suggest otherwise. The overture began to play, introducing many of the key scenes to come. They looked at their programs and read, The Disappearance of the Lamb, The Mothering Place, The President in Evening Coat, The Appreciation Cake, The End of Childhood . . .

Music for a while, the mother sang to herself, *shall all your cares beguile* . . . Another phrase came to her and through it she tried to hold on to the shrinking world before her, framed by red velvet curtains. *Music . . . source of gladness . . . heals all sadness.*

If she was sad, she was not cognizant of it. Still, thinking about the play before her about to begin, tears streamed down her face.

The dog Shimmer, though he wouldn't be needed until the third act, bounded onto the stage. Let him run outside until his time has come. And the same for the Hamster Ball lovelies. Release them into the meadow and into the sky: the Dall Sheep, the Gray Goose, the Arctic Tern, until the end.

The Grandmother from the North Pole sat beside the mother for a moment and handed her a bowl of cloudberries. The mother smiled at her mother and accepted the deep blue bowl graciously and fed a few to the child who was growing restless.

Just then two children holding a banner appeared on the stage and recited:

Welcome to our play.

The banner read, *Scene 1—Pastoral, Spring.*

It's a Pastoral!

Someone turned on the fog machine.

No, it's a ghost story.

Frogs could be heard.

A dream within a dream . . .

The curtain opened.

figments

GHOSTS GATHERED IN the early hours while the mother and the child stretched a mesh between two poles at the pond. They had come, as they did many mornings, to extract water from fog. Though they were far from the sea, the mother heard the doleful sound of a lighthouse and felt the eerie piercing glow coming from it. After the net was secured, the mother and child sat in the grass.

If the child were a monkey, she might take the mesh to the tallest trees and install it there. If the child were a monkey, there would be cymbals and a little hat and an organ grinder. Many people do not realize that a little organ grinder monkey, not the chimp or the ape, is the next smartest mammal after man.

After a while, the pond slowly came into clarity, and the sun came up. It is strange the way one state is always bleeding into another.

Frogs are a sentinel species. The skin of a frog is permeable. Recently, frogs have been growing longer legs or extra legs. Boys catch these frogs in boxes and bring them to science class.

Frogs can be said to have beautiful voices, especially at mating season, but one part per billion of weed-killer in the water shrinks the voice box of the male frog, and they cannot sing their song so well. The earth was turning from one kind of place into another. This frightens the mother who knows all things must change.

She looked at the monkey, now a child again.

All the frogs in the world were singing their crooked songs in the fog. The child did not think the songs crooked, she thought the frog songs lovely. They were the only frog songs she had ever known.

THE MOTHER DIRECTS the child to the eyepiece of the microscope. Ordinarily, if you cut open a bee, its insides viewed under a microscope appear white, the mother said. But these bees were black with scar tissue and disease. Everything you can think of is wrong with them, including new pathogens never before sequenced. The mother knows well that there is a trigger that takes an otherwise borderline population and throws it over the edge.

The mother opens the Report on the Status of Pollinators. It is said that pollinator decline is one form of global change that has the potential to alter the shape and structure of the terrestrial world. They were a people at risk. The disappearance of the adult bee population presaged the human disappearance.

A drift of soldiers came up and over the hill, babbled into their radios, and then vanished.

The tortoise, untroubled, looks up and slowly says, the disappearances have happened before, and will happen again. The truths of the universe are so profoundly concealed. The mother and child hung on to his every word. You've no need to worry. And with that, its great liquid eye shut.

EXILED FROM CHILDHOOD, but in the constant presence of it, the mother felt covetous of the child sometimes because the child still had childhood, and to the mother, childhood was no longer accessible.

Even the mother's mother, the Grandmother from the North Pole, was not young anymore. The light was bright late into the night in summer at the North Pole. When the North Pole Grandmother came with a platter of fish preserved in vodka and lingonberries, the fish had a face on it and the children ran and hid. The candles were lit then and there was juniper and holly.

The child was busy in the corner making a sculpture of a rabbit out of a carrot. Next she was sculpting a boat. On the table sat the Red Book of Existence. Even the child will one day die. It takes three cups of salt to cure a fish. The mother tries to remember being small, not as an adult remembers, but as a child, though it is hard. She would like to fit inside a thimble, and someday she probably will.

There is a casket the size of a walnut shell that waits in the garden. There is a husk. There is always the sorrow of the last morsel of fish to consider. Many of the children are still hiding in the garden. When she was little, she remembers going into the sewing box and taking out her favorite thing: a pincushion encircled by Chinamen. When she was small, she remembers the bright thimble and the way it looked like a castle on her thumb. The Grandmother from the North Pole was there then in the next room where she could hear her preparing the fish.

Lingonberries are something else she remembers. While the mother reaches to remember, the child wishes she had a picture phone so that while she talked to the Grandmother from the North Pole she could see her face and watch her white hair blowing in the wind.

The lifespan of a North Pole Grandmother is eighty-three, the child reads.

THE MOTHER HAD no use for computers and could not accompany the child as she entered the world of ciphers and shadows and glyphs, but the Grandmother from the North Pole, who loved nothing more than the future, gladly went wherever the child took her and was always happy to be able to learn something beautiful and new. The child put her grandmother's hand on the cursor, and enigmatic, translucent fields were revealed.

It was marvelous, she thought, floating in the digital universe. At these times, above all, the Grandmother from the North Pole thought it was wonderful to be alive.

A blue multitude of children huddle around her. They've just come in from the blueberry patch. See them now as they dose off with their full buckets: Lars, Bibi, Ingmar, Anders, Sven. Baby Inga must be at home, or maybe she is not born yet.

Before the screen's deep glow, the Grandmother said, I should like to write the Book of Wonder before I die, and her eyes sparkled.

IT WAS A privilege to live so near the river, that is what the mother always said. Silt passed through them some mornings and the mists worked themselves into the ways they thought about things. The child found fish in her pockets and river rocks in her pockets, and the sense of weight and immensity filled them, and many days they walked immersed in water and water-song.

There was swell and verge in the world. In spring, the banks surged. In the winter when the river froze, the mother and child read about how once cakes of ice were cut from it and stored in small icehouses. The river fed their notions of spaciousness and hope. They imagined carrying great cakes of ice in the shapes of hearts to the neighbors.

They would put the cakes on a baby's feverish head. Or preserve a fish for the Christmas Eve dinner.

The child was thankful that the mother treated the river like a god. Some Sundays, they would spend the whole day lazing on its banks. They found fossils and slate and shale, and trains went by, and people from the city could be seen blinking in the windows. Then all was quiet again, and the train, sleek and fleeting, was gone. The child grew sleepy. The river made everything in the Valley radiant, even at night.

At night, the mother said, the river crept into their beds, and they could wade out until it was over their heads, and at that very place in the river there would be a birch canoe waiting to meet them. The child loved this part most of all, floating in the boat, and waving to the people on the other side who waited. She thought she could even see a girl about her age.

Before the mother and child arrived, the Indians had already lived here for thousands of years.

THE MOTHER WOKE the child before dawn and told her that she was to quickly dress because they would be going with the elders today on a bird-watching expedition. The child liked the sound of it: a bird-watching expedition. The mother loved bird-watching because it fostered the things she valued most: attentiveness, patience, care. What should have been a white stripe on the head of the smallest bird in the deepest wood, if one looked carefully and was very quiet and did not move, was actually orange because of the abundance of berries in the bird's diet at this time of year. So much, the mother thought, depends on this. This watchfulness. The mother liked standing there in the dew in the sweet fleeting early hours of the day. What could be held could

be held only for an instant—all the rest was held in the mind. A sighting, then a flitting away. And then the linger. That dream. It was a
beautiful, prolonged instant, this being prepared, ready to let whatever
flew into the field of vision be caressed by the eye.

When the child awoke that morning, the mother had handed
her a bird atlas in which to make notes and record the names of
the birds she saw. Standing in the meadow, suddenly and with great
force the child was overwhelmed by the desire to fill the entire bird
atlas. She was taken aback by the feeling—she had no idea where it
had come from. She tried to quell it, for otherwise she would have to
run around and shout with glee, which might scare away the elders
and the birds.

Mostly they were very quiet, but sometimes the elders made
sounds—phisshhhhhhh and phoshhhhhhh—and this seemed to call
the birds to their sides. The child liked the sound, and she thought she
would try it at home when their cat Bunny Boy was in the house.

There! Over there! a woman said in a hush—a momentary silhouette on a dark branch—there! It was the Ovenbird. You could tell by
its song, *teacher, teacher, teacher,* it said.

Where? Where?

So little so drab so gray—or green, impossible to see.

Later when they were out of the forest, she would hear about the
enclosed nest that the little bird would build. I should like to see the
covered nest of the Ovenbird, the child said. Someone else spoke of the
courtship rituals of the Woodcock.

In a great and mysterious turn, one of the elders took the child's
head and pointed it upward and to the left. The mother gasped, remembering how round and perfect the child's head had been when she was
born. It had seemed to her like a planet. One of the elders spoke of

the Sphinx Moth. It was very quiet, and when someone spoke, it was always in a whisper, and what was said sounded like a secret. Another bird flew by. *There!* someone said. But she could not rescue the bird from the distance.

One of the elders, a woman without binoculars who led the way for a while, had fallen behind.

I can't see a thing anymore, she whispered to the child, but I like to come nevertheless.

She took the child's hand so as not to stumble, and they walked a little further, into a place of improbable darkness. The woman who could not see anymore phished and phoshed. Her eyes were the same watery blue color as the Grandmother's from the North Pole.

THE MOTHER RECALLED the Arctic Cloudberry—rare, brief of season, difficult to pick, unlike anything else. And how the Grandmother from the North Pole would make a Cloudberry Cake. Cloudberries were always the Grandfather from the North Pole's favorite. Grandfather was said to have made Arctic Cloudberry cordials back home. The mother recalls currents and lingonberries and elderberry saft.

She would like the child to write the names of the berries in the atlas. She would like the child to keep track for her. Cloudberries grow in the remote fir and silver birch forests in the north or in the far bogs. They can also be found in the mountains of Lapland. In late July they appear on the forest floor, and by early August they are gone.

THE HONEYBEES HAD disappeared three years ago now, but to celebrate the child's birth, Aunt Eloise made funnel cakes shaped like beehives nonetheless. Happy Birthday, she sang to the child, and while she sang Uncle Lars did a sprightly dance. The cakes were curved, and all agreed they were most splendid in all the Valley. She made tiers of hives, replete with little marzipan bees. Everyone sighed. They were the most beautiful cakes anyone had ever seen, and Aunt Eloise and the child closed their eyes and pictured the bees.

After the candles were lit and the song was sung and the child had made her wish, it was not long before a single bee—regal, gilded— landed on her birthday crown. And then another came. And then another.

Word spread quickly as Aunt Eloise had a talkative streak, and before long, beekeepers all across the country came leaving their offerings for the child.

The beekeepers traveled a glowing corridor to the child's door, holding cakes they themselves had baked. They moved as if through a golden tunnel, or a honey lozenge, to the child.

The mother, drowned in amber, accepted the offerings on behalf of the child and quickly closed the door.

Bees use the sun as a compass. They search for the place of continuous nectar flow, and all season beekeepers from across the world left their farms and made their way to the Valley.

A wooden aqueduct holding aloft a fleet of six beeswax boats floated by.

A golden halo of pollen appeared to hover above the child's head.

THE VIRGIN SMILES at the mother and child. She wants them to come to the clearing in the forest, to her shrine near the hive. She is holding a honey cake. There will be three schoolchildren there to play with, she promises. She is wearing a beekeeper's suit. Gloves and a hood. With a smoker she puts the bees to sleep. Come to me.

WHEN THE MOON was full and the weather was right, she would invite the child out to the night garden. The garden at night scared the child who was afraid of the dark, so she would always stay inside. It was time again for applying the fish emulsion, the ritual feeding of the roses with the bodies of liquidated bass and trout and sunfish. It was quite a sight—the mother working through the night.

When the child looked out the nursery window, she saw fireflies plastered to the outline of her mother, and she watched her like that for a long time. Small things of all sorts seemed to attach themselves to her and cling. When the raccoons came, as they always did with their awful tiny human hands pressing, the child would be jealous and she would try to force herself out the door.

Come see the Luna Moth, the mother cried with delight, but not even that enchanting, silk-producing creature with its huge pale green wings could entice the child. Instead she held vigil at the screen door and waited for day to come. From the door, she could hear the mother singing, "Tomorrow will be my dancing day," and it soothed her.

And in the morning, resplendent and smelling of fish and roses, and wiping away bits of fur and fin, she would bring the child out into the daylight to live their daylight lives, and the men and the boys would follow them, and hum and trip and fall around the mother, and touch the child's hair, and this alarmed the child for they lived in a household without men or boys.

How sad are the men, the mother thought, in love with fish and figment and oblivion and the night.

THE MOTHER WAS drawn to the glow of the votives and she would kneel before them, and the child too loved the small flickering flames in their cups.

Once after Midnight Mass, the mother told the child a story of when she was a girl. She had never forgotten, though it had happened long ago now. She was out late, when all of a sudden the dazzling body of a wolf appeared on the path. The silver fur. The sleek head. She motioned to it, ablaze on the trail, and slowly neared it, and her hand slid beneath its head. How to describe such velocity? How to describe this passage in the night? This transit? This portal? He had carried her across the threshold and introduced her to the other world. Never had there been such an initiation as that. Thinking about it, even now, she shuddered. She had never told a soul.

For a long time she forbade herself from even uttering the word "wolf."

That night they put a candle in every window and waited.

oracle

BUNNY BOY, THE cat who had smuggled a tiny rabbit into the house without being noticed, now munched on it in the corner. When the mother saw it, there were rabbit pieces still in view, but the next time she checked, they were far and few, and then finally it was as if no rabbit had been there at all. Where did you put that rabbit, Bunny Boy? the mother hissed, as she lifted a rug and peered under chairs, but if it was there, even a whisker, she never found it.

Somewhere in the house what is left of that rabbit is stashed away and hidden. Somewhere, while the mother and child sleep, its carcass is turning to stone.

THE CONCRETE RABBIT appeared to the mother the next morning. See what you've done Bunny Boy, the mother scolded—now we have to live with this hare, standing erect, holding a basket, guarding his kind forever, in all seasons, in all weather, night and day.

But despite her dismay, after a while she and the child found themselves going to the rabbit with their troubles, their thoughts, their ideas, their dreams. They brought him water and they washed his feet and they moved him when it was sunny and put him under a tree. They brought him lettuces and carrots. In April or March, they set before him little Easter chocolates. But no matter what they did, the rabbit's expression did not seem to change.

After a time, when the neighbors got wind of the rabbit's existence, they began to sneak over to visit him with their petitions. Soon, word of the rabbit traveled through the Valley, though what he signified, no one could be sure. An old woman who visited the rabbit wished to conceive a child though she was a hundred years old. A man, who loved a woman who did not love him back, became a regular visitor. A mother whose child had disappeared rubbed the rabbit's paw. Widows, in increasing numbers, sat by his side. All day a steady stream of Valley folks made their way to the place. The Concrete Rabbit listened. They called him Sir. The pilgrims thought that indeed Sir did love them—how could he not?—they who came with every problem the flesh posed. They felt great tenderness and pity coming from him, and because he never closed his eyes, he always appeared attentive and empathetic. Who ate the chocolates they brought him, no one knew.

The child danced and played near the rabbit, though her feelings were decidedly mixed. In the back of her mind, she feared the rabbit might take the mother away somehow. Weren't rabbits known to be wily? Weren't rabbits the sort that would want to share the mother— something about those silky places on a rabbit's underbelly made her wary. What if the mother just walked to it of her own accord and forgot to look back and joined it in the concrete world? The child might be forced to perform a Concrete-Rescue, which was never easy.

In the night, when the moonlight illuminated the rabbit, the child worried—but in the day, the worry left her.

The Rabbit Oracle stood silently in the now green grass, and the child danced and marveled at all the garden deities: the Turtle, the Frog, the Mantis. In many ways it was an extreme life. From the tree, an idolatry of birds. A charm of finches and meadowlarks passed, a bevy of deer, but unmoving at the center was the silence of the Sir. Fearful is how the mother felt standing on the spongy warm earth next to him.

THERE WAS A knock at the door. Who's there? Before them stood a man defanged. He wore no sandals; he carried no moneybag, no sack, only a small box of teeth, which he rattled. It was the Toothless Wonder.

Can you direct me to the Rabbit Oracle? I have heard he can be found under a woodbine, shaded from the sun where gentle breezes blow and there is a most pleasant fragrance.

Where are your teeth? the child asked. He laughed and she saw the cavernous black at the center of the human. Teeth! he said, amused. What kind of Toothless Wonder would I be then?

THE MOTHER PUT the Concrete Rabbit in her yellow wagon. She was going to wheel it in the night while the rabbit's disciples slept. It was high time for the rabbit to dispense its wisdom elsewhere. She walked as far as she could possibly go while the child counted alligators and waited for her mother to return. At 3,745 alligators, the mother peeked her head in and announced she was back. She had found a lovely grotto for the rabbit, she said, in the nearby town of Warren. They could visit it, the mother promised, it wasn't far, though she had no intention of ever visiting the Sir again. Enough was enough. They drifted off together in the child's bed that night and had a peaceful and dreamless sleep. No one was watching them with concrete eyes, or listening with unnaturally long, erect ears, or holding a basket. It was a long time since either of them had slept like that—the sleep of the dead, as the mother called it.

In the morning, a few people gathered under the child's window. Someone was tossing Bunny Boy into the air like a ball. The mother was prepared to accept condolences. Yes, so sad, quite sad, perhaps he'll turn up. But when she looked out the window, the rabbit was back.

THERE EXISTS IN the human world a Child-Mother Proximity that must always be maintained no matter what, and the mother and child adhere to this equation.

The Vortex Man pulls down the blackboard. Observe, he says, the increasing proximity of the child to the attachment figure even now as they casually make their way to the lake. Note the investment in keeping the proximity within an acceptable and bearable distance. See how if the child gets too near, the mother demurs and retreats slightly. A marvelous thing!

The white fox is drawn to the tundra, and the mother to the river, and the father is drawn to the fog. In the Child-Mother Proximity Equation, one is always calibrating the Greater and Lesser Proximities like the Antilles. My Aunt Tilly was always leaving, and luckily she was childless, the Vortex Man roars.

As the Researchers have noted, the Vortex Man continues, whether a child moves toward a mother by running, walking, crawling, shuffling, or in the case of the Thalidomide Child, rolling, is thus of very little consequence compared to the set goal of its locomotion and namely its *Proximity to the Mother*.

One has to call up the Science in these matters, the Vortex Man says. Infants are biologically predisposed to stay close to their mothers, or be killed by predators. The survival of the genes the child is carrying is paramount.

Behold the Child-Mother Proximity—a precious measurement, unlike any other.

As for the Mother-Rabbit Proximity—that was altogether another matter.

THE NEXT DAY, Bunny Boy deposited a full-length hare on the porch directly in front of the door. If the mother had not looked down, she would have been raised several inches above the ground when she stepped out, borne aloft on its body. The hare was perfect in every way—brown, long-limbed—except for its face, which was not there. The mother screamed and the child ran to her, and elbowing her mother aside, she looked down and then pointed to the meadow where its ghost had already arrived. There beside the Concrete Rabbit stood another rabbit, nearly identical, only whiter. It stood straight up and its ears stood straight up and it seemed to be listening. The mother noticed it carried what appeared to be a little basket. Look, the child said. No, I don't see it, said the mother. Multiplying Concrete Rabbits in the field frightened her.

The mother looked down at her dress, which was gleaming white, and washed in the Blood of the Hare. The rabbit's blood was poised to relinquish liquidity, assume a solid shape, and never leave her side. Hard bits of rabbit attached to her. Look, said the child, but the mother refused.

THE SOLDIER, SHOCK-HEADED with locks of white, having seen appalling things, *atrocious things really*, he whispered, weeps on the bridge.

May I help you off with your shock head? the mother said, and he turned his gentle face to her. His face was mild, but his eyes were wild. The mother thought she had never seen such a strange person in all her life. And in the glade the mild soldier multiplied.

A DEPRAVED GROUP of moneylenders and other high rollers had made for themselves a bronze bull and a molten calf and were worshipping them. Their golden hoofs, their gleaming haunches. Just another day in the Valley, the mother quipped as she ushered the child by. Everyone wanted everyone else to love its little molten figure best.

Meanwhile, the war droned on. Attempts were made to measure the mothers' tears as they fell to the earth and drenched it. The Concrete Rabbit shunned the molten calf, who in turn shunned the cricket. In every village there were living sacrifices and the great sadnesses of rabbits, calves, crickets, and mothers. Death bells sounded from every mountaintop.

IN THE GREEN glade, soldiers were tumbling and falling off their horses and getting back on again, and falling again, and the mother and child wondered how they ever got anywhere or won anything, until they considered that perhaps the rules of battle included falling on their heads, or walking on their hands upside down, or any number of topsy-turvy actions, and that the battle always ended with everyone falling off their horses and laying side by side. The victors indistinguishable from the vanquished, and all of them lying in the green glade.

IT WAS SPRING and the Risen-Again children were descending en masse from the hills. When the mother had fair warning, she would dive into the bushes and hide, but sometimes there was just not enough time. Ambushed again, the mother thought, damn. She'd like to live in a Risen-Again-Free Zone. It was her goal.

The child, who was ordinarily mild-mannered, grew fierce. *Do not wish the Risens away!* Eight children were coming to play. There was Ezekiel, Nathan, Rebecca, Hannah, Jeremiah, and so on. These could be friends for her. Friends, the mother said. Friends? The mother began to laugh, and once she began she could not stop. Sometimes the child hated the mother so much, it frightened her. Some days the feelings were so explicit that she had to cuddle up with the mother a long time to find her way back to her.

Good morning Nathan, Ezekiel, and Jeremiah! Good morning Simon, Grace, Prudence, Elizabeth! What astounding feats have you accomplished today? Though it was only eight in the morning, the boys reeled off an impressive list from the homeschooled wee hours.

Wouldn't it be nice, the mother thought to herself, to live somewhere without fear of looking out the window and seeing Risen Agains waving, pontificating, and spelling everything? Matheletes, Champions of the Spelling Bee, Latin scholars. So what, she said to the child, if you can't spell profligate or nematode or marsupial?

The mother never understood why they were always quoting Scripture out of context. The use of that, she could not see. What the little Risen-Again brood could not know was that the mother, of course, could quote Scripture with the best of them, if that was what she chose to do. Then the mother got an idea.

O deliver soon to me, the mother prays, the likes of Rebecca and Ezekiel, Simon, Jeremiah, for a Bible-bee! Bring them soon to this bloodstained door.

The Rabbit seemed not to approve.

THE SHEEP KILLERS were her friends, and so the mother refrained from saying things she might have said otherwise. Being friends with someone, the child would learn, had as much to do with not saying things as saying them, and it made the world seem even more lonely when she thought of that.

The Sheep Killers had come from the city, and they had thought killing sheep was the right thing to do. It's only right, they said, if you are going to eat meat that you should be responsible for where that sheep meat has come from and what that meat has gone through in its life. This was considered acceptable dinner conversation. Uncle Lars could not agree. He looked sheepish and he piped up, I most certainly do not need to know, and it left a bit of a pall over the proceedings. Out the window, a bucolic scene unfolded before them. Sheep punctuated the pasture, and it was pleasant to watch the various patterns they made throughout the evening.

The Sheep Killers liked city music, and while they were doing the chores, they played city music to the sheep. All in all the sheep had a pretty good life, even Uncle Lars had to agree: outside all day with the sweet grass and breezes on Curly's Corners Road above Tivoli. It was the best view in the county. Look at them! And Uncle Lars drew the sheep in their slippers smoking pipes with their little sheep aperitifs, on a cocktail napkin.

The Sheep Killers did not like to say "killed"; they liked to say "processed."

IN HER SLEEP now, she hears the black wing-beat. And in the morning when she awakes, the Red-Tailed Hawk circling above with its gimlet eye on Bunny Boy. Now it is a world where birds eat cats, and not the other way around. Now it is the season for the "time is out of joint" speech. The mother snatches Bunny Boy and cradles him in her arms, and she does not duck or cower even as the hawk dives at her. The mother, with the force of her Motherhood, a force which is something like reverse gravity, compels the bird back high into the sky and then pushes it away entirely. This time they are not forsaken; the mother's powers are still intact.

Later when the Grandmother from the North Pole hears the story, she says quite plainly that it should be perfectly obvious: the hawk had not come for Bunny Boy of course, but for Miss Frosty, the cat from next door who often appeared in the yard. She is emphatic—that hawk was coming for the old lame one. Ask not for whom the bell tolls. It tolls for Miss Frosty!

MORE AND MORE, she was a transparency through which things passed. The self was a window that glimmered, the world outside wavy. The split maple tree had opened something in the mother that had remained closed down in her a long time. Be that as it may, the child wanted the mother to play with her.

She imagined that the thing that had eluded her for so long might actually be within reach—had been there all along: not hostile, not reluctant, not deaf, just as the poet had said, but she could not see it— nor did she wish to. They took out the Tinker Toys. Today it would come no closer.

ONE HUNDRED MILLION years ago, flowers appeared on the earth. Shortly after this, predatory wasps evolved into bees that fed on those flowers anew. The bees had left the hives, and they had not come back. Everyone on earth mourned their disappearance. What's that? the child had asked. On the horizon, a force of human pollinators could be seen.

The mother understood that the day that people were hired as hand-pollinators would mark the beginning of the end. It would not be long now until they too would perish. She said it out loud. Destroyed will be our remembrance from the earth.

absence

I T WAS NEVER easy being a baby—being a baby meant being at the mercy of almost everything. Things appeared and disappeared before a baby's eyes, and there was nothing a baby could do about it. The baby's task was to become a master of the unresolved absence. Oblique is the angle, fragile is the whole setup: crib, changing table, layette, human outlines, mother figure.

Because objects came and went all the time, a resourceful baby might make a wooden spool attached to a string that she could control simply by pulling the string or letting go. A spool so cool, so predictable, so easy to maneuver. So much better than the massive face that came and went at will and crooned peekaboo. Who is that? Uncle Ingmar, no doubt. The spool so much better, more solid, more comprehensible than the whims and figments that otherwise pass before an immobile baby's eyes.

A baby grown into a child will often still find the spool very useful. And even that child grown further into an adult might find that the spool is a very handy thing to have indeed. First many men were being lost at the front. Then, many men were being lost in the rice paddies or in the bamboo. And now on the outskirts of the ancient city, men and women and children were being lost again. In fact, not a day had passed in the history of the world without men and women and children lost somewhere. She reeled the spool out and it was gone. Then she reeled it back in. It was fun to play a frightening game. It was also fun to play a game where there would always be a satisfactory ending. Coping was what the child learned to do. There was a steady crown of stars around her mother's head, though the mother could not see or feel them, and so to her they were of no use. But to the child, the stars were everything. The mother proper would come and go, but the stars remained. That is what the child learned to do. Whenever she wanted, she could close her eyes and see stars, or a glove, or whatever she needed to see. It was a neat trick.

A band of itinerant magicians were making their way to the Spiegelpalais. Now you see it and now you don't, they liked to say. Jugglers filled the void with brightly colored balls for a moment. For the duration of the evening, there were white lights and libations and song. Still the men were being lost, in and out of war, everywhere you turned.

THERE IS A gloom in the day no one can shake. On the horizon they see a toy tractor enlarged to life size—all green except for black tires, a farmer astride it, waving to the neighbors perhaps or to the children, or to something that is not there.

She once saw a boy painted bright white sitting on the floor playing with a toy truck. The truck was rendered in precise detail, but the boy was formless, amorphous, lost in play. Little crouching boy cast in stainless steel and painted white, mesmerized by his toy truck. Bending down to him, the child tries to see the look on his face, and she is surprised to see there that he has no face at all. All of the boy has gone into the truck, she thinks. There he is: in the grooves of the tires, the shining fender, the intricate steering wheel, rendered in the greatest of detail. He's emptied himself there into the machine.

He's an abstracted boy; he's not like the Boy in the Glen, who dances with panpipe in the wolf hollow and is filled with music. The space between the huddled boy's hand and the truck take on a burden of almost unbearable weight. Still the child sits near him and puts her hand on his painted steel shoulder—hoping to help him, with whatever it is that is the matter.

THE MOTHER RECEIVED a telephone call from her sister Inga. The sister had some bad news. The child had never seen her mother listen harder to anything than she listened then. The listening had a hard, smooth quality to it, like ice, only hot. After the mother hung up, she curled into a ball and she did not speak or move for a day and a night. The child watched her mother curled up like that, and she thought about nests and she thought about shells. She felt so alone she did not know how she would bear it—and she felt worn by silence and the duration of time.

After a day and a night the mother finally uncurled, but the child saw the mother held something still clenched in her hand. When the mother saw the child, she wept and she opened her hand. In her palm she held the left ventricle of a human heart. The child took the left ventricle of the heart from her mother. She walked down the hallway and she laid it in her bed. Although it had looked blurry and ruined on the screen, here it did not look bad at all. She was happy to have it on the pillow next to her. It cast the room in ruby light. After pink, red was her favorite color. This way, if anything went wrong, she would know right away. She thought of her aunt seven and a half states away. A kindle of kittens appeared under the bed. A clowder of cats soon came to join them outside under the sill. After a while, the child fell into dream. Helpless and blind, the mother cat licked the kittens until they began to breathe. There was mother's milk for all. Then the mother cat went outside again with the others.

Everything seemed contingent on this arrangement: the clowder under the sill, the kindle under the bed, the ventricle next to the sleeping child, slowly repairing itself.

THE SOLDIERS WERE battling sleep, the most formidable of all opponents, and with their rapiers they sliced the heavy air. The soldiers in endless procession walk through the somnambulant world, singing as they go, an antidote, they hope. It was an invisible adversary and therefore the most dangerous of all. They talked back and forth on their walkie-talkies and gave each other pep talks, but before long, they had found a nestling place and they all curled up like babes together and succumbed.

THE GRANDMOTHER FROM the North Pole came to dispel myths, to correct misconceptions. For instance, she says, if you throw a baby in the ocean, you should not worry because a baby will always float. Its head is rounder and lighter than an inflatable beach ball. And it possesses a supreme swimming memory from before its birth. Besides, the mother chimes in, if a baby doesn't float, there's always a lot of commotion and someone goes and saves it. I love to see them bouncing out there on the event horizon, the Grandmother said. Such a beautiful thing!

A BABY SAILS like an inflated star craft high above the ocean, swooping and diving, skimming the surface and then flying back up.

AND THERE'S GRANDFATHER, she says, sailing smooth and straight. On the pale blue. His sails are puffed. He's still handsome.

MUSIC MOVES THROUGH the left ventricle. And the curtains blow in the breeze.

THE CHILD PUTS the ventricle in a doll's cradle, attaches wheels to it, and paints it blue. From her book she knew about Permanent Doll State, and she hoped the heart would not lapse into Permanent Doll State forever. The Grandmother from the North Pole reassures her, and points to the sky.

THE CHILD SITS high, high up and looks at herself in the mirror. There is something unnerving about a child dangling in the air while a hand bearing silver airborne scissors glides by. She is having her first haircut. The mother watches as the curls fall in slow motion to the floor. So many things are always falling. The tables fell through the floor, but that is another story. The mother and the child missed already the falling hair and all the feelings they had no names for.

In the Valley, the Palatines dreamt of building boats, but the boats would not float, so they turned to coffin making, but lost heart after a while and decided to try their hand at tables. The Palatines loved tables as all men love tables. They loved tables as women love linens. Tables were a place to plan a strategy, arm wrestle, or drink a stout. But something was wrong with the tables.

The tables were too heavy to lift, and they had a habit of falling through the floor like boats of stone. With coffins it did not matter how far they fell into the earth. In fact, the farther a coffin fell into the earth the better; this way they could layer the dead and the dead would not be quite so lonely or sad. Galileo tells us that the tables fall at the same rate as the child's hair. The deeper the coffins sank, the more pleased everyone was with the arrangement.

Sitting high, high up in that little executioner's chair, the scissors and the child gleam. Some men, but not all, revere war. The dead in the Valley lay in layers. The mother gathered the child's hair and placed it in a glassine envelope. There it will quietly lie through the years of peace and through the years of war.

How many years would tresses fall? Falling on human time. The mother bends to the ground and collects the hair of the young men who will not come home again.

The child's hair fell a long way to the floor that day.

THE MOTHER FOUND the men named Martin to be the best read of the men, and she preferred to have them for her friends, but they were far and few in the Valley. After the Risen Agains, and the Witnesses of God, the next most popular sect was the disciples of Baby Gabriella, or the Gabbies, as they were called. Whether Gabbies was a derisive name or not, she could not tell; she did not like to think about them. None of the groups read a whit as far as the mother could tell, though they all held books.

There was a city, she knew, filled with reading men like her friend Martin, but it was hard to reach now, so instead she cut off her hair and put it in a Lucite box and left it by the door. The child hated when the mother cut her hair, but the mother promised her it would grow back on the third day. Our passage on earth is brief, but to make up for it, things happen at a dizzying rate. The number of miracles is inexhaustible and never used up, the mother says. That's just the way life is. On the porch, the Lucite box began to breathe.

She hoped this might attract wise men to her side. But wise men were scarce in the Valley.

She might have liked a life where people read books and where many faces would come and go. She missed the big and beautiful city sometimes, and the Towers where Martin worked that had once presided.

A PIKE IS swimming in the bathtub. A chicken foot is sticking out of the sink. In every room, there was singing and dipping and whirling. These are scenes from the men's childhoods, and they created the deepest of longings in the mother. Kippered herrings passed before her eyes. Shining fish in their skins of gold. She names all the men Martin as they pass, after her friend Martin who had once delivered the news in his cupped hands. This is what he said, and she has never forgotten that cupped-handed gesture: the fetus is not in danger.

The mother closes her eyes. Many years now had passed since the emergence of cinematic time. This made her smile. Anytime she wanted, she could see Martin again, or if she preferred, the long line of Martins walking, or the child Martin, all alone leaning over the bathtub to pet the bright pike.

SHE PICTURES HERSELF climbing floor after floor with the men, higher and higher up into the sky. Books line the walls on every floor, and it occurs to her this must be a library of some sort, or some other kind of repository. When they get to the top and stand on the curving roof, she understands it to be the city she once loved, and she looks out and she is filled with joy. How beautiful you are! she calls out.

Far below is the vortex: a commotion without sound, some sort of drama, hundreds of fire engines and ambulances rushing to the scene.

The mother remembers standing high, high up, atop the beloved city. The mother remembers smoke, so much smoke, and at her back a searing heat. Between the mother and the ground far below, a force field now makes itself known and beckons her irresistibly to the street. The force becomes a pull so enormous that the mother names it Gloria so as to better withstand its call. She tries to step away, though all she wants is to move toward it now.

IN THE WEE hours, the mother, woken by a sound, followed a small flame into the Vortex Garden. There, before much longer, she would abandon herself to it—its blue heart, its heat, its light. Here, despite the advice of Cecil Peter and the elders, she would allow herself to burn. How exquisite is the sensation, the pull of sleep and smoke, the reduction to ash. What the bat had said was to prepare, and the flame had concurred. Who was the mother in the face of such directives? She felt herself dissolve in fire. She understood it in an instant. Soon they would be taken.

THE HOUSE SEEMED to grow light, and the air took on a peculiar quality—sparkly, as if you could see the bright molecules that made up the light. It looked something like pollen to the mother, and the mother was perplexed. The child wore a gleaming white dress and a veil and shoes with diamonds on the toes. The mother hoped it was not the child's wedding day already. The child was still young, of this the mother felt certain. She took a few steps closer, and let out a sigh. It was the day of her First Communion. She was receiving the Body of Christ—that was all. No cause for alarm, she supposed. She could see it now. The bread, the wine; no cause for concern there, she guessed. There was no bridegroom yet to speak of.

But the long pine casket—who was that for? She did not know. Oh, it was not a casket after all, but the tall box the grandfather clock had come in from the North Pole. The mother laughed as the girl came closer. There were still many years together left to them.

T HE GAP IN the life expectancy was widening according to the morbidity table. It was another part of the National Nightmare. Socioeconomic disparities declined in tandem with a decline in the mortality rate. The child did not quite understand what this meant. She always thought of tandem and bicycles as going together.

There was an island that allowed only bicycle traffic on it. The child sent away for a brochure. She and her mother might ride in tandem on a bicycle and breathe in the sea air. What could be better than a bicycle built for two? A bicycle was a good thing except that sometimes you saw things you did not want to, along the route. Poor people who were hungry and without houses, Witnesses of God with butterfly nets, or psychics with their useless bits of free-floating information about your past lives. They always wanted to tell you that you were once a peasant in Russia or a soldier in the Civil War, or that you had perished in the South Tower.

The mother was hoping that she and the child might live a long time together. When they pass the soothsayer in the bushes, the mother snarls, I was not a little girl in a babushka two centuries ago. Past lives are no comfort to her. I have this one little life, and the morbidity table, and the sea, and the sky, and the breeze, and the birds, and the bicycle, and the trees, and she opens her arms wide. Luckily the child is in the back to steer.

A SEA BREEZE blows and light pours through the chambers of the heart. Aunt Inga falls asleep.

THERE HAD BEEN a time once when the mother had a friend. Implausible as it seemed, they would go out to the bar on Ladies Night and have drinks with salt lining the rim in shapely glasses. Aside from these times with the friend, the mother had never drunk this drink, or any other. The friend had a small son, and she would bring him along to Ladies Night with her, and the mother would bring the child, and the children would play while the two mothers chatted and laughed and licked the salt and drank the drinks.

One night, the friend told the mother that even though she was only thirty-two, she had been diagnosed with a serious illness and that there was probably a gene from thousands of years ago that could be traced back to a small European village that was responsible for it. The mother, who had been a nurse before the child was born, had an inkling of what the gene might be, and she went home and prayed. Then she called her friend on the phone.

The mother apparently did not understand other people well, even the friend. The mother, without realizing it, had activated a peculiar mechanism in the friend, and by the time she hung up, she realized that there would be no more room for friendship. Never again would they go out to the bar for drinks and laugh and chat.

The mother thinks there are not enough human tears for certain kinds of sadness. When the mother sees the friend now, they wave to each other from a distance, but they are unable to cross the circle of salt each has drawn around the other.

From her memory bank now, she remembers the laugh that once came out of one of the ladies' mouth at the next table at Ladies Night. The laugh was coming out of the lady's mouth, but the mouth was taut and unmoving, and it seemed like it must be some sort of trick mouth or artificial mouth, but still sound came out of it, and words. When the mother asked her friend, the friend said casually that this was a result of the Plastic Surgery. She was very matter-of-fact about it, and the mother had liked that. You never knew what you might hear or see, she thought to herself. This was the very reason that the mother and child did not often go out to a restaurant or a bar. But it was different when she was with the friend. With the friend she felt protected.

LITTLE VORTICES BECAME big vortices, and the forward-going band of soldiers on horses began to turn in circles, faster and faster, and were carried up by the high and whirling winds into the sky where, frightened, they cried out for their mothers.

CECIL PETER CAME in breathlessly and announced that the New Age of Funnels had definitively arrived, there could be no doubt. He drew mad spirals with chalk on the path and shouted as if otherwise he would not be heard. It frightened the mother to see Cecil Peter like this. How many able-bodied men had been taken and how many were yet to be taken? he bellowed. He pointed to the flame perched on the mother's shoulder, which he could not brush away no matter how hard he tried. Watch out with that thing! Cecil Peter said. The mother looked around her. For now, though Cecil Peter carried on like mad, all seemed calm and bright.

EVEN THOUGH THE winds were all around, and near her ankles little vortices whirled, the mother went in search of a piano for the child. There was a simplicity and directness to the task that she liked very much. It was obvious to the mother that if you didn't learn to play the piano, your life would be less complete and your world diminished. She closed her eyes and began to envision the piano. She did not worry so much about its elegiac qualities: the dark mahogany or the ivory. Besides, hardly any keys were made of ivory anymore.

Before long, a piano became available in the town of Kinderhook, and the mother made her way to it. When the woman with the piano opened the door and saw the mother, it was as if she knew her, and she hurried her into the drawing room with scarcely a word. Drawing room is short for withdrawing room, and it was a place where ladies once went after dinner while the men retired elsewhere. In the drawing room, the woman played the nocturne now.

Later she explained that she had had a son once who loved the piano, but that he had lost his hands in the war. The keys had been refurbished with his finger bones, which the war had sent home in a box. His wedding ring was kept in a saucer on the piano top. The mother braced herself for the rest of the story, which had been foretold in the nocturne.

Eventually, the woman said, a world where her son could not play the piano became a world impossible for him to live in, and he left this life.

She began again to play.

A keyboard of bone makes a sound like no other.

IN THE AGE of Funnels, the Vortex Man ruled, and the mother felt a certain awe when she thought of him there at the center of the whirling world. Though she could not exactly see him, she liked to think of him as a large fellow, wearing a crown and seated on a throne at the core of the Vortex. Conversant with danger and the depths, but a ballast, nonetheless, a guide in dizzying times.

No matter what wind whipped around them, or what the spinning suggested, the Vortex Man remained calm, fixed, solid, jolly even. Such was the mystery of the Vortex, that while all whirled with unfathomable energy, at the center it was still and mild.

She loved him: part wizard, part professor, choreographer, director, smoke artist, misanthrope, a monster, some said. Now the mother was hearing things: Destroyed will be our remembrance from the earth, he bellowed. It was night. Hello, she called, but who could hear her?

Sometimes, she thought his face must seem patient, impassive, serene, in waiting. Sometimes she imagined it as condescending, bemused, intolerant, or worse. Other times, it was possible to see strength and wisdom. More and more, people attempted to make their way to him through high winds and treacherous terrain, braving tornadoes, hurricanes, sunspots, cyclones, black holes, and even ether, the fifth element, to be by his side.

NOW BEFORE HER in the seductive wind-ridden night, the wolf stood in dazzling moonlight. Its silver fur, its sleek, streamlined body. Its snout. The glowing head. If it was an apparition, it was a sly one—and masqueraded as real, and suggested only solidity and magnificence. There was an unearthly quiet. She stood in a thicket of emotion, blinded by its beauty. Something wild moved through her and she shuddered. She remembered when it had turned her long ago from a child into a woman overnight and carried her over the threshold. The wolf darted away now. If the child had been present, she might have named it Jet.

How remarkable is the world, and all its creatures, and the magnitude of the feeling. The force of arrival, and the force of departure. And the way the space, made radiant by the wolf, retained something of that charged, majestic quality, long after the wolf had passed.

conflagrations

THE NIGHT OIL Man came to check the propane tanks and hoses and lines that ran into the house because the mother was certain the house was about to explode. The Night Oil Man had claws that were black from oil and curved. He was muttering because it was the center of the night and bitter cold, and though he was on call, he clearly had other places to trundle toward at that hour. The child remained asleep in her little firebed, and the mother saw no use in waking her. In the flammable world, it was better for the child not to move a muscle, and if she was awake, she might toss Lamby into the air and they might go up in the conflagration. Earlier, the mother had moved the child's bed with the child and the lamb outside onto the grass under the stars into the garden. If the child woke up she would be scared, but it was better than being blown to smithereens, the mother reasoned.

When the Night Oil Man returned from his inspection, he was angry, for he found nothing at all that might have signaled trouble, no cause whatsoever for alarm, and no reason to justify his being taken away from the thick of his Night Oil wife and the night.

At that moment, he might have strangled the mother or violated her in some unspeakable way, at the very least, were it not for the child whom he saw all of a sudden outside asleep in the little makeshift trundle bed under the stars. Seeing her from the corner of his half-closed, blackened eye, he hunched over her, and cinders dropped from his hair. Instead of squatting above the mother with his night oil grunts, the house exploding around them, he smiled at the child and the lamb neatly tucked in.

At this time, no mention was made of the smell—not the smell of the Night Oil Man, nor the smell of the child. The child was wearing an amulet containing the aromatic Oil of Wintergreen, an oil known in the Valley for warding off bats.

The Night Oil Man patted the child on the head, sneered at the mother, and made his way back into the night.

Before he left, the mother pressed a spare amulet into his hand. Despite the reassurances of the Night Oil Man, the mother put up her umbrella and held vigil all night at the mouth of the house, and waited for day to come.

A SMART BOMB was falling directly at her, but she was smarter, and she caught it and she held it in her arms and she rocked it and soothed it, until it was detonated and rendered harmless. The mother appeared meek and mild on the outside, but she was fierce and brave inside. She wrapped the bomb in swaddling clothes: her eyeless, soulless, inanimate child—so that another child might live.

IT WAS JULY, and the Headless Horseman Fife and Drum Corps was making its way across the sheepfold. The children were Grinning for Cheese and playing Hoops and the Game of Graces. It was a splendor

to watch them on the lawn with their circles and ribbons and slender sticks, and the gaiety and laughter delighted the mother. On the
Croquet Lawn, a Punch and Judy show was being staged. Chimneyside
Tales were being told. There were games of Shuttlecock and Nine Pins.
Bells rang. Some who came were walking on stilts. Others were spit-
ting cherry pits, trying to go the distance. Little children were making
dolls of cornhusks. The child sat next to the loom with her lamb. On
the Bleaching Field, skirmishes between the Redcoats and the Patriots
were being reenacted. At noon the Freedom Pole was raised, and at
four the effigy of King George was strung up and hanged. The boys
beat it soundly with sticks.

Effigies in fact abounded in the Valley. It was a valley of fewer and
fewer men, and more and more, the women and children were asked
to chase figments out on the memory field.

After the last tale was told, the mother noticed that there was
some small calamity occurring in the bushes, and she rose to see
what the commotion was. It was not enough apparently that King
George had been strung up and hanged and beaten. Seven small
boys had dragged the entrails of the King furtively into a wooded
enclosure and were huddled around it. In the enclave, the boys were
beating and battering the very daylights out of what remained with
sticks.

In their fervor, they did not notice the mother. One boy who had
been appointed Guard, so as to ensure no one came to take away their
cache, had gotten caught up in the enthusiasm of the moment and had
deserted his post.

The mother, as she got nearer, felt as if she were seeing through
a veil something of the shrouded part of humanity, something at the
very heart of life's darkness. Mysterious are the days. Not far away,

a small faceless cornhusk doll reached for day, or her mother, now a husk as well.

The boys bent over the wreckage and worked at it with unbounded passion until even the entrails of King George were no more. The mother knew that soon enough, the boys too would be gone without a trace.

NEWS TRAVELED FAST of the teenager's drowning in the Palatine Lake at the edge of the village. No one knew why a healthy young man on a clear summer day should have drowned in a lake.

Hundreds of years before, the Palatines had come to this place to build boats, but they discovered that the wood was too heavy and their boats would not float.

The Great-Grandfathers in the Valley recalled the ice harvests. Next winter, a church will be built on the ice at the very place the boy bobbed up, and all will lift a crystal glass to him. The boy will not come back. He sank—no one knows why—like the Palatine's wood.

Wunderbar, the Palatines will exclaim, looking at the magnificent glittering monument to their drowned son, but after that, an irrepressible gloom will enter them, and their hearts will grow heavy and sink. They had not realized how much they missed the Rhine.

Come summer, the palace melted, they will wish they too could go home, but there is no way back. The lake where the boy drowned will seem to have closed up around him, but that is not exactly the case. The water will retain the information of the boy's body for a long, long time. And next to that memory, the people will stay.

THE ASTRONOMERS FOUND a new planet; it was situated in the Goldilocks Zone, they said. The Goldilocks Zone is a small, hospitable zone of possibility in the vast burning and freezing cosmos where life might actually be sustained. It is not too cold there; it is not too hot—it is just right.

The astronomers could barely contain their excitement for their new planet, and they named it Gliese, which sounded to the child like *glissade*, and she dreamt of water, the origin of life, and rock, and sandy beach, and a thousand streaming living organisms.

Water is so important—we can't survive without it, even for a few days. The mother thought of the world of thirst, and the work of human hands, and the miracle of water and desire.

THE CHILD DREAMT of a beautiful lake, and the mother dreamt right along with her. It's very blue and deep, the child said. It's fed by warm and cool springs. At night it is as smooth as silk, and no bats skim the surface.

There is a beach, and on the beach there are many children, and they always invite the child to play the circle game, or the game where they would say again and again the name of Marco Polo, the Venetian explorer who traveled the Silk Road.

The mother kept the child tethered to her by a silk strand of the most remarkable resiliency. There was a special gland in the mother's abdomen. The silk the mother produced was not only flexible, but it stretched to accommodate the farthest places the child would ever want to go. It was extremely durable, and as long as the child was alive, it would be there for her: smooth and strong, and with a lot of give.

Every night the child would spend a few seconds of dreamtime sharpening her teeth in preparation for the day when the silk tether would have to be severed. Only at the very end of the child's life would her teeth be sharp enough to break it, and by then it would be almost painless. For now, the mother reeled the child in, but gently, almost imperceptibly.

Marco Polo traveled the Silk Road and reached farther than any of his predecessors—venturing even beyond Mongolia into China. He passed through Armenia, Persia, and Afghanistan over the Pamirs and all along the Silk Road to China. He was the first traveler to trace a route across the whole longitude of Asia, naming and describing kingdom after kingdom.

The airport in Venice was named after Marco Polo, and one day, after the mother had died, the child would go there. On the outskirts of Venice is the Lago di Garda. It is said to be one of the most beautiful lakes in the world.

GLIESE'S STAR WAS cooler and smaller than the earth's sun, but it was also much closer. A year passed there in thirteen days. In the paper there was a drawing of a child standing on Gliese, and behind the child was an enormous sun setting. It is only 120 trillion miles away, the astronomers say, which is not really so far.

THE ANGELS OF Death flew over the boy's head. Three girls with their backpacks sat near his bed and took turns holding his hand. Surely, surely, he thought, if there was anyone out there, he would have heard, and it was by far the worst part of his short time on the planet that he had not made contact with those in other galaxies. Yes, he was only nine, and perhaps he would if he could only live a little bit longer. A number of distant civilizations could have developed and perished while flooding the cosmos with signals which have long since passed, or will never arrive in time.

Give me a sign, the boy says, and waits—and in the distance Gliese shines.

SEVEN ASTRONAUTS SLIPPED into unconsciousness—so said the report, and their bodies were whipped around in seats whose restraints had failed. The astronauts had continued to work as parts of the shuttle, including its wings, were falling off. Multiple failures of the smallest and largest sort had been set into motion. Helmets meant to protect them battered their skulls, but neither helmets nor spacesuits mattered in the end, for the crew had been subjected to five separate lethal events.

The breakup of the module and the crew's subsequent exposure to hypersonic entry conditions were not survivable. The mother thought of that word, "survivable," for a long time, and it filled her with awe.

Yes, the Gliese dreaming boy thought, there would be winds, shock waves, and other extreme conditions in the upper atmosphere. The craft went on a nauseating flat spin. Surely, the boy thought, the loss of cabin pressure had asphyxiated them within seconds.

THE PRODIGIOUS PUPPET-GOD and his Puppet Circus had come with its radical Utopian Vision in cardboard and cloth. There would be workshops, the poster said. At the workshops one might learn how to make effigies, father figures, giants for rallies, table heads for families, etc. Their mission: International Understanding through the Art of Puppetry. Their second mission: to honor all the disappearance when and where it occurred with small puppet actions. Tonight the Divine Reality Comedy was scheduled—and next week, the Everyday Domestic Resurrection Pageant. A smattering of applause could already be heard.

THE MOTHER BAKED an Appreciation Cake for Cecil Peter and his wife Wise Jean, who had saved the house once more, snuffing the flaming Swedish candelabra in the hall that she had left burning brightly while she went to the art exhibit at the child's school.

The child had done a drawing of an angel and had wrapped it in red cellophane, and in a certain light, it looked to the mother as if the angel were catching fire.

Angels can be weird, the child wrote under her picture, *but they have beauty inside.*

The mother did not particularly like to bake, but the cake for Cecil Peter and Wise Jean turned out to be exceptional. It took up the entire kitchen, having risen so high and grown so large, she told the child, because it had been made in gratitude, and its enormity surprised even the mother who, whenever possible, tried to keep her emotions in check. It grew so large that by the time Cecil Peter and Wise Jean and all their relations arrived, they had to cut themselves an entrance out of cake to get in, and all then understood well the importance of Cecil Peter and Wise Jean to the mother, for there is something definitive about an entrance made of cake.

The mother hugged Cecil Peter's wife Wise Jean, who, having dozed off in her chair, had seen the fire in a dream. When she woke, startled, she whispered to Cecil Peter to check on the house up the hill right away. Wise Jean, who was a volunteer firefighter, was blessed with extra vision, and Cecil Peter, who could always be counted on, nodded and was there in a flash.

Come let us dance, for time is short! The mother sang, and the child played the bone piano and the family danced like dervishes, and the house stood in all its glory, securely on the far side of the char.

When it was late and the family of Cecil Peter was sated and the child's shoes showed wear from all the dancing, they wrapped what remained of the cake in shining silver foil, and the child put a fancy red ribbon on top to signify the fire, and the consensus was it looked like a space capsule, and they lifted it into the mother's yellow wagon. It rivaled the moon in its brightness, and as it traveled down the hill, the moon did call to it, and the family of Cecil Peter and Wise Jean, including all their children and grandchildren and nieces and nephews and other relations, began their glinty way back down the hill.

What a night, the mother thought, and while they made their way home, she thought of Cecil Peter who fell from an apple tree as a child and hurt his arm; Cecil Peter who had been Apple Tree Cecil, then Falling Cecil, then Cecil of the Gangrene. Like a saint the mother shuddered; now he was Cecil the One-Armed Handy Man, filled with cake, and celebrated for saving the house from cinders again.

rose

FOR YEARS THE Queen stood in the darkest part of the garden. Over time she grew more and more weak as she reached for the sun. She had been a regal rose once—tight, beautifully shaped, upright, tall—and when the old cherry tree that shaded her finally fell down and light flooded in again, her natural beauty once more began to flourish.

The mother had always watched the Queen but had never given in to her many demands. She had observed her struggle with a kind of detachment, noting: tall, gangly, remote, prone to thrips. As the child followed her mother on her rounds, she could not help but notice that every other rose in the garden was lavished with attention: water, light, food, deer repellent, insecticidal soap, compost—but not the Queen.

The rose is the most precious of all flowers, the mother said, for out from its stem of thorns blossoms the sacred heart where the red cross of Mary's son is forming.

The mother remembered now the men who carried heavily thorned roses into battle, where they perished.

But what about the Queen? the child asked. Where is her food? Where is her compost? Why do you pay attention to everything but her? Even the Monkshood you have doted on, the child says. Why the Monkshood?

Because it is a living thing, it must be revered as such.

Yes, but what about the Queen then?

To tell you the truth, the mother says, I am a little ambivalent about the Queen. I have some ambivalence.

What's ambivalence?

It means you're not sure, the mother says.

Maybe that's why the bat came, the child said. Your ambivalence about the Queen.

The mother looked at her curiously.

How can you not be sure about a rose?

YOU GAVE ME too much medicine tonight, the child says.

No, I did not.

You did, you already gave me two teaspoons and now you have given me two teaspoons more. Before I know it, you will be forgetting the two plus two and giving me two teaspoons more. You must hear the ambulance going by. You must see the men in white coming now to the door. They are here to rescue me.

No.

You must have some ambivalence, the child said.

I SAW A bobcat in the grass. Or a mountain lion—some big cat, the mother sang. And a giant Blue Heron!

You did not, the child said. Without me? Not without me!

I did.

Remember the lake, and the Venetian explorer?

I do.

And the beautiful blue tether made of silk?

I do.

WHEN THE MOTHER gets dizzy and has to go upstairs for a minute to lie down, what is left is this: on one side of the kitchen door is the child alone finishing her papier-mâché vase, and on the other side of the door is the head of a squirrel on the welcome mat, the only part of the squirrel's poor anatomy Bunny Boy has left behind. There was a ferocity in ordinary things and suffering around every bend. The mother closed her eyes and saw its gray head blooming, crimson roses streaming from the neck.

The whirling mother upstairs recalls the green rain of frogs last spring. At night the night creatures had come and eaten off their legs, leaving their torsos for the mother to find the next morning, their hearts still beating.

But today while the mother is dizzy, the child does not know about the squirrel just feet away on the other side of the door, or the rain of frogs, or the real reason for the mother's vertigo—her beautiful vase is ready—and when she sees the mother descend the stairs restored, anything in the world can be weathered.

THE VIRGIN APPEARS to the mother and gestures for her to come into the forest, a place the mother loves to see the Lenten Rose.

The mother shakes her head no. I'm not ready yet.

The Virgin smiles and around her a little fawn prances.

Above all, the mother wanted more time. She sat at the edge of the dark wood and wept.

EVERYONE IN THE Valley knew that the man drank, and that sometimes his eldest daughter would come by to check on him, but lately she came less and less. During moments of enthusiasm, the man had kept a vegetable garden, but the garden now had gone to gloom, and if you did not know there had been one, it would have been better, because then it would just seem like another sad patch of land and not a garden that had been taken back while the man sat inside. It was particularly sad to think of that: the time when the man still had enthusiasms. The child felt that she understood something about the man who lived in the closed house and could never come out. The child heard that he liked to drink, and she left bottles of water by his door in case he got thirsty.

People in the Valley sometimes talked about him, but it was usually in the past tense, as if he were already dead. The man had been a baby in that house, and he had not begun drinking yet, and he was not already dead. Someone had cared for that baby. The Valley must have been even more beautiful then—so expansive, so wide, so pure, so many places to roam. Someone lifted the baby toward the impossibly blue sky. He had been taken out for fresh air and sunshine and walks. Once someone had taken a photograph. It showed a woman pushing a black perambulator, and inside it, protected from the sun, was the man.

A THREE-RING CIRCUS of sorts had made its way to the Spiegelpalais, and the child watched as it slowly assembled. Hildy the German Juggle Boy, Tavis the Silent Clown, and Rosalie's Racing Pigs—they were all there. Even the Dock Diving Dogs featuring Hanson's Hounds. In one corner a Mad Science Millennial Chess Match had been set up, and the child, who excelled at chess, sat down. And in the rafters above their heads, already caught in the kleig lights, the Flying Child.

THE CHILDREN FROM the city had come for the day, and the neighbors invited the mother and child over as well. The mother and child brought them a bouquet of roses from the cutting garden.

The children from the city had roller blades and wheelies and cell phones and did the newest dances, and they taught the child all the moves. They also talked about skyscrapers and anything else the child wanted to talk about. The child liked the oldest boy most, and his rollerblading, break dancing, and skyscraping stories. The day was hot and the children swam and played, and they liked each other very much. In the garden, the children from the city were astonished by all the heart-shaped leaves there were to find. When it was late in the day the children went into the barn, but the mother forbade the child to go up to the barn's loft with the oldest boy and his sisters.

She was unequivocal about it. There were days like that where the mother possessed such a terrible incandescence that the child had to look away from her or be burned up.

Under no circumstances may you go into that barn's loft, the mother had said, and the child thought to herself: bat face, fish emulsion, vapor—for vapor is what the mother was, everyone could see, and what the mother fought so hard against being.

Why must she be so unfair? the child wondered. Shouldn't she be allowed to do what other children did? Shouldn't—but before she could complete her thought, the boy, twelve, began to fall, and continued to fall in what seemed slow motion, through the barn, having stepped on a rotted floorboard.

Next a helicopter came and took the boy away creating its own weather: heat, wind. After that, back at home, every box started to look like a receptacle to hold a falling thing: the dollhouse with the roof that could be taken off, and the piano bench that opened, and the rain barrel.

Certain things, once seen, cannot be unseen. She felt the world had changed and it would not change back.

Now she cannot stop seeing boys falling from the rafters. She lines the floors with shoeboxes. Children are falling from the sky all the time. She lines the earth with anything soft. She looks out the window and sees the mother is in the garden. Cut flowers were the most beautiful, the mother said, because they live such a brief time.

THE MOTHER'S GARDEN unnerved some who saw it because it seemed to exist always on the edge of disarray, barely contained, at the place where any moment, it might be reclaimed. There was something exciting about this cusp to the mother, that place in the day where at any moment the garden might return to chaos, but did not. It held its own. Looking down from the second-floor window, she could see its architecture clearly: the boxwood, the dwarf spruce, the pergola, the birdbath, the circle of stones.

She loved what people thought to do with the small plots of earth allotted them. She was making a pattern, a design, a dwelling, a haven for their small time on earth—that much was clear from her perch.

Even though the child was holding a stone, she easily rose up two flights to the window where the mother looked out. The mother waved, and on the Aging Stage, she cast herself centuries into the future where she could see that a few rocks they had arranged in a circle remained. Another mother and child had unearthed them, and for a moment, they had intimations of a garden perhaps that once existed, and they reached back toward something ineffable but real, holding the rock the mother and child had once chosen for the circle and caressed.

Further even into the future, when the circle is taken apart and the rocks have scattered and gone back to the forest, something still of the mother and child has been left behind. For a moment it stayed in her, the full weight of the feeling, of what survives, a momentous feeling, a rock in the forest that someone had once held; it was a prolonged moment, momentous really, and then it was gone, and the mother resumed her day. Only figments of the feeling remained in her after that—flight, design.

Something about this comforted the mother. All effort passes, everything of us and who we were disappears as though we never existed, falling back into obscurity. What remained was perhaps an intimation.

The universe is drifting away from, not toward, the center of gravity, though no one knows why. It was all right. We will not understand it, not in a thousand human lifetimes.

THE CLOCK ARRIVED from the North Pole and the next day the mother swooned in the Children's Garden, and for minutes in a row she could not be revived. This terrified the child who stared at her mother even after she had gotten up and was talking again. She had left an indent of her body in the Lamb's Ear. Though the wooden box the clock had come in was shaped like a coffin, it was too narrow and too long to hold the mother comfortably. Still, it might have worked in a pinch. It lay now in the clover with her name and address on it.

THE BOYS WERE up at the top of the hill throwing Frisbees in the last moments before they were called back to the skirmish. When summoned, the boys rolled down the hill like little rag dolls. They tumbled into the vale where the mother and child tried to help them up. They had little smiles on their faces and they said they were just having a Tumble Down, and that they would get up soon, but not yet.

THE CAT LAY in the catmint and the bee was in the beehive and all seemed right with the world. The schoolchildren were in school, the painter was painting, the farmer was farming, and the drinker was pouring a drink. Only the lover, returned from the war, and renowned in the Valley for his love, was trying to find his way beyond it, because as his beloved had told him it was necessary for her to leave, and she would not be coming back.

The lover went out to the garden. He knelt down and it looked as if he might be praying or staking the tomatoes. There was a secret sadness in all things that he would never understand.

The mother walked in the Sterling Forest, recalling the story. It was a long walk, and ephemerals covered the forest floor. The next September, the beloved would be trapped in the burning tower, and she would not make it out.

A fox crossed the mother's path. The bee burrowed deeply into the heart of the rose.

dream

S LEEP WAS A biological imperative for every creature on earth. It
was essential because it did something the awake brain could not
do. The mother knew as she watched the sleeping child that the brain
was taking what it learned during the day and placing it into more
efficient storage regions. To consolidate all the memories, certain genes
up-regulated during sleep and got activated. Memory tracks were laid
out, categorized, distilled. The brain synthesized some memories during the day, but these memories were enclosed and concretized in the
night. Synaptic plasticity strengthened connections, and it was a beautiful thing. In the night, new inferences were drawn leading to insights
the next day.

The limbic system, she knew, amps up during REM sleep, and the
brain's emotion streams fear while rational thought is dormant. The
secondary Visual Cortex, striving to decipher, ricochets through it. In
REM sleep, a small region in the brain that paralyzes the body is alive.
Immobile, the streaming video of one's life passes by.

The mother loved the drama of the night. Had she not had the
child, she might have been a Scholar of Sleep, she thinks, a Professor

of Sleep, or at the least, a Sleep Advocate, tirelessly working for the Rights of Sleepers in the hospital's deepest recesses.

In the night, the sleepers might be closely monitored and observed, and experiments might be conducted. The object would be to scramble, detoxify, and discard old fears, so that there was room for new ones. Circadian rhythms could be measured by testing saliva. Open your mouth; sleep researchers might serenely take a swab.

Dreams take the day and cannibalize it, using real life, such as it is, for props and spare parts, defanging fear—making it stupid, useless, harmless. Close your eyes, says the mother to the child. Everything was changing. Sleep was the ingredient for change.

Melatonin, as a child grows, makes it harder and harder to go to sleep early—teenagers need as much sleep as toddlers but cannot begin their descent until midnight. It's science, the mother says.

The child loves the idea of it—that she one day might be the one to keep the night vigil, while her mother sleeps.

VOCABULARY IS SYNTHESIZED by the hippocampus early in the night. During slow-wave sleep, the motor skills of enunciation are processed. In slow-wave sleep, we practice our French. Auditory memories are encoded across all stages: the song the bird sang, the music from chorus, the piano lesson, the mother's voice.

Memories that are emotionally laden get processed during REM sleep: the mother upstairs dizzy, for instance, or the way more and more, the Grandmother from the North Pole seems to tip away from them on her axis.

The more you learn during the day, the more you need to sleep at night, and earlier and earlier the mother and the child grew sleepy.

A WOLF DRESSED in a tuxedo with the moon under its feet, and on its head a crown of twelve stars, rose in the sky. What to make of this wolf in a prom outfit surrounded by a halo of stars? the mother wondered. Emblazoned behind him was Jupiter, larger than it had ever been, closer to the earth than in all recorded time.

Next a red dragon with seven heads and ten horns and diadems appeared in the west. Its tail swept away a third of the stars in the sky and hauled them down to the earth.

And after that in the east: Mr. Min. How are you doing, Mr. Min? He waves to her and motions to the box he holds.

What an unusual night, the mother thought to herself.

When the visitations were over, she sloshed through stars, back to the house, and wiped the florescence off her feet before entering the room where the child was sound asleep, dreaming. The wolf stood over the child's bed. Sleep spindles and the presence of Complex K told the mother that the child would not be waking for some time yet.

THE NEXT MORNING, Mr. Min appeared again, tapping the mother on the shoulder. What is it, Mr. Min? He asks if he might take the bats that are asleep beneath the mother's shutters. Be my guest, the mother says. Curled into small balls, he plunks them in a bowl; there must have been a hundred. My son, he says, he loves them very much.

Come, Mr. Min, and pluck the sleeping bats, the mother whispered. Come and pluck my sleeping bats from underneath the shutters for your son. He smiles and is gone. Gone to pluck the bats and plunk them in a bowl. His son, he loves them very much.

As THEIR FRIEND down the road grew smaller inside the dark house, the hole outside grew larger and deeper. Mute boulders had been excavated and served as a reminder of the severity and silence at the heart of the earth. Just when it seemed the great cavity could not get any bigger or deeper, it was lined with concrete. At the time the concrete was still wet, the man inside could still walk a short distance, and he went out into the day with his wife and infant son so that they could press their hands into the smooth wet surface and make a permanent imprint of their lives together. A little while after that, the hole lined with cement, along with the family's hands, was filled with water.

The man's wife dips the baby again and again into the blue, and the baby squeals with delight. Often the priest comes now to talk with the man, and afterwards the priest walks out to the cement cavity filled with water where the woman and baby are waiting.

THE PAINTER TOLD the child: she remembered that after her father died, she would watch the train each day on the horizon depart at 9 AM, and that she could still see it crossing the horizon at noon, that was how vast the world was, and it was not until 3 that the train disappeared entirely. That was what life was like on the Plains. I was a small, magical girl, she said, with a wand that could not save my father; he clutched his heart, and the world was flat and wide and the train was so tiny and the horizon was a hovering stripe.

For years she painted the blue horizon, multiplied. The painter takes the child's hand and they move through rooms and rooms of stripes. It took a long time—almost my whole life, but finally I found it: the grid; and the child saw stripes that moved back and forth and also up and down. And that is what I wanted all along.

The Mourning Party moves along the grid now to the Spiegelpalais. It's a strange diagonal step we take, they say, strangely cheerful, but a bit bewildered, the invisible father leading the way.

MR. MIN APPEARS again, some miles away. He has come with his cages to catch the woodchucks because woodchucks, Aunt Eloise says, are the kind of creatures that can take down a whole barn if you let them. How many can you catch in those Have a Heart Traps? Uncle Lars asks.

Oh it depends, says Mr. Min. The lady said to come and trap them. The lady says she is at her wit's end.

How much to catch them? Uncle Lars asks.

Fifteen dollars each, says Mr. Min.

Uncle Lars can't complain.

Aunt Eloise had called to have Mr. Min come and trap the varmints in his very nice Have a Heart Traps and take them with him, but when the varmints were caught, Aunt Eloise was away.

In the cage, the woodchuck is making a tunneling motion. After a while, exhausted, it stops. Uncle Lars looks at the large face of the creature that fills the cage. On the radio someone is saying the war is botched, there is no way to make any good of it.

Mr. Min is getting out of his truck; he's brought along his grown-up son—he loves him very much. Mr. Min, where have you been? The woodchuck has been in here a long time, Uncle Lars says, pointing to the cage, and with that Uncle Lars hands the cage to Mr. Min.

What will you do with him now? Uncle Lars asks.

I will let him out in a green, green field, some miles away from here, says Mr. Min.

And what happens out there? Uncle Lars asks, lighting his pipe.

Out there? says Mr. Min.

Out there, says Uncle Lars.

Out there he will have no place to go. The others will shun him. And eventually he will die.

Uncle Lars blows some smoke into the cage, and thinks awhile.

How much would it cost to let that woodchuck go? asks Uncle Lars.

Right here?

Uncle Lars looks around and nods.

Fifteen dollars, Mr. Min whispers. On one condition.

Yes?

You won't tell the lady.

Uncle Lars winks.

And that is what it was like with Uncle Lars and why the child loved him most. He always asked one question extra.

UNCLE LARS SAYS the soldiers on the green, green grass are only children. Boys in helmets, they might easily have been playing football. When day is done someone throws a last ball, and they take off their helmets, then lie awhile on the green, green grass and fall asleep. They are not expendable fodder this time. Their lives are not sacrificed for a few meters of land.

THE LADY CALLS Mr. Min one day to retrieve his cages. She is pleased with how many woodchuck faces she has seen, and she is happy that so many have been released into a green, green field far away. She has seen not hide nor hair, she says, since Mr. Min has been on the case. She shakes his hand goodbye. In the driveway, she sees a large, slumped shape in the front seat of his truck. I see you have brought your dog today, Aunt Eloise says.

No, Mr. Min says, that is my son. I love him very much.

THE CHILD STANDS on a vacant stage bathed in white light and makes her petition to the Grandmother from the North Pole. I wish you were here, she whispers. I feel in my body you are due. Light floods the child. It's the distances that make it so hard. I need you so much closer, she says. She stands for a moment longer, all alone, holding her box of melting snow.

THE ICE LOSS was contiguous to the Bone Loss. There is a sadness that is spreading. The Grandmother from the North Pole, on the move, leads the delegation that brought the consensus of Ice Loss and Bone Loss to the President. The President said he did not believe in the loss, and he walked to his jet plane. The Grandmother from the North Pole blocked the entry to the jet and offered her needle-thin arm to him as proof, and she jutted her pointy hip at him, and then her even pointier other hip. No one give up the ship, she cried, and they moved into the White House and waited for the President to change his mind. Hour after hour they wait. He sits in the rose garden in the dark holding his mother's ice-cold hand.

He will ruin the whole planet if you let him, his mother says.

EVERYTHING WAS RETURNING to funnels and everywhere there was proof of it, the Grandmother from the North Pole told the child.

Just look around. The Grandmother thought that in this new Age of Funnels, Presidents should be made to take lie detector tests on a regular basis, and along with all the other pledges, they would be required to take the Doctor's Oath: *First Do No Harm.*

THE MOTHER WARNED the child that they would be seeing unusual things, and at the H sign, she seemed to tremble. The mother had said that once she possessed a nurse's demeanor, but that the nurse's demeanor had left her. The child in turn thought that once you have a nurse's demeanor, it never leaves you entirely. The H, the child surmised, must stand for Hospital, as they walked toward the front door. Earlier in the day, the child had heard the word distend—but she did not know what it could mean—then she heard the word lesion, and then the word occult. The psychic landscape grew desolate. What next? the mother wondered. She did a little dance for the child in the reception area. The child was not used to seeing her mother this way.

The child noticed how the letter H was shaped. A bridge united two parallel lines, which would otherwise never meet. It calmed the child to carry the image of the letter H in her head as they now ascended a white elevator.

Upstairs, their friend, all bones, was curled nearly into a complete circle now.

The mother said that she had not meant that the child see this so soon: eventually, yes, but not today. She unfolds the picture of the gallbladder the man had drawn on a small paper a few months before. They had thought that that had been the problem. But the doctors had been 100% wrong. (She had gotten that from the child: "100 percent.") The gallbladder had nothing to do with it.

While the mother sits at the man's bedside, the boy wanders down the hallway. On her walk, the child sees a small boy who had swallowed a dime holding up the extracted coin in a glass jar. In another room, a blue light is being shone on the abdomen of someone's grandmother. In a third room, behind drawn curtains, a father sobs. The mother had told the child that when she was still a nurse, she once saw the doctors drill through a small skull. She never forgot that. The mother remembered bits of bone flying in the room.

Once long ago, they had to return the heart to a child's body after they had repaired it, stitching him back together as neatly as they could. Though he was her brother and his name was Lars, everyone who saw him called him Frankenstein, but at least he was alive.

When the child returns, she and the mother stand before the body of the man—what body there is—so many bones on a plate, a continually warping harp. The man is a magnificent and terrible instrument from which music now originates.

When the child is dismissed again, she continues her long walk down the hall. There is an old man asking for his mother; a child in a paper dress holding hands with another child in a paper dress; there is a boy gasping in blue diamonded pajamas; a belly dancing lady; a child with a red balloon; a black cat at the foot of a bed. The child walks and walks, and it seems as if the walk might go on forever down this endlessly elongating hall, but then all of a sudden she is at the last door.

When she looks in, she sees it is the Virgin, resplendent in a mantle of blue, standing in a grotto, next to a waterfall.

THE CHILD KNEW things it was impossible to account for, and this frightened the mother, for she feared, having already learned the lessons this life had to offer, that she would be taken away. Now the child is holding a bird in her hand like a statue at Versailles, and she has a star at the top of her head. In dreams, the child stacks the crypts of Europe and she tells the mother not to worry; it makes a swift and neat pile. She pulls a curtain or a tarp over them, and she assures her mother there is really nothing there to fear. But the mother fears the tarp and the martyrs that are quite obviously underneath it. Why are they calling her? And the flagellation, and the starvation, and the levitations, and the seven states of grace, and the Virgin and the fawn waiting in the wings, and the incense lantern and the smoke . . .

BUT FOR THE smoke, so dense, so dark, they might have jumped into that blue lake named for the explorer and survived. It's very deep. The mother is dreaming. And no bats skim the surface.

IN THE MORNING, the child announced that she was going to cut her hair and donate it to the wig for the Virgin. This frightened the mother who did not understand why the Virgin needed a wig. She remembered the child's first official haircut, and she wondered how in this brief passage it had come to this. The child's hair had fallen from a great height that day, an unspeakably dark cascade, and the mother had been there to catch it. She wanted to hold the child now by a long braid, a different tether altogether, and keep her close to her, but already the mother knew that she was no match for the Virgin, who waited patiently in the alcove for the plaits.

THE CHILD HAD made up her own language and was now speaking it in front of the mirror. What if she was speaking in tongues? the mother worried. In a bag with a target on it at the end of the child's bed slept the hair to be given to the Virgin for a wig. The mother feared that the child was going to be taken and turned into a saint, and she did not want the life of a saint for the child. The Virgin was coming to get her—the one the mother was asked only to protect. The child was too young to be taken away or to become a saint. The mother could not bear the idea of the tears of blood, or the flagellations, or the visions. For a moment she thought of Saint Stephen, the first martyr, holding an open book that supported three rocks, the instruments of his martyrdom. Maybe she should take the target bag while the child was sleeping. Life was already hard enough.

The mother was determined not to let these intimations get the best of her—she would not be intimidated. She would stand up to all the angels with their herald horns, and all the lacerated saints, and the Virgin herself if it came to that. During Mass, she kept the child close to her side to protect her from the endless petitions, the bombardments of light, the bats, the exactitudes and beatitudes and plentitudes and indulgences, and during Communion she implored the three-personed God to leave the child alone.

Each week when the Mass was ended, she hurried down the aisle and she put up her black umbrella to shield the child from the Light of Christ. They were alive, and not in any way would they be pulled to the other side. The people of the congregation thought that the mother had gone mad since the appearance of the bat, but the mother didn't care what they thought.

CECIL PETER HAD always said to place human hair on the sills at night for protection, and the mother now consented. But at night, she thought she could hear someone taking it away and collecting it in a bag.

THE SOLDIERS DRAG their rucksacks through the mournful terrain. Aspects of the slain, still intact, follow them, the remnants of their day. Perhaps it is they who have come in the night, having mistaken the child's hair for that of their German maidens.

THE MOTHER'S HAIR lines one of the small tents at the Spiegelpalais used for sheltering the sleeping Aunt Inga. It breathes well, all agree, and holds up in every weather. Aunt Inga dreams peacefully. And a velvet curtain blows in the breeze.

IN ONE CORNER of the tent where Aunt Inga slept, the mother thought she saw a particularly blue patch, and she went to it and stood there a long time, and the berries fell dull and sweet into the bucket. Row after row of dusty silver blue berries called to her. For a moment the invisible God was made visible.

She had picked berries there forever, it seemed. She thought of her childhood now: a beautiful blue mountain seen through the parted black curtains. Lars, Anders, Ingmar, Sven, and baby Inga. She loved the sound as the berries fell—dull and sweet into the bucket.

AFTER THE OTHERS had left she and the baby remained behind. She wanted to swaddle her, here among the blueberry bushes, to protect her, her little sister. It was getting late.

Each beat of the heart is triggered by a surge of calcium ions that cause millions of overlapping filaments in a heart cell to pull against each other and contract. What would happen, she wonders, if white dwarfs—small, dense, dying stars, emitting axions, could attach their luminescence to stricken cells? What a beautiful world that would be, the mother thought, and bathed in moonlight and still holding the baby, she fell asleep.

SHE STOOD HIGH, high up atop those towers now and looked out. It was one of her favorite spots in the world. When the mother was pregnant with the child she would often come and admire the world which was so blue and so wide. She was tired, having come directly from the night shift, but the view always soothed, and the height.

blue

THE MOTHER UNDERSTOOD more than most about the ways that people got sick and then got better, or got sick and then continued to get more sick, because of course she had been a nurse. In the neo-natal unit where the mother was often stationed, there were always many blue palm-of-the-hand babies to nurse.

Sometimes the child wished they could keep one of those babies, but she worried that it would need a lot of attention and she would lose her mother to it and she might end up hating the little palm-of-the-hand baby who needed only love. The child was so lonely some days that even a little sick palm-of-the-hand baby would do. She didn't think the mother could take care of two children anyway, though it would be nice to have a little company. She would make the baby little dolls out of hollyhocks. She would make a tiny doll bed out of a walnut and some straw.

If the baby got sick, the mother would know what to do, how to wrap it up, and if it stopped breathing and turned blue, she could always put it under grow lights on stainless steel trays where it could be warmed, and the mother would breathe on it for extra protection and she would make it a tent out of her hair like the tent for Aunt Inga.

THE BOY IN Room 11 had been the only child of the three to survive the operation. Even though they had had wheelchair races in the halls in the days before, the other two children had died. When the boy who survived got home and was well on his way to recovery, he said, now I must live for three people, and an unimaginable darkness entered him.

The Boy in Room 11 was always a fighter, his mother said, but since having his chest opened and the blood field exposed to air, something had changed. He lived now in constant terror of invasions and contagions: attackers, burglars, rapists—those who might violate, dismember, or take something away.

After the surgery, the mother had handed the boy a glass hammer. She wondered now how things might have turned out if instead of a hammer she had handed him a sapling; instead of a sword, she had handed him a raft; instead of a stone—a pear, or a guitar, or a thread.

NO ONE COULD tolerate the girl in the newspaper's death from an undiagnosed, treatable form of diabetes after her parents chose to pray for her rather than take her to the doctor. There was too little insulin in her body, the autopsy said, but when opened up, all that could be seen was that she was overflowing with prayer. The prayers could be examined and dissected, but the God had already exited the body, leaving behind the wreckage. After the autopsy, the child's sweetened organs were placed in a glass jar as a lesson for all.

When the girl in the newspaper at last finds her way out of the jar, she is miniscule, a fetus in fact, but all her organs are back, and she crawls to the best of her ability to her parents and nestles in the crook of her father's arm awhile, and then moves back to her mother where it had all begun, and burrows herself into the porch of her ear.

Who's there? the mother whispers.

At the Spiegelpalais, a little master of ceremonies appears from beneath a tent flap: once I saw a deer no more than twelve inches tall emerge from underneath a rhubarb leaf, somewhere in the Andes, and I caught it and brought it back for you to see today here on display! And he places the tiny deer on a little amber block, said to be a million years old.

The little master is lonely even now, surrounded by Atlas the Dwarf, Quasimodo, the Half Man–Half Woman, and the Bearded Lady. He's come now to fetch the little fetus girl, the child says.

Who's there?

The praying mother feels more and more as if she is being called, but by whom she does not know. She experiences a strange somber sound in her left ear—a plaintive sound that no matter what will not leave her now. Those who remember the girl in the jar, and the mother standing over her, look on now with a special pity reserved for a certain elevated category of tragedy. Who's there?

The sweetened fetus falls into unconsciousness. The mother bows her head.

DOWN THE HALL they were dislocating the football playing boy's hip in order to shave the bone, which was growing like a tree inside him. But the muscles of a boy who plays football are strong, and so are the bones, and it took a long time to pry the bone from its socket. When they were finished prying and shaving, they put big screws in to hold the hip together.

IN ROOM 13 a man had been diagnosed with a condition character-ized by periods of irresistible sleep, and more and more, the irresistible sleep overcomes the man. Sleep-induced paralysis makes it impossible for him to move. Frozen, he awaits reanimation. Sometimes the man is not 100 percent asleep, but somewhere in between. Strong emotion makes the man's body go still—they call it the Stillness—and at this time, he is both somewhat awake and somewhat asleep.

The part of the man's brain that maintains wakefulness is now being stimulated in the room adjacent to where another man is shrink-ing into a boy. When the legs turn blue, she will know it is almost over for him. The mother tries calling her friend the Blue Man now in an attempt to prepare herself.

Around almost every corner whole lives, hanging in abeyance, await transformation.

A powerful sedative known as the date elixir is being administered to the man in Room 13. Among daters it is known to cause dates to become drowsy and consent to a variety of acts they might not otherwise.

For reasons unknown, the date elixir seems to revive the man in Room 13, which is the exact reverse of what it does for the dates. Beside him, in the chamber, a herd of anesthetized women slumber, but not the formerly sleeping man, who steps blithely, no one knows why, over them.

The mother has heard that in the case of the Seven Sleeping Sisters, seven single-cell parasites entered their bodies, and when these bodies encountered the Sleeping Sickness parasites, the single sleeping cells would change shape, and then change shape again, so they were in disguise and the sisters' bodies could never recognize them. The Seven Sleeping Sisters slept soundly now in the Spiegelpalais, along with the dreamers in the Blue Ward, where those who are blue due to the smoke inhalation are kept.

As the mother has always maintained, there are any number of miracles that have always happened, are happening now, and will continue to happen in the hospital. It was what drew her to it in the first place.

THE CHILD HAD wandered up to the Dementia Unit where Oscar the Death Cat, who had the uncanny ability to predict the exact moment of death, was said to roam. The dying, right before death, turn a bluish color, the child had heard. Oscar is never wrong, the nurses say, as they make their rounds. The child follows Oscar as he passes those with days to live and moves to the one with only hours, drawn to the imminence. He arrives a few hours before death; he leaves a few minutes after.

Never underestimate the power of cats. They are tuned permanently to Alpha, the psychic station—divination is their gift; witches love them. The metabolism as it changes has an unmistakable aura. Who knows what Oscar gleans from the dying? Perhaps he assumes the soul into his corporeal being for comfort. Perhaps he is the barge from one shore to the next. Those who can no longer move open their arms, miraculously. Stop here, they implore. Those, too far gone to speak, somehow manage to say, stay with me, with utter clarity. Oscar, Oscar don't pass me by again today, the woman begs in a direct address. And yes, the child notices, her legs do seem to have a bluish tinge.

SHE TRIED TO breathe. Many times she had stood high up and looked out, atop those tall windy towers. A window on the world—she gasped for air. Cecil Peter said not to worry—it was only the Blue Madness passing through her.

tooth

Look how blue, the Bay of Fundy! The Grandmother from the North Pole tells the child that the Bay of Fundy is an extremely beautiful and environmentally fragile part of the coastline, and she brings it up on the screen. There, the Grandmother from the North Pole says, she has seen whales. Only four hundred right whales exist in the Northern Hemisphere, and that is where they congregate and she counts them.

Once, blue whales filled every ocean on earth, the Grandmother laments. Now there are only a few, and she awaits their blue visitation. They are so enormous that when they come, she will see them easily from her outpost at the North Pole.

Whales sing above the frequency of the human threshold for sound. Their song moves through the speed of water four times faster than in air. Yes Sven, once blue whales filled every ocean on earth. Now she puts her ear to the emptied ocean. A melancholy sound, a dirge can be heard if nothing else.

Uncle Sven tried his whole life to catch a whale to no avail. All his life he held 180 decibels next to his puny chest. What can withstand

the navy's sonar? Uncle Sven reasoned from his infinitesimal ship. He
tried to make a noise that would stop the whale—*Little Sven, you
know better.* All his life he tried. Sven, his one small soul suspended,
laments. The muting effects of water. Little Sven, the Grandmother
from the North Pole says, you know so much better than that.

The blue whale can accurately map the soul, though the soul of the
sea is out of reach. Sven turns on his little sonar. It has been said that
a blue whale can build in its mind's eye a picture of the entire ocean
simply by sending out a sound and registering its echo.

The Grandmother from the North Pole knows that the blue
whales killed by whalers can never be weighed whole. The heart
alone is over a thousand pounds. Extracted, it sings above the human
threshold.

A BLUE MULTITUDE of children just back from the ocean huddle
around the mother—Lars, Bibi, Ingmar, Anders, Sven, and baby
Inga—and she sings to them a whale song and pats their heads.

It is believed to be the largest animal ever to have lived.

THE MOTHER THOUGHT it was one of the great unspoken strange-
nesses—the inaccessibility of the present—where the child ran toward
her on the green grass. So coltish, that day on the lawn. The image
indelible, but also vulnerable and porous, permeable, open to bruising
or injury. And a medium girl here now, and at the same time a baby in
her carriage under the same tree and a toddler toddling on the green
grass and a teenager, suddenly sullen, and a grown woman now walking toward her mother who has not aged.

Everything was fluid, nothing was fixed, nothing was in the
moment, in the instant—or by the time the instant was upon her, as it

approached without notice, it was already gone, had in fact serenely passed by without pause or fanfare. How incidental and how momentous at the same time.

On the Aging Stage the child is a toddler, or the mother is a child, and the Grandmother from the North Pole is young again. Only to die. Even the future seems in memorial, taking on an eerie burnished quality as if it has already passed. Every moment frays and unravels. The child's child running in the grass. The mother picks her up, but already her skull is covered with moss.

These errant visions. This striving on the Aging Stage after multiple girls in the grass, the Easter egg hunt, the croquet on the lawn, the time of the Communion, or the day not yet here, when the violinist will show up and open his case, shaped like a little lady, and play. Or the soft sutures, furrowing suddenly the grass where they will lay Bunny Boy to rest one day.

NOT SO FAST, Bunny Boy says. The concrete rabbit in purple garments plays a herald horn. Not quite so fast.

TO TAKE THE heart out and fix it, they had to break the child's sternum. The heart taken from Uncle Lars floated above the mother's head like a red balloon, and she followed it for the duration of the surgery, wherever it led her. She was just a girl, and she wandered over hill and vale and grassy slope.

How nice to see you, Mr. Min! What are you doing here? He too has been following the red balloon, he says, along with his son. But the mother must have gotten confused, for no Mr. Min was with Uncle Lars then when he was a boy in Minnesota, and Uncle Lars was all grown, and his heart had been put back a long time ago now.

HUMAN BREATH IS pressed through the valve—the origin of music. *My Darkling*, the mother whispers, petting the child's head. Tears and seawater wash the valve clean.

BUT WHAT IF time was all around them and they were swimming immersed in it? What if the past hadn't vanished and the future didn't eradicate? And it swirled everywhere around them?

The Vortex Man lifted his head and seemed to smile.

What if Oblivion did not pull at them, did not summon them; what if it just stayed in its place, somewhere offstage, or waited in the wings of Uncle Ingmar's shadow theater a little while longer?

UNCLE INGMAR PHONED to say that the other Ingmar—the great filmmaker—had died, and with that, a small essential light in Uncle Ingmar went out forever. He felt he was the director's invention, the director's confection, and now Uncle Ingmar wondered what was left for him. Film was more solid, Uncle Ingmar always said, and reality more remote.

A part of Uncle Ingmar was disappearing now, unable to sustain himself without the other Ingmar. And most fittingly, with that, Uncle Ingmar's cell phone connection went dead. The mother was not concerned, for she knew Uncle Ingmar would turn up like every year—with the snow.

CECIL PETER SAID that the Age of Funnels always brought madness when it returned, and this time would be no exception. In the pastures the mad cows lowed, and in the rafters the bats chittered, and on the horizon the vanishing men increasingly lost their way and their teeth, and the women, dizzy, swooned a little, and small vortices followed them wherever they went.

The child too was losing teeth. The Toothless Wonder worked hard trying to get the teeth from the mouth of the child, but the mother no longer opened the door. The mother recalls when the child lost her first tooth, and that for a long time she carried it around with her everywhere in her pocket. It was something wonderful to hold: smooth and sure and white—a trinket extracted from the great whirling of time, which spun around her. In the increasingly remote place the mother inhabited, she could carry a tooth, and it served as a souvenir and a talisman and a way through.

More and more the mother found herself in an interim place. She could not get herself to cross over, but neither could she go back. On such days, the tooth was just the thing.

EVERYWHERE THE MOTHER went, she carried the first tooth in her pocket, but one day when she went to feel for it, the first tooth was gone. She was certain she had had it still in the blustery garden, and in the root cellar, and in the smokehouse, so she must have dropped it, she reasoned, in the parking lot of the Stop & Shop.

At night the mother went out into the supermarket parking lot and divided it methodically into quadrants, then took out her broom and carefully began to sweep, the child all the while asleep in her car seat.

The anguished mother, night after night, lights the lamp, sweeps the macadam, and weeps. Never again, she vows, shall she take a tooth, detached from the child's head, out to the Super Stop & Shop.

IN THE BLUE Park, the Children of the Spectrum feared the sliding pond. They did not care that a box of sparkle awaited them at the bottom. Heights frightened them. The laws of gravity frightened them. They traversed an arc, a continuum that moved from cautious to more cautious to most cautious, from less fearful, to mildly fearful, to paralyzed with fear. Fear of the sliding pond can be attributed to the abnormality in chromosome 15, some members of the community speculate. Yes, and there is always the possibility of Fragile X Syndrome, the mother says.

Take care when walking between the frogs after the rain in spring. Take care when holding the too-soft hand of your grandmother. The Children of the Spectrum moved along a trajectory of carefulness. The mother thought it wouldn't hurt for more children to be more cautious and less careless in all things.

Blue, removed, fearful of the sliding pond, the child didn't mind; the child liked the Children of the Spectrum. She did not want to give them the Horse Cure or the Smiling Cure or the Chess Cure like others did. She would sit, if they came, a long time by their sides.

I N THE FACE of the Blue Madness, she thought of the mother she
might have turned out to be in the great Midwest with an apron full
of palm-of-the-hand babies and wee ones, and how when the funnels
came up, she would just stand there with the whole clan until the very
last moment. The funnel would be coming right toward them, and
she'd open the trapdoor every time with only seconds to spare.

Despite the child and all the palm-of-the-hand babies, of which
there are many, the mother's solitude is cosmic: a force field, and
everything is engulfed by it. She was hypnotized by the funnels, she'd
say—all that swirling, and she would tilt the babies' heads toward the
green light, and she would hold the child's hand tightly.

In the face of the whirling world, the mother, with resolve,
thought maybe they could tack a few things down, or make catego-
ries, or make lists in order to better manage the chaos and the solitude, which were mounting, and this the child approved of, and the
mother felt soothed. She closed her eyes and behind them a wall of
rain began to fall.

Tears

The mother recalls the magnetic water city—but whether she had produced it with her tears, or it had produced her, she could not say for

sure. For the weeks she was there, she never stopped weeping. She recalls water flooding the streets, water turning the girls round and round—and those extravagant fountains. If the insatiable city had produced her, a weeping woman, in a place reliant on weeping for its existence, so be it.

She thought of the painter Titian, and she thought of the painter Tintoretto, and she thought of the Lago di Garda. Perhaps she was part of a larger design she would never see or understand.

All she knew was that she shimmered.

Some days, the mother had the distinct feeling that she had been painted into this ravishing scene, thousands of years earlier, where she had been left to wait. Only today, in the small library, when the child turns the large beautiful pages of the art book, running her hand over the painting, and murmuring says, *look!* does the mother come to life.

Look!

The people who had assembled in the meadow gasped. The very letters that spelled Spiegelpalais above the mirrored tent seemed to have caught fire. The children climbed the fire truck's ladder, rung by rung by rung.

At Last the Shark

At last the shark, suspended in a vitrine of formaldehyde, had arrived. It had made its way from across the ocean to the Valley and would remain at the Spiegelpalais for an undisclosed period of time. Many who flocked to the verdant Valley in summer came to view the shark suspended in liquid.

When you visit the shark, the paper had advised, visit it with an open mind. It was meant to be viewed as a work of art, and it was titled The Physical Impossibility of Death in the Mind of Someone Living. The mother and child walked gingerly into the tent. A blue light filled them. In the large tank, nothing moved. The child pressed her hand to the place of the shark's mouth.

Everything in the world is a substitute for every other thing in the world. Today the mother was quite certain that whatever had once happened to her, whatever she had survived, whatever had brought her here to the Valley, whatever allowed for this—the Spiegelpalais, the child's hand in hers, the other hand of the child in the shark's mouth, the shark suspended in its glass case—she was inordinately lucky. Like the shark, she was floating too, outside time, outside space, at the mercy of a merciful universe.

The child thought this was by far the best art show she had ever been to.

A human skull encrusted with diamonds was promised at the Spiegelpalais next.

Next

At the edge of the meadow, a battalion of small children carry a heavy fire hose and put out the fire that has unexpectedly begun in the left ventricle.

Divinity Basket

She wanted to order the man who was her friend a Divinity Basket, with flowers as white as the resurrection, but in all the Valley, there were no white flowers to be had.

Since when are there no white flowers in summer? she wanted to ask the florist on the phone. Since when is a town bereft of flowers in summer? Summer, he says, and even though he is a small businessman, his voice drifts, and he says summer as if it is a question. Yes it is summer, the mother states plainly.

All of the flowers the town possessed within its borders had already been used up on the man who had once shown her the drawing of the gallbladder, the florist tells her.

Now the season will not hold. The path she walks slips back into winter. Like those moving paths in the airport, she now seemed to be moving without taking a single step, toward the funeral home, a place she does not want to go in such a hurry. She worried that cold and flowerless, she would arrive too quickly now to her destination. With or without flowers, the family must arrive to greet the body first.

Standing outside in the chill, the mother thought maybe they should all let up on the flowers a little. Maybe he will suffocate under so many flowers. In the end he was as thin and light as a harp, and perhaps not able to withstand the weight of so many flowers. Had anyone thought of that?

Blind

Before she went blind at the Spiegelpalais, the artist had spent a good deal of time scouring the Valley, traversing both the hills and vales in search of a cardinal that had met its end. It was against the law to shoot or otherwise harm a songbird of any sort for any reason in the Valley, and as a result, each day the artist's search had grown more and more desperate, as a cardinal was imperative to her next work of art. Though she had ordered hundreds of artificial cardinals over the Internet, not a single one of those cardinals as it turned out would do. She put out an announcement: if anyone in the Valley happens to find a dead cardinal on the path, et cetera.

Awhile back, Jean Audubon, having captured a Golden Eagle, tried to smoke it to death by setting a coal fire under it and putting it in a closet and covering it with a blanket, but four hours later when he checked, what he saw was an eagle glaring back at him, *bonjour!* The next day, he added sulfur to the rekindled fire, and still after many more hours, a glaring, living bird greeted him. Finally he had to resort to five stilettos through the heart, all the while being careful not to ruffle too many feathers.

Don't forget that Audubon was French, and to look at a bird that hard, and to draw and paint it feather by feather by feather, was to remove five stilettos from its heart and bring it back to life five times over, the mother thought. If you are Audubon, the moral is that try as you may, you cannot kill a Golden Eagle. It is still there; it is always there, radiant and waiting when the mother and child open the book.

Imagine then that astounding red bouquet brought to the door by the artist's aging feline, Birdy Boy. Incredulous, the artist's assistant snatched it from the jaws of the cat before it became red pieces of bird. Still warm, it seemed to beat like a heart. What an astounding gift—that shock of red—the first thing the artist saw, upon waking that morning. Who can believe—it is not a dream—it is in the artist's hand, this small, perfect, astounding red corpse.

The law, as you might imagine, prohibits the stuffing of songbirds in the Valley for any reason. It is quite simply against the law to bring a dead songbird into a taxidermist in the Valley to have it stuffed. If you happened to come upon a dead songbird, you will need to send it to another place altogether if you would like to have it stuffed. Before the artist went blind, she wrapped it carefully in white paper and placed it in a shoebox and sent it to Texas: that riot of red feathers and perfect cardinal beak and head. What a work of art it shall be, the artist cried with glee as she danced in her circular room and prepared herself to go to the Cabaret Rouge that evening at the Spiegelpalais.

Music

The casket holding the harp was lowered slowly now into the silence. It had been laid out on a smooth, white satin pillow, and the people in the Valley shuffled past it and mourned the end of music.

Precisely a week after they watched the harp—all that was left of the man, lowered into the earth in a box—the small, sad entourage traipsed across the field to witness the unveiling of the new fire truck. It was noon and twelve bells sounded, and the chicken was cooked on the grill, and the living went about the things the living do. Wise Jean pointed to the new fire engine that lay covered under a black tarp—a large and jarring shape on the landscape—and the mother balanced a small flame quietly and waited.

At last something was said over the loudspeaker, the people drew close, and the great shroud was lifted with a drum roll. There it was before them: red, shiny, bright, several stories high. Everyone gasped. It was a wondrous sight: its tires the size of a human child; its body impervious and strong. For a long time no one moved. Then all of a sudden, the children ran to embrace it as best they could. They rubbed their hands along its smooth, gleaming surfaces. The chief rang the bell, and the truck, although stationary, seemed already in motion. How much we miss you, she thought she heard someone call out to the new fire truck. And the women wept. How strong you are, and how brave! The truck, she understood, was an obvious stand-in for the man.

Something inside the mother was burning. Today there was no way around it. She wondered if you dug a hole to the perfect center of the earth whether it would be possible to float.

Fire

The ladder is lowered and the children climb up one by one by one. They lift in unison the heavy yellow fire hose and point it as best they can at the towers in the distance, which are on fire.

lamb

THE CHILD'S LAMB, her most precious possession, had disappeared. It had been sitting on a small desk atop a high pile of books the last time anyone had seen it, its arms, as always, extended.

The mother remembers thinking the day before that because the little lamb had been loved so hard over so many years, it had grown lighter, as light almost as a feather, and hollow. Its little teal blue T-shirt. Through love, its interior had been assumed into the body of the child, and only the exterior shell remained. The mother's fear was that now the child could float off too. In the night, the mother made a second tether, this one out of satin ribbon, to keep the child here awhile longer. She thought of all the things that could no longer be held by the earth, utterly exempt from its charms, things with reluctance the earth gave up, or the sky attracted.

The child was always trying to understand the science of things. The rational explanations for what seemed extraordinary, outlandish occurrences. She thought there must be some sort of magnet in the sky, and that the earth's pull loosened once a day and allowed certain things to lift entirely off the planet. There was a vulnerable second in every day, a wobble, a warp through which things escaped. Otherwise, the disappearance of the lamb was intolerable to both the mother and the child. The mother could not see living in such an inexplicable place. The child wished the sky might have assumed the Toothless Wonder instead. Why Lamby?

Soon it would be the fifteenth of August again, and the Virgin would be assumed into Heaven. The Virgin looked beautiful every single time her body was assumed, but Lamby went up without even a single sighting, into thin air, as they say. Poof! Just like that.

She would like to inquire about the magnet in the sky. If the soul is flat and metallic and spins like a disc, then what does that mean for it? She wonders if rain strengthens or weakens the attraction between two poles. The day Lamby disappeared, it never stopped raining.

The mother wonders what makes the child stay on the Ferris wheel and not fly up. Sometimes children too must be assumed, the mother thinks. When the mothers sitting in the park close their eyes for a nano-second, that is when the slippage occurs. Lost forever in the blink of an eye. She wonders what makes a girl stay fastened to the earth. What makes some girls stay fastened to the earth, and not others. What happens when some children go up that way, never to be seen again? All that remains is the vacated space and the mothers who did not keep their eyes open.

The mother decides it must be one of the Luminous Mysteries. What brought Lamby to them, why the child loved it above all others, and why it had to disappear like that. There was no other way for her to think about it.

☙

WHEN THE CHILD thinks about all the things that get lost or forgotten, she thinks that someday there will be no one alive who will remember Lamby, or the Grandmother from the North Pole. This, more than the mother's death or even her own, pains the child.

☾

THE VERY NEXT Sunday, the magnet assumed the baguette that the mother and child had gotten at the bakery for the Sunday breakfast. It had been lying atop The Poetics of Space, a book the mother was reading. The Law of Funnels suggests that not the lamb nor the missing children nor the baguette is coming back.

☾

IF THE MOTHER and the child flew high above the world in an airplane of some sort, they would see below them a field of wool. The clouds are like that. They bring back to people the things they most deeply love. Slowly it would seem from that height that they were traversing the entire body of the lamb.

It might take a human lifetime to traverse that enormous field of white; it might take more courage than they can muster to traverse the body of the lamb, the mystery of absence. And still what would be known?

☾

THE WORLD REARRANGES itself every time she leaves the room, and she is constantly returning to a changed place. The child's lamb is gone. The mother stares into the space it is missing from. How to say how upset this makes her, she cannot—with the child feeling so terribly bereft already. Still the mother feels herself emptying too from the space. She puts little fishing weights in her shoes, just in case.

She noticed how precious things were often taken by the magnet. She wondered about the equation between here and there. Even when a thing appeared to be right there before one, it was already in the process of being taken. If there were only some way to recognize this in advance a little better. She thought she had noticed something strange about that lamb recently.

She stared into the space above the desk a long time. Presence informed the absence, and absence the presence, and each was haunted by the other.

When the painter Pierre Bonnard worked, he told his model that she was not to sit still, but to move around the space while he painted. He wanted to paint both presence and absence, the model concluded. The mother continued to look at the place where the lamb had once been. The space so charged, so precious, that for a time, it burned so brightly it almost flickered. She remembered how after the towers fell, you could still see them in the air where they had stood—everyone said so. She noticed now the way the space and her certitude always seemed to be shifting and fraying.

The space vacant now. Lamby's arms extended, his eyes forever open.

∽

IN DESPERATION, THE mother filled the windy room with plush, adorable animals—small and large, all colors, all sorts—but never would the child find anything that could compare, and never again, as she said, would she be 100 percent happy.

THE CHILD SEES wings behind the mother's head, and the mother being carried away. She asks her whether she has been to the doctor lately, and right before she falls asleep, she says, you would tell me if there was anything wrong with you, right? You won't leave me here alone.

THE CHILD HAS learned to play some songs on the piano. She played Mary Had a Little Lamb and made up new lyrics calling to Lamby, who once would sit on the bench next to her.

EACH NIGHT, THE child tried to solve the Mystery of the Lamb in her sleep. One night he was sitting on a bench waiting for a bus. Another night he was digging with a silver spoon in the sand, looking for something on a smooth white beach. He hadn't gone far.

THE MOTHER ASKS the child if she would like to talk a little bit about Lamby. The child says she does not want to talk about it because talking makes the feeling go away or change, and she does not want it to change or go away. The mother does not understand where the child gets her wisdom. It has always been there.

⌒

ANOTHER NIGHT, A little girl named Wyo appeared at the side of the child's bed and said, where I live there are people called Sheep-Eating Shoshone. Just so you know. And she left her a map.

⌒

EVERY STORE THEY saw they would go into, and in every store they would pick up every comfort object, that is what the child called them, and they would place the object into the crook of the child's arm in the hopes that something somewhere in this world might console.

⌒

THERE IS A planet the lamb may have gone to, the mother thought. Yes, Gliese, the child says brightly, the planet in the Goldilocks Zone. The Goldilocks Zone is the most plausible and hospitable zone to sustain the life of a little lamb. They imagined a lamb, billowy, tufted, floating up to it, assumed into the air. It sounds like a perfectly lovely planet, the mother said, and she thought to herself: there is an incalculable amount of hope in the world.

⌒

EVERYONE COULD BE found nowadays. No one was ever lost anymore. In cars there was a global positioning system that told you exactly where you were at all times and exactly how to get to where you were going. The Grandmother from the North Pole and the child thought this was a wonderful thing to have, but the mother was not so sure. You could have a woman or a man as your GPS Guide, and this guide would patiently tell you where to turn, though never why.

She pictured the planet encased in satellites like a woman's head in curlers, and in every car, voices.

If you messed up, the man or the woman would patiently recalculate, and as many times as you lost your way, it would not lose patience. On long highway stretches, you would not hear from your guide for a very long time, and that would make everyone lonely.

෧

BECAUSE OF WHAT happened to Lamby, when the helicopter came down so low it seemed it might land on her head, the mother ran for the cat, imagining that he was going to be the next thing taken from the child. For what was the likelihood of a helicopter hovering low like that on a perfect clear sky, out of the blue?

Only later when the mother sees the hummingbird extracting nectar from the newly opened rose does it occur to her that perhaps the helicopter had in fact come for the child.

෧

NEXT TO THE concrete rabbit, barely discernible, a Praying Mantis led the prayer. Mantis, the mother somehow knew, derived from the

Greek word for prophet or fortune-teller. Where is her lamb? the
mother demanded.

&

SHE PREPARED THE porch: rearranged it, put flowers out, swept.
They made a Welcome Home banner, though they did not spell it out;
to others they did not want to appear to be waiting. If Lamby was
going to come back in the conventional way, he would be wrapped in
brown paper and string, and left on the porch by the post person. He
would come like this in an ordinary way, on an ordinary day. She liked
to think without fanfare: something long awaited was coming at last,
something much anticipated was going to arrive.

&

AFTER MONTHS HAD passed and Gliese had become permanently
fixed in the child's affection, more news arrived. It seemed that Gliese,
in the Goldilocks Zone, that most perfect and hospitable of all zones,
had but one small problem. Gliese, with further investigation, was said
to be tidally locked. Tidally locked, what could that mean? the mother
wondered. It meant Gliese could not rotate; it could not turn. The
planet, quite simply, is not believed to transit its star, the newspaper
stated. As a result, one side of Gliese eternally faces its sun, in perpetual
daylight, and the other side forever faces away, steeped in eternal night.

One side is far too hot to be inhabited, and the other side is far, far
too cold. Still—and the mother looks out into the slip of space the little
lamb disappeared into—there remains a slender crescent where the
two hemispheres overlap, and where these hemispheres overlap, there

is hope. There is a small space called the Glisten Zone, the mother says, where something or someone may still live.

The mother is a beautiful star, hot to the touch, radiant beyond belief. When the child turns away, she is draped in darkness, and when she turns back, she catches fire. The child is burning. Freezing and then burning, and then only burning—caught in the incineration—until she is a ghost, a specter, and her hope falters. The specter chatters and babbles in her sleep. She does not rest. She finds and then loses, finds and then loses that thin sliver. Where is her lamb?

☙

THEY COME SWIFTLY from the ends of the earth. None of them grow tired. None of them stumble. They never doze or sleep. Not a belt is loose; not a sandal strap is broken. Their arrows are sharp, and their bows are ready to shoot. Their horses' hoofs are as hard as flint, and their chariot wheels turn like a whirlwind. They are looking for her lamb. There is nothing they will not do for the child.

☙

ANOTHER MOTHER, CLEARLY a more mindful mother, had an arsenal of identical monkeys exactly like her son's beloved monkey Zippy. They were hidden away in the event that the real Zippy disappeared. The more mindful mother had a stack of extra Zippys in her bedroom closet, and one day while her son was playing Hide and Seek, he came upon them—an improbable pile of monkeys in the closet.

What on earth are these? the boy asked, horrified. These are the other Zippys, his mindful mother responded calmly, upon which the boy began shaking his head back and forth, back and forth, back and forth with great consternation.

This is the good Zippy, he said most emphatically, and these— *these, these, these* are the no-good Zippys, and straightaway he was gone. After a few hours the boy emerged again, having built a house of cardboard for the no-good Zippys, and he dumped the monkeys inside and he made a sign for the door that said, Home of the No-Good Zippys. Such was the story the more mindful mother told the less mindful mother when she heard of the lambless child.

Regardless of the reception of the no-good Zippys, the mother wishes she was a mother like that one, a more mindful one, and that she had a roomful of good or no-good Lambys in a quiet pile by her side.

The more mindful mother got the less mindful mother to thinking of Other Mothers and Mother Substitutes and As-If Mothers, ones who might guide the child through fraught terrain. An As-If Mother would come in handy too, in the event something ever happened to this one.

That night she dreamt of a cupboard full of Lambys, but the next morning when she went to the cupboard, the cupboard was bare.

Ꮙ

IN A ROOMFUL of extra Lambys, she might, after the child was asleep, toss them into the air and watch them: their white bellies skim the ceiling and billow and then fall. This would give the mother a happy feeling. She might love the extra Lambys in the night and play with them, in preparation for the day when the real Lamby returned.

She wanted the child to know that Infinite Grace was available to them. It was only a matter of being open and ready to receive.

SO MANY THINGS were going on in the backyard. The children were following the squirrels with notepads, noting where they hid their nuts, real and otherwise, for the winter. Hiding nonexistent nuts was nothing new to the squirrels. They did this routinely to protect their food from thieves, but when the squirrels saw the children with notebooks, their fake burials increased. Squirrels are smarter than they look and understand a marauding child very well, thank you. Squirrels understand the intention to steal. This suggests a Theory of Squirrel Mind, the eighth graders noted.

Next door, cameras were being put onto the heads of sleeping deer. Everyone wants to see what a deer sees and where they go when they go away. Had she known this before, the child might have put a little device like that on Lamby's head.

Down the road, little location devices, very tiny, were being placed on the heads of anesthetized crows to show where crows go. Everyone loves a bird's-eye view from time to time.

IN TRYING TO think about where Lamby went, an exhaustive application of logic to all available possibilities should be employed. One must follow every thread. Trace every step, inch by inch, point by point; blindly exhaust the search space completely. Such a process is known as Ariadne's Thread. It permits backtracking, reversing early decisions, and trying alternatives. Yes, the mother thinks, all quite sensible, but we have little interest in the truth if the truth will lead us in a disheartening direction—all we want is Lamby back.

☙

THE MOTHER AND child walk through the sacrificial world. There appeared a mark of rabbit blood at the door. The mother places her hand over the mark, and the blood shines through. A great price will be exacted and a small reward will be doled out in return. Who looks down on them? the mother wonders. They step over the threshold of blood where the cat's catch of the day lies splayed and faceless.

Some cultures believe that stepping over a threshold of blood brings lifelong luck; others believe the luck is in a swarm of bees or in a vanishing lamb.

torch

THE MOTHER HAD been under an inordinate amount of stress, and it made the Leprosy appear. Actually it was not Leprosy, it was something called Shackles, but it covered her face and head and she looked like a Leper, as the Risen-Again Children duly noted, and her suffering was extreme. The doctor said she might go blind, or she might go deaf from the Leprosy that had come from too much stress. After the pain subsided somewhat, the mother began to resume her life, and she could hear, and she was not blind. And though she still had a bloated, swollen monster head, there was the matter of back-to-school shopping to do.

The mother and the child went to the shoe section of the large department store and sat in the children's section and waited for someone to help them. When the stack of boxes tall as a skyscraper came toppling down, the mother started to cry. Probably the mother was just tired. She put her terrible head in her hands, and when she looked up, there was a small coven of children pointing at her, gasping and then running away.

As news spread throughout the first floor of the department store, more and more children came to do their gawking. It was always the same: her head in her hands, then her head up. When her head went up and she looked right at them, they would run away, screaming with glee. Head down, head up, gasp and run away, gasp and run away.

The child, however, did not notice. She was oblivious to the commotion and remained deep within her shoe trance.

The child, as any child psychologist will tell you, cannot, no matter what, afford to see her mother as a monster. The disintegration of the core narrative is at stake, the psychologists might say. The mother smiles from inside her crusty head and helps the child with every buckle and every lace, buckle after buckle, lace after lace, shoe after shoe.

The child saw only that her mother was tying the laces of the most wonderful sneakers in the world, and that they lit up and had princesses on them, and that her mother was beautiful.

THE DEAD BIRDS, still warm, have been arranged from warm to warmest on the path by Bunny Boy. The mother is getting fed up. Isn't there a primeval forest, isn't there a deep unconscious better suited for this sort of thing? Why this path, the path she must walk day in and day out, to the mailbox, to the car, to the world at large, littered with the newly dead, still warm? Along with the birds, the path has become more and more crowded with the things she dreads; but it is okay, she tells herself, it is just something else to bear.

On the path now, a jar. On the path a glove, a stethoscope, a briefcase, a silver basin, a pair of gleaming scissors, a doll's head, a torch.

There is a wilderness deep inside her, a place she now no longer allows herself to go. It might frighten the child and the child might then disappear. More than anything, she knows she must stay close to the path.

If the wilderness wants to come, it must meet her more than half-way; it must come to this path now, from which she will not veer.

EACH DAY NOW, the schoolgirls appear on the path with backpacks and sharpened pencils. All they want is to resume their studies. All they want is to go to school again. The mother motions to them to come, and she hands them a book and tells them to take a seat.

THAT NIGHT THE mother sees in the distance a flame and she tries to walk to it, but no matter how far she goes, she never arrives. The mother becomes tired and decides to sit in the meadow and watch the flame from afar, as it is her job, she knows, to keep track of the paths of fire whenever possible.

IN THE ANCIENT world, a torch has been lit on a mountaintop, and soon it will be traveling across the world to the Olympic Games, and the announcement is made that the entire sojourn will be projected on a screen at the Spiegelpalais.

The Mother Flame, origin of fire, shall accompany the Torch on all its travels. The Mother Flame cannot be extinguished. She is stored in an official lantern and is always there. Yes, the mother thinks, she is just like any mother.

Keeping the Torch lit will be the responsibility of ten flame attendants who attend to the fire twenty-four hours a day. The mother and child will sit in the front row of the great theater transfixed. The Torch will ride on a camel and on the Concorde and in a North American canoe. The child will keep close track of its itinerary. The newspaper fears for the Torch and its mother because GinGin, the place that is the Torch's destination, is controversial on more fronts than one.

THE MOTHER AND child bring their trundle beds to the Spiegelpalais as they do not want to miss even a second of the flame's transit. Most times it is only the mother and the child who are there holding vigil, and they wonder where everyone else is. A place of fire is being prepared for them, the mother surmises—what other explanation could there be?

☙

THE FLAME SITS in its specially designed charter plane, glimmering in the corner. Security is high. The mother and child eat popcorn and stare at the enormous screen, riveted. The Torch and its group of round-the-clock guardians often take up residence in the most chic hotels. They all go to the hotel bar. The bar patrons sense something glowing in their midst, but they know not what.

At night the Torch sleeps in a lantern along with its mother, who sleeps beside it. It stays in a single room each night with three watchmen, one of whom must be awake at all times. At night there are the wonders of the world and constellations, falling stars, and from their trundle bed they observe the heavens through the Spiegelpalais' skylight.

At Gethsemane, despite the assurances that they would stay awake with Jesus in his darkest hour of need, the apostles fell asleep. When it comes to the Torch, a world of sleeping potions and conspiracies and dastardly acts orchestrated from somewhere else does not sound so far-fetched.

☙

THE FLAME COMMEMORATES the theft of fire from Zeus by Prometheus. Look, the mother cries, it's Paris! If there is a place in the world the mother would like to see before she dies, it is Paris. In Paris, black banners are hung on Notre Dame and the Tour Eiffel to greet the Torch. French protesters attempt to steal the flame, and the flame is extinguished five times. But you cannot kill fire, try as you might. The resurrected flame cowers, and eventually the Torch is driven by bus to the stadium.

ର

WHEN THE FLAME arrives in the City of Saint Francis, accompanied by dignitaries and protected by riot-ready security, a round of photos is taken and then the flame retires.

ର

THE VORTEX MAN appears from inside the whirling world. Hold on to your hats! he cackles. The Torch, fed by the Vortex, blows furiously in its cup.

ର

THE CHILD IS mesmerized. Protesters announce their desire to kidnap the Torch, to take the flame hostage—every mother's nightmare. The Mother Flame fears that if the Torch is captured by protesters, there is always the possibility that the Sympathy Syndrome will set in, and if this occurs, she may never see her little flame again.

It is called the Sympathy Syndrome when a captive begins to sympathize with its captors and begins to do uncharacteristic things of all sorts because of its deep affection for its newly bonded attendant.

The child wonders if the flame is captured and begins to sympathize with its captors, and if it heads up the liberation of TingTing, GinGin's enemy, and breaks from its box, whether the earth will be consumed in fire. The child thinks she should number her worries, but before long, the child is asleep and the mother is left to track the flame.

The next day, the mother, whose tears are flammable, looks at her dry-eyed and tells her it is not for her to worry about.

෩

THE CHILD IS packing her backpack for the day. It is too heavy, the mother says, and she takes out all the items—the pencil box, the calculator, the complete works of Lewis Carroll, the Piglet, the wooden rosary, the lip balm, the photograph of the Eiffel Tower—and she rearranges everything and puts it back. The child finds that just because of her mother's touch, the objects have lightened, and smiling and weightless and worry-free, she rises up, and heads off to school.

෩

THE TORCH WOULD like to climb Mt. Everest and cares nothing for Doomsday Predictions or the Sympathy Syndrome. In its mind, if a flame can be said to have a mind, the flame is free.

The mother, for one, thinks all fire should be treated with respect.

Through the skylight of the Spiegelpalais, the child sees three silent astronauts from GinGin making gestures. They're tethered only tenuously, it seems, to GinGin anymore. They are looking for Torch, they say.

☌

WHEN THE TORCH appears again, it is in India, and the mother imagines it might mingle with the fires of India, a country that in her mind is always burning. She imagines the Ganges sometimes when she and the child go to their own river, and all the small pyres.

The baby flame, enormous, licks the edges of the glass. Some days there is nothing more the mother would like than to be stored in a jar by the door, there for the child to feed from, if the situation becomes dire.

☌

ONE OF THE school girls had a squished eye and had to have a series of eye operations to unsquish it. Back in GinGin where she was a baby, she lay in a bed, in a row of beds, in a room of beds filled with girls that they must have forgotten to touch or turn over. And because no one had remembered to touch or turn them over, their eyes had squished into the beds.

The GinGin astronauts were going to a new planet. Don't forget to hold the girls when you get there, the child called after them. Don't forget to turn the GinGin girls in their beds! Otherwise they will have squished eyes, and it is not so easy to unsquish them. She felt the air above her dense with stars and birdsong, and above that the lonely transit of planets, and the men starting over again.

On the new planet, the astronauts call back, we have no intention of holding the girls or turning them over. Not for all the tea in GinGin are we going to touch those girls.

☾

THAT NIGHT, AFTER the screen went dark in the Spiegelpalais, the mother looked up to the skylight. Behold the bat, she cried! O winged wonder! The only mammal besides children able to fly. O faceted scapula. Behold the sternum, the rib cage, the robust clavicles. O Flying Fox. O Prodigy! Behold the tree chreub!

At dawn, the artist's cardinal, emblazoned, alighted for a moment on a mulberry branch and then flew away.

☾

THE RAINS CAME and many funnels swerved into them and the world was shaking, and they were afraid. *Hold on to your hats!* There was nothing the mother and child could do but take cover next to the giant screen in the cavernous, emptied space and wait. The screen flickered and gave no clues and then grew dark, and for a full twenty-four hours, nothing could be seen on the screen. Petitions were sent to the Vortex Man, and they must eventually have been heard, for at the Fortieth Hour, the screen at the Spiegelpalais at last filled with light.

☾

EARTHQUAKE KILLS TENS of Thousands, Many of Them School-children, the screen reads. *GinGin Grieves, Suspends Torch Relay.*

The mother bows her head as if bludgeoned. She and the child fall to their knees.

ᕲ

DEAD SCHOOLCHILDREN ARE strewn across the debris. Many others are trapped. Everywhere there are fingers and feet, and mothers clawing the dirt. Crushed in the shoddily built schools. The earthquake struck at 2:30 when the children were still in class. A mother is screaming in the ruins. Her only child has vanished into the chaos, and she cannot find her. Textbooks and backpacks are everywhere.

The children are extinguished. The mother cowers as rescue workers search for survivors on the screen, and she puts her hands over the child's eyes. It is the rule that a couple is allowed one, and only one, child each. A stack of only children in the rubble of the schoolhouses across GinGin Province. Maybe children are alive in the rubble, the child says. Maybe the parents will dig them out with their fingers.

Tie the mothers tightly together to calm them, an official is instructing. A distraught mother abruptly turns. She thinks she feels her child's presence like a wind at her back.

The mother and child stand helpless before the enormous screen. A large crane outfitted with floodlights arrives to lift massive slabs of concrete through the darkened, smoldering terrain, where the only children do not cry out any longer. Parents build makeshift shrines and place photos of their children at the death place. Some burn red candles or paper money to send their children into the Afterlife.

The screen at the Spiegelpalais says that the Torch will be revitalized after the proper term of mourning. It is promised one day that it will appear again in the City of Forests.

And with that the screen goes black.

༺

THE MOTHER AND child hobble home as best they can, but they don't get far before the earth opens up before them. In all that darkness they stand before a vast canyon of light, and for a moment, the ancient maple flashes before the mother's eyes. Where are we? the child asks. But the mother says nothing in return. The canyon is filled with dump trucks and cement trucks and small fire engines and police cars performing their tasks—they look like toys from this vantage point, and they mesmerize the small boys who have materialized from the outlying gloom. The mother and child stand at the top and look into it for a long time.

What can be seen now, without the Slurry Wall, and what has been hidden for millennia underneath the great metropolis astonishes them. Look, the mother says and she takes the child's hand, and gingerly they begin their climb down the steep ravine, hundreds of feet below the sea. They sense the dead are all around them, and they see what remains, as they pass archeologists sifting the debris. In the subterranean world, the workers hand them the remnants: a shoulder, an ankle, a few ribs. Maybe they should turn back, the mother thinks. Still, there is no question of turning back. The child points. She sees that piles are being made now: computer parts, electrical wire, carpet. Someone tries to hand her a bowl of two hundred bone fragments. Are we dead? the child asks.

Dread fills the mother, but still she is compelled forward. For a moment she hesitates, torn as to whether to bring the child further down into the canyon or to leave her near the anthropologists at the rock ledge and retrieve her on the way back, but by the time she formulates a plan, it is too late. The mother has no choice, as the child seems to have folded herself up and attached herself to the wall of the mother's womb. Though she cannot see the child, she knows she is there, and the child's little heartbeat gives her the courage and the momentum she needs. She takes a few more steps. As briefcases and cell phones and jewelry and dresses are being excavated, the mother bows her head. She doesn't know what to do. She can't look or look away. The child peers through the ruby scrim of her mother's body as they continue their descent. They pass, along the way, battalions of vanishing men.

Who goes there? And the mother's voice echoes in the space. Deep within the earth, plant material has been compressed for millions and millions of years into nuggets, and the men, who have gone to retrieve it, begin their way back up. They pass the mother and the child going in the opposite direction. Come with us, the men say, but the mother shakes her head no. They shrug and ascend, soot-covered, holding their illuminant—something from the center of the earth that glows. We could bring you back up, they offer once more, we know the way. The mother thinks there is a kindness to them. But she shakes her head once more. The vanishing men hand the mother an ember and are gone.

The mother continues her grave descent. They see extravagant rock striations from the last Ice Age and pause. The mother puts a hand to the gleaming boulders—so cold to the touch, so strange, and all memory of the Valley and the life above begins to fade. It's beautiful here, don't you think—irrefutable as it is, and so quiet, and so dark.

The child urges the mother not to linger, and the mother understands, though she fears that she soon will reach the point of no return.

The way is steep, and the mother's footing is unsure. She wonders why they did not go back with the men.

She sees swirling concentric rings now, and she realizes she is far beyond the Ice Age all of a sudden—the rocks more ancient than those marked by glaciers—and with this realization she plummets, and her ember goes out.

At this point, she turns on the miner's lamp she been wearing all along on her head. The lamp lights the cave nicely, and she points out to the child the minerals and the essences. Look, she whispers, look. They have gotten to the place where the rock layers run vertically now instead of horizontally.

Five hundred million years ago, in this very place, the North American and African continental plates slammed together with unimaginable violence. This consoles the mother who knows that they are small and their lives insignificant, and that one day all the catastrophes will be erased. Astounding reds and purples and greens open up for the first time in millennia, miles below the wounded site.

If this is the Afterlife toward which she was being pulled with such magnetic force now, if this was the place that had been beckoning them from the very start, she wanted no part of it. Still—the colors . . . I wish you could see them, she says to the child. She was fearful of the void, fearful of the drop—and then suddenly not. If there is only meaninglessness in the end, only nothing, only welter and waste, she did not feel it.

She looks far, far up to the surface and sees now two shimmering ghost towers of glass, casting their twin shadows before her.

When she called for the child now, the child did not answer. She had dissolved back into the mother's body entirely, and with this, the mother felt more able to face whatever it was that was here. She stood at the beginning of time, at the bottom of the canyon. She was being bombarded by light. She had not died here. She had lived. She had lived to give birth to the child. She would stay alive for her, and for all the children. She could see it plainly now. Never had anything been more clear. She had been summoned here to the depths of the earth, to the origins of the world, the beginning of time, to receive this message. She felt at the infinite mercy of the universe. Somehow she had survived. She closed her eyes.

the red book of existence

T HE MOTHER WAS entranced with the large red book with the gold embossed letters, and from it she read out loud to the child thinking it might help soothe them a little. Though on the surface the child did not seem in need of consoling, the mother understood what the child could not.

In the book it said everything in the world is made of quarks and electrons, which are energy waves, and that these energy waves have the potential for taking form. Solidity, or the appearance of solidity, is something conjured by stimulating our sense receptors and ultimately creating an image in our brains. Each of these swarming particles exists as a shimmering wave of potential until its wave function collapses (caused by such things as the presence or absence of the observer). The mother leaves the room to get a biscuit and the child is desolate. She did not move her head too much so as not to disrupt the receptors, for what would she have if she does not have the mother?

It's mind out there in front of them—it's the only place the world and its images and tactile impressions exist.

That night the child thinks that when the mother leaves the room, she is no longer anywhere at all. That she no longer exists on any level. She can't keep her mother together. And the child too has no color or form unless particles interact with the mother's consciousness.

Tell me we exist, the child begs.

Silly girl, the mother whispers.

You should have never opened that red book with the gold letters, the child says.

Though it could be worse, the child supposes. Of course it could always be worse.

She will live with the appearance of solidity if that is what is asked of her—perhaps she was already doing it. They move through the enigmatic world to the hardware store at the edge of town. Everything is exactly the same as it was before they opened that book. She shall believe it: the five packages of nails on the shelf, the tower of light bulbs, the man behind the counter who holds a metal box with a lock on it, the Spiegelpalais in the distance, and in the middle distance three GinGin girls with backpacks, and now too close for comfort, the Toothless Wonder.

She didn't want to be stranded on the wrong side of the stability divide.

The mother smiled.

That night, the mother sits at the end of the child's bed. She looks at the child: shiny, bright, emitting photons, packets of electricity and magnetism. She concentrates hard not to take her eyes or mind from her, even for an instant.

IF ALL THE people in the world perished and the world returned to welter and waste, what she would remember best from that desolate place would be the Super Stop & Shop.

She liked going to the grocery store. She liked to go alone, but she liked it equally when the child accompanied her. The child loved making lists, and they would reach for things and put them in the carriage and check them off the list. It made the mother feel efficient and a definite part of things to do this. She liked driving the carriage, standing behind it, moving purposely down the numbered rows.

She also liked looking at what all the other people were doing. She liked the way they picked up certain cans or bottles or boxes, the way they would turn and examine them for dates and codes and counts. Sometimes she heard someone in an aisle talking on a telephone to someone at home to ask if there was enough butter. She thought it was a lovely question. And that there was someone there to answer it.

A riot of color and sound and sensation would stream toward and past the mother in waves. The abundance always made her a little woozy. If there were any one place in the world where the lecture about the starving children would make sense, it would be here, she thought. She had never seen so much of everything. In the vaporous frozen food aisle, she pauses.

No matter; today she is part of the give-and-take. The cat food quandaries, the price of coffee, the coupons, the two-for-ones. The child is not afraid of the disembodied voice checking them out, and so she will not be either. It is part of the human exchange now, and the computer voice intones in a friendly way, it is true. She notices that the Other Mothers enjoy turning the pages of the tabloids and so she tries it, and it's not bad. It passes the time, while the voice checks them out, and she waits.

ALL THE MEN were vanishing in and out of wars. After a brief experiment in which women were allowed to go to war, the decision was

reversed, and it was legislated that women, who were responsible for
the replication of the species, would go to war no more. And so an
edict was issued, and it came to pass in the Valley that for every man
there were two hundred to three hundred women. Surely, the child reasoned, there would have to be a stepmother somewhere for her friend,
the Girl with the Matted Hair.

THE SOLDIERS TALK about riding the wake. Some of the soldiers
are crouching in a foxhole. Women are throwing bandages and roses
at their heads. Some of the soldiers' heads, they notice, are flowering
red with abandon. Some of the soldiers are asleep. Others are turning
to vapor.

INFANTS ARE CONVINCED that when their mothers leave the room
that they have disappeared and are gone forever, never to return. When
the child looked at her mother, she did everything in her power now to
keep the outline of her solid and continuous and separate. She could not
have her turning into birdsong or branches, or pond or stars or smoke.

    What kept the mother together on many days was the child's
application of the Flicker Fusion Theory. In the theory her mother
came together beautifully, fixed for extended moments at a time. She
flickered, but then held, and then later would begin to flicker again.
But it was the holding that was miraculous, and it brought both child
and mother great joy. It was sad that the child had to resort to this, the
Flickering Mother thought, and the child too thought that sometimes,
and yet for those moments when the mother was held in perfect stability and presence, it felt like a supreme blessing. It was best to look on
the bright side, the child always thought that. As a result of the Flicker

Fusion, she and the mother possessed something that other mother-child states could never provide. As for the sadnesses—well, with the sadnesses they had made their amends.

There was always the Persistence of Vision Theory, the child reasoned when things got too difficult, the retina retaining the impression of the image even after her disappearance. This way, in long retinal waves the mother would remain for prolonged periods of time. Such were the ways the child would compensate for the times the mother would go off-again/on-again, off-again.

She knew never to take the solid world for granted because that, in the end, would be a source of much heartache. When the Disappearance Threshold had been reached, when the sense of absence seemed unbearable, when the Flicker-Off became more frequent and prolonged, the Persistence of Vision Theory was the natural theorem to apply. It pleased her to know what had to be done.

Still, the solitude of the night continued.

ON THE DAY the child came into language, she spoke elaborate sentences in an instant and the mother was afraid. No baby babbling or preliminary words had been heard, and there had been no practice or preparation on the child's part. Just like that, one day, when the mother came into the room, she found the child speaking perfectly formed syntactic units, carrying their burden of meaning and desire.

The child said first how happy she was to be there. And the mother smiled sweetly. The very next words the toddler said were that she had come here from Heaven and that God was waiting for them. He could not wait much longer, she said, and they couldn't live this way forever—between worlds, floating.

From time to time, the child went on, she would see God while sitting in her car seat in the car. The mother at these times would stop the car. She was not floating, and she didn't care how long he waited; she was not going to budge.

Soon enough—not even a year had passed—and the child had forgotten all about what God had said in the car seat and about Heaven and about the hovering in-between world, but the mother never forgot it, and sometimes the child begged her to tell that first God story, which she had once overheard the mother whispering to Father Ted. The mother was not sure she wanted to be the repository for a story such as this, but after much badgering, the mother always relented. Still she longed sometimes for the days when the child was a wordless creature and did not ask the mother to hold such things for her.

Now they were exiles in language together and forced to make the best of it; now they would have to make small reductive signs for the oceanic ways they felt inside. Now they would have to sputter after the wolf and its majesty, and the river, and the fire. But beside this world there was another world that there were no words for.

The funnels would come quickly now—all the dark diminishments, the mother and child, caught in the high winds. The mother could not blame the child for learning to speak. The child was exhilarated and did not see or feel what the mother did. The child was enlarging and talking a blue streak. She could not blame the child for going forward: talking, walking, going to school. Bringing home the child with the Elephant Trunk, and the Girl with the Matted Hair, or telling the God story. It was not really her fault.

God was pulling at the child, asking her to bring the mother home. Instructing the mother to get on with it now.

Still, the mother implored the God to *leave the child alone.*

THE JACKAL LEADS the deceased before the scale. He weighs the heart (left tray) against the feather of Ma'at, the goddess of truth and justice (right tray). If the heart of the deceased outweighs the feather, then the deceased has a heart that has been made heavy by evil deeds. In that event, the god with the crocodile head and hippo legs will devour the heart, condemning the deceased to oblivion for eternity.

And that indeed, the mother says, is a long time. The War Crimes President is moved into the withdrawing room with a heavy heart. The jackal snatches the heart and puts it on the scale.

WOMEN IN VEILS moved through the Valley now. There had always been veiled women in the Valley, draped in black, and now as the vanishings increased, women mourned in greater and greater numbers—but these veiled women who moved through the Valley were new. The new women came from far away, though from where, the mother could not say.

One of the women in veils breaks from the group and walks down the path to the mother. She might have been a kind of beekeeper had there been bees. For the first time in a long while, the mother was being pulled against her will toward another human being. What do you want? she asked. Each night when the mother awoke, the veiled woman would be sitting at the edge of the bed, next to a chittering bat, beckoning.

THE CHILD WAS doing a report about a faraway land. The child asked the mother what she knew about it.

Music and singing and dancing are forbidden there. Write that down, the mother said. It's something I know for sure.

I won't. I won't write that, the child said; it's too sad.

LISTEN, THE MOTHER whispers. At the end of the corridor a dirge could be heard moving through the left ventricle. Give us the courage to enter the song, the mother said, and they fell now with grace and resolve and some fear into the darkest of dreams:

A young woman from Punjab and her baby trail the mother and child, and no matter what the mother does, she cannot completely shrug off their shadow. Even though she does not understand why this young woman and infant boy from a distant land must follow them, she tolerates it—they must be looking for something very important, she reasons. Or perhaps it is simpler—perhaps they have been drawn by the great silver river, like so many are drawn. The woman from Punjab mutters sometimes, sometimes sings in an incredibly lovely voice, sometimes wails, but all without sound, and the infant boy cries at times and sleeps the rest of the time.

Inevitably at some point in every day, the young woman from Punjab and the baby appear, though some days it is very late. Sometimes the mother goes to look for them and if she cannot find them, she goes back home and waits for them to come. She knows it must be a far place they journey from; her hunch is Punjab, though she cannot be sure.

She notices that more and more, the woman, when she arrives, is crying. The mother remembers how difficult it was when her own child was a baby, and she also understands how difficult it must be for them to be so far from home. If she could only verify their existence, then perhaps there would be a shift in their rapport, in their relationship to one another, in what could be communicated. The mother does not dare ask the child about them, as she is not prepared for the answer the child will give, and also she does not want to hear what it will sound like to ask the child casually, have you by any chance seen the woman and the baby from Punjab today? If the young woman and baby are invisible, it is not on the mother's account. Some days she sees them everywhere she looks. The baby seems to know sign language, as so many babies seem to know these days, and the mother feels he is trying to tell her something urgent, but she does not know what.

And then they are gone. They do not come back again. A year passes, and the mother opens a newspaper and reads about a woman from Punjab who moved to New York when she was six, grew up, walked in the American summer, had a son, and one July morning, distraught, killed the baby and then herself. The mother is horrified when she reads this, but she is also a little bit relieved. She gets on her knees. She feels an inexplicable gratitude. Because of what the shadow mother from Punjab has done, this mother will not be required to.

She and the child will be spared.

THE CHILD IS running toward her with such velocity that she has broken the sound barrier. She is shouting something to the mother, but the mother can't hear her. Her arms are open, and she is filled with joy. No one has taken them away. No one has asked them to leave or to die. Nothing else matters but she and this child running through the breathing world. The child does a little song and dance. She loves her Fippy. It was the favorite part of her body—perfectly pink, and a little slippery. The child does a Fippy Dance.

Dance, the mother says, for there is not one day that is promised to us.

THE CHILD TOLD her mother that she had been invited to a swimming party to celebrate the end of summer. The mother pictured the beautiful blue cavity and the children jumping into it again and again and again. When she closed her eyes she saw before her a continuum of jumping children. All the usual suspects would be there: the three schoolgirls, the Boy in the Glen, the Boy with the Elephant Trunk, the Girl with the Matted Hair.

The mother supposed they too could go. She much preferred children under the water than above it. The children looked to her like flowers underwater: graceful and silent, their tendrils elongated, undulating.

SHE TOOK THE child in her arms. She thought of a blue chalice that held time, floating, suspended overhead, protecting and holding them. For a moment in this radiant Valley, time seemed elongated, and everything stayed exactly the same. She knew it would not last long—possibly only for as little as a fraction of a second. It was a strange feeling. They made their way up the hill for the last time of the season. The summer now was winding down. Soon the blueberries would be gone, and the apples would appear.

18

WHEN THE CHILDREN were small, they would often play their grave resurrection games back behind the prickle bushes at the Winter Bear Montessori School. Each day after graceful walking and practical life and blue line work, the two girls would venture out after snack to begin once again to concoct the Mother Potion from scratch. The potion, as the Girl with the Matted Hair said, would save once and for all the mothers who had died or were dying. Otherwise, the Girl with the Matted Hair said, they would die for good, and they would never come back. As it was, the Girl with the Matted Hair's mother had died when she was a toddler, and ever since then, she had worked night and day to find the cure for that.

This sort of project enthralled the child, and every day at recess she and her friend collected and assembled a wide assortment of ingredients and charms: rose thorns and wishbones, robin's eggshells and goose's eggshells, scrunchies and ribbons, knee scabs and matted hair (for DNA, the child said), chestnut casings, glitter glue, butterfly wings, birchbark, and other forest charms. Ten dandelions—nine discarded, the last placed in a vial of rosewater; eight hairs from the tail of a black cat dipped in clay then burned to an ash. Chewed grass from the grave of the schoolmaster. They sewed a magnet into a mother's dress and slipped fish lures into the hem. They obtained a dead wren and sent away a black lamb, for a little black lamb foretells mourning garments within the year. They tied mint around their wrists while skipping. They mixed chamomile and mud with salt and silt and tears into a poultice and stirred it with a Hawthorn branch. Spells and banishments were many. The child carried elf stones in a velvet pouch and waited for a four-footed beast to pass in order to animate the charm. Before the magic words were spoken into the well, they covered it with a wool shawl. Lavender plucked on a Sunday night they pounded with a stone that never was moved since the world began. When the child, who was gathering thistle, had her back turned, the Girl with the Matted Hair snuck up on her and sank her teeth into the child's arm. There, she said, the blood of a child! The child screamed and drew a circle on the ground and said the magic words, and a fire rushed up from the earth and a flood of water, pure and bright, sprang from her side creating a mote, separating now the child from the ring of fire. It all occurred so fast that the Girl with the Matted Hair at first did not know what had happened. That was fantastic! She shouted and began to applaud. She had always suspected that the child carried the water charm inside her, and now it was verified.

Sometimes the child would carve a little figure out of a carrot from her snack for her friend, and the Girl with the Matted Hair would put it in her pocket. Together they wandered past the prickle bushes through the vale of tears, over the river of sleep. They crossed the bridge and saw Billy Goat's Gruff and the place of the trolls, the witch's den, and they went down to where Rumpelstiltskin and Rip Van Winkle slept, and past that to where the mothers slumbered.

Awake! the Girl with the Matted Hair commanded at the Place of the Slumbering Mothers.

෨

As it happened, the Girl with the Matted Hair's mother died when she was only eighteen months old. She had been so young that her age was not even counted in years yet. How is that fair? she asked, and a fury filled her.

Some days, the Girl with the Matted Hair forces everyone to pet the dead crow on the path, to pet the feral cat or the mange of the dog—to put their faces close to the white moths that come from its bark—its circus of fleas, its clown cone collar, its disturbed sleep, but the child refuses. How is that fair?

Shunned by her mother, forsaken, on these days the girl felt mocked. She held a bouquet of crow feathers in her fist.

෨

Yes, but I do not have a father, the child said. All I have is a Glove!

True enough, the Girl with the Matted Hair says, but a father is not an Absolute. No one absolutely needs one. The Girl with the Matted Hair looks to her forlorn white-maned father on the periphery. And it was true in the Valley that with each passing year, there were fewer and fewer fathers to be had. Sometimes a Glove is enough, she said. Sometimes a Glove will suffice. A father isn't a Necessity. A father isn't a Requirement. The child shrugs. The potion: shed skin of snake. River water taken at the place it changed from fresh to salt, the rind of the elder tree, the carcass of the crow, the blood of a child. She ran a silk ribbon through a bowl of milk and then suckled the tether.

෨

THE GIRL WITH the Matted Hair had already begun going far off in an attempt to assuage her grief by the time the child met her at the Winter Bear School. Soon enough, Resurrection Science would become all the rage, but it wasn't yet. In certain ways, it could be said that the Girl with the Matted Hair was in the forefront of such science.

ᘒ

AFTER HER MOTHER died, the Girl had begun to display Matted Hair. Someone said it was her father's fault for never combing it, but the mother did not think that that was the reason, and sometimes on particularly difficult days, the girl grew a pelt for additional protection.

At the very least, the child's mother might offer to drag a brush through that thicket of hair, that wilderness of grief, that sorrowing. Poor Girl with the Matted Hair (no mother), the others whispered. If her mother were alive, she would have licked and licked until the fur was sleek and smooth.

Everything would have been different then.

The child admired the pelt. It was cool in the summer. It was warm in the winter. In the rain it was like a raincoat. Those who might try to break her spirit or her resolve or her heart, it frightened, and they would not come near. And she could always wear it when she visited her mother's grave, which was when she needed the most protection of all, and there it served as a kind of armor. Even though she pretended otherwise, she could not take it off—a pelt was permanent after all. The child did not mind her friend's pelt. The child was impervious to pelts.

ᘒ

THE GIRL WITH the Matted Hair lived some distance from the child, and so there was always the matter of transporting her, which the mother happily did, and sometimes on the way home when the children sat together in the backseat and chattered in their own language saying boden and pish-pish and wimple, and the child would sniff the girl hard—the forest and wind and sadness on her skin—and like a mother monkey, she would pick the nits from her pelt.

The girls spoke in their code in the backseat and dreamt their dreams and planned their plans. This was in the time that they were still mini-bodens, and not bodens yet.

ON THE DAYS the Girl with the Matted Hair came to play for the whole day, they would build a tent together out of the mother's diaphanous clothes, and when it was time for her to go home, she would hide in the crimson recesses of the house and she would not come out. At these times, when the Girl disappeared, her white-maned father wept because the story was that the Girl with the Matted Hair resembled exactly his deceased wife—but weeping did no good. After the house was searched, her white-maned father would roam the forests disconsolately looking for her. The child knew that the Girl with the Matted Hair would leave her baby teeth sunk into the trunk of a tree and they shone in the dark, and at night the child could always find something of her friend again that way.

ON SOME DAYS the girl felt mocked by the world, and mocked by the mothers and mocked by all the girls with mothers, and with extreme reserves of rage, she would turn on the child's mother, and pouring out the potions, and destroying the endless offerings, she would peer out at her and say, *not a single mother will be saved today.*

Forsaken, she had been forced by their existence to the place of the humiliated. By the time the mother and child had met the girl, she had already made several forays into the forest.

She pronounced it definitively; she could locate your utmost fear. *Not a single mother will be awakened by any child today.* The mother pats the Girl's head. If she could help to wake her mother just once, even for an instant, she would—there would not be a moment's hesitation.

Still no one who was there will soon forget the Girl with the Matted Hair glaring that afternoon in front of her pyre, stating most gravely to the mother, you are getting sleepy. On these days the mother is cursed, and she whispers and hisses from the cursed place where she is negated, cancelled, erased. Some days the Girl with the Matted Hair would put a Frozen Charlotte spell on the mother and bring her to the infirmary and wait until she was pronounced blue and dead. Nonetheless, the mother would rise up from the shabby hospital where she had been placed in a row of Charlottes, frozen solid. I've had it, the mother says, with the Furies today, and she gets up effortlessly. There's a flame at her shoulder and she rises as she always does, enormous and bright from the curses and cold, uncondemned.

I've had it with the potions, the cold, the sleep, the spells, she says, and she gets up and walks out, just like that.

☾

THE GIRL WITH the Matted Hair eats from a bowl like a small dog, too hungry to hear the admonishments. Doesn't your mother feed you? the mother asks. Hasn't anyone taught you how to eat?

As for the orphans, the mother does not know what to do about the orphans. The world is full of problems she does not know how to solve.

The GinGin girls long for the Starfruit Tree and the Scholar Tree. Understandably, the mother says, patting their heads.

☙

FOR THE GIRL with the Matted Hair, it was the unresolved absence that proved so difficult. An absence where the mother continued to reside—a space in the Girl that had never been sufficiently emptied. It was an absence always on the verge of filling, always on the verge of presence, always at the precipice, always at the cusp; the Girl with the Matted Hair, in a perpetual state of longing and hopefulness and sorrow, set out. She was tired of waiting. She knew where she had to go.

☙

SOME DAYS THE coast seemed clear; the mother thought at last she could walk around without worry—free of sad and longing children, or enraged and spiteful children who wished her nothing but harm. At last the mother thought she was safe. She imagined a place free of the world's harrowing grief, where everything was accounted for and taken care of, where all seemed right with the world, and that is when the Girl with the Matted Hair would appear. What was hard was not the appearance of the girl, whom she had grown to love, but the mother's assumption that she would ever be safe.

☙

THE GLOVE MARRIAGE is named for the custom of allowing a bridegroom's glove to stand proxy at the wedding in his absence. In the absence of the beloved, it is always possible to wed a glove by proxy. If the woman accepts the proposal, the bride can hold the glove instead of the groom's hand at the ceremony.

☙

PUT THE LID on the pot to ensure nothing climbs or flies in or that no one comes and steals the meats, the Girl with the Matted Hair says, tapping her on the shoulder. The sect members are gathering in the glade right now, she whispers.

☙

THE SECT MEMBERS gather in the glade. They inquire after the Rabbit and the other deities in the Valley. They fear the Mantis, they despise the Dormouse, and so on. After they gather in the glade, they make their way to their Pyramid. They meditate on the Seven Aphorisms. They contemplate the Bog. Where is Bog Belly by the way? the mother suddenly wonders. They speak of making the Secret Nectar. They stand in their sacred circle of mummified pets.

When no one is looking, Bunny Boy or Bog Belly, as the mother sometimes calls him, examines the corpses: a cat named Mimsy, a Doberman named Butch, Felicity, the guinea pig.

Meanwhile the members meditate on the Third Aphorism: Nothing rests, everything moves, everything vibrates.

Everything vibrates?
Not Mimsy, Bunny Boy thinks to himself.

☙

FIVE YEARS PASSED, and the Girl grew and the matted hair was not quite so apparent to human eyes. Civilized, to a point, she put away her witch's brews and began to search on Match.com, and PlentyofFish, and Cupid.com, and Chemistry.com, and LavaLife for a stepmother. She hoped her white-maned father might oblige.

19

RUMOR SPREAD IN the Valley about the Girl in the Reading Trance. There was a girl, it seemed, who couldn't get herself out of her book. She sat in the front of the school bus and sometimes she waved to her classmates as they got on and off, but she herself didn't move, and though she recognized them as they came and went, she could not make further contact with them.

At night while the others slept in their beds, the girl stayed on the bus in the bus field, and the next day she would wave to her classmates again. Only when the book was over did she get up and stretch her legs a little and get off the bus and look at the stars. Then the girl, lost in the book, accompanied by her dog Shimmer, would jump and play and run by the river.

The next morning the girl would begin another book, and even though it was the same book, each time she read it, a different story emerged, or something she had not seen before came to the fore— for the right book and the right girl are endlessly replenishing. It was the magic of the girl and the book. The children grew old and were replaced by other children, who passed her and waved and grew old, but the girl in the book was eternal and eternally new, and forever all things were possible.

THE PIANO TEACHER arrived all right angles and flying hair, and the child immediately adored her. The piano teacher stood stern over the child and divided the air into beats and measured phrases, and the silence was flooded with music and numbers and beauty. On some occasions, the piano teacher had to stop the child from getting up and dancing. She pressed with her long fingers on the child's shoulders every time it looked like she might rise up.

More and more the mother felt she had to struggle to stay alive in any room, but not in the room filled with music and the child crooning and the lithe fingers of the piano teacher. In that room for a moment all human genius moved through the child, who was belting out the Ode to Joy as she shimmied on the bench.

The piano teacher revered the great composers and had spent a lifetime with them. The child recognized this from the moment she had stepped into the house. Like the great river, it was a privilege to sit next to her. She handed the child Twinkle, Twinkle Little Star, a child's version of Mozart to play. Some things vanish, the mother thought, but not all. A few things will never die.

And one day, the teacher said, she would teach her to play Bach.

AT FIRST ALL the children flocked to the side of the tiny crushed girl who was their classmate. In a matter of a weekend she had gone from a tiny, running, laughing girl to a tiny crushed girl in the hospital. The first word had been in the form of a cry heard ringing through the stables. One of her horsey classmates had gotten the news first.

The helicopter came and took the girl away. She had fallen off an enormous horse. As if that were not bad enough, the enormous horse had then fallen and landed on top of her. Word from the hospital where she lay in a world of white was that there was to be one operation and the possibility, sometime later, of another. After a long time, the girl returned to school and the children fought to be near her, to wheel her around the periphery of things and to slip her sweets. They knocked each other down trying to get to the little broken girl first.

Later the children learned from the tiny girl that before she had gotten on the enormous horse for the last time, she had developed a fear of horses, a horse phobia, but her mother urged her back anyway because that is what one did in a new country such as this. The mother who was from a different, sadder country encouraged the girl to get back on the horse, as it was, she said, the American Way. In her first country, it would have been okay not to get on the horse again, but here it was not an option. This made it all the worse, somehow.

And it was only a matter of time before the children tired of the tiny crushed girl—in part because it is how children are, always ready to move on to the next thing, and in part because the tiny girl in her crushedness was becoming a tyrant. No one could give her what she wanted, which was two legs walking again, and so she would demand other things, and after a while when the children saw the big, slowly moving wheels of the wheelchair, they would pivot away and run in the opposite direction before the tiny girl could spot them. Increasingly it was only the girl, her mother, the teacher, and a tiny horse, which had somehow insinuated its way onto the crushed girl's lap.

In the solitary, increasingly hostile place she finds herself, she tries to recall a time only a short while ago when she felt impervious to pain. In her mind she goes out into the fields in search of an echo from her other life. She works to recall when she had friends for real, and there was pliable ground. Pity this suddenly isolated, crushed child.

She yearns for the time before her mother failed her, the time when she ran in the field with the others, the times before she was not broken or crushed—still a whole girl.

THE TEACHER DESPISED the children, a fact that the mother was well aware of, and now the first Parent-Teacher Conference was upon them. The mother entered the room and sat in the small chair and waited for the teacher to speak. All was silent. She had drained the room of all ambient sound so she might hear more precisely every word the teacher had to say.

The teacher believed it was her task to point out what she perceived as the weakness in each of the children and locate it for the parent. She would call one child disingenuous, another dimwitted, yet another ingratiating. She despised each child in his or her own unique way, and she was determined to find a way to slip this disdain casually into the conference, as they sat across from the other on the small chairs. Gleefully the teacher would wait for the perfect chance, the exact right place so as to create the maximum possible shame in the parent. It was this utterly mesmerizing moment in each conference that the teacher lived for; it transfixed and sustained her.

The mother sat silently waiting for the inevitable pronouncement, but while she waited, she isolated the skinny, mean-spirited teacher on the ever-darkening stage of her psyche. Soon in the quiet, the teacher began choking on a fishbone and was forced to excuse herself. While the mother waited, she focused on the small Bunsen burner in the back of the classroom.

When the teacher returned, the mother began her polite inquiry. Where most parents were rendered helpless in the face of the teacher, the mother enjoyed such encounters, as she was not reluctant to assign the word evil where it applied. Identified as such, the mother serenely proceeded.

Woe to the teacher who abuses her station, the mother thought to herself. A teacher possesses great power and so had to be held to a more rigorous standard than others in the community, and as such, a teacher's trespasses when they come are far greater than most of the trespasses of others. She holds a child's life and self-esteem in her hands, and as a result, a teacher must always be prepared to pay. Please rise, the mother commanded her, and the teacher, caught off-guard, got to her feet.

Isolated that way and standing against a blackboard, the mother took away her poker and eraser, her pink slips, her dunce caps, her reason to be. Woe to the teacher who abuses her station. It is unpleasant, the mother thought, but sometimes necessary, to watch an entire teacher go up in flames. For a moment the teacher stepped behind Miss Archway, the headmistress, her firewall, who had come in to help, but alas, to no avail.

No one knew why the South American doctor had appeared in the Valley and was sitting on a twirling seat at the diner next to the mother and child unless it was to deliver his soliloquy, which he now did. He was one of those Doctors without Borders doctors, and he did not know what he would do now that he had seen what he had seen in the borderless world.

The Doctor without Borders on the swivel seat in the diner seemed to be spinning faster and faster when the mother finally looked up from her teacup and said, look, slow down. He seemed more hyperactive child than doctor, and she imagined after all he had been through that he was probably going mad. Clearly he had spent a long time in the various denizens of disease throughout the world. He could not look at this child without seeing the other children, the ones with hallucinations and deliriums and fevers and tremors, wide fluctuations of pulse and blood pressure—everywhere he saw their seizures, their delusions: their fear of water and their fear of air. The ones said to be possessed by demons, the ones bitten by bats. She heard a kind of falsetto coming from somewhere deep within the tin of the diner and then a whooshing sound.

The Age of Funnels arrives in many guises. The anti-cyclones have come! he shrieks. Already whole villages have been swept away. One hundred thousand people at a clip! And with that the doctor spins away.

Demented, spacey, he calls out from what was once Burma, *Can-You-Still-Hear-Me?* His swivel seat still madly spinning next to the mother and the child who is stirring her chocolate milk. *Yes-We-Can,* the child calls through a paper megaphone.

CASPER THE BABY, along with Igor the Giant, appeared one evening at the Spiegelpalais. Casper was sleeping and Igor was dispensing leaflets and singing a gentle song. Igor's heart, the leaflet said, weighed a full pound and a third. When he saw the child, he showed her the baby and then gently cooed. Why is it giants are always gentle? the child wondered, but The Guinness Book of World Records had nothing to say about the gentleness of Igor. They cared only about his height, and his girth, and the size of his hands and his feet and his head. The mother, who kept a record of such things, said she prized Gentleness above all.

OKAY BUNNY BOY, the mother says, making little strangling motions as he runs triumphantly in. Do not ask what he carries in his mouth. It is always something different. PUT THAT DOWN, she yells, or I'll throttle you.

THE WARRIOR CHILDREN from suburbia's darkest heart were coming to the country day school to display their expertise in Tae Kwon Do, an ancient art of war.

The children looked a little sickly, the mother thought. They seemed to move through a chemical haze of performance-enhancing drugs and pesticides that were the minimum requirements for life in their excellent, leafy, perfectly serene wonder world.

There is something wrong with children from America's very own heart of darkness coming to the Valley in busloads and putting on shows, the mother thought. There is something wrong with children saying Yes Master, No Master on a stage. Prowess in combat is not something one should display. Public censure should rise up at these sorts of shows.

A Black Belt means that you have become impervious to darkness and fear. In the upside-down and backward world where they all live now, the warrior children who excel at unarmed destruction styles from three rival Korean villages are raised up on the shoulders of the others and praised. It should be remembered that Tae means to destroy with the foot, Kwon means to strike or smack with the hand, and Do means an art or a way of life. Tae Kwon Do: the art of destroying with the foot or the fist.

Where, she wonders, have all the Scholar-Fathers gone? And the Scholar-Artists? As always she has an insatiable hunger for the Scholar-Artists. Even one Scholar-Artist, amidst all these fists, in a time like this, would go a long way. There is something obscene, the mother thinks, about a display of this sort of prowess, especially when the country is at war.

At the end of the Tae Kwon Do show, the mother felt the need to make a small speech. She made her way to the stage. Couldn't these children find something better to do with their time? she wondered. It made the child remember the other time the mother had felt compelled to stand up. It was in church after the singing of the Battle Hymn of the Republic at the end of the Mass on the Fourth of July. Didn't they know there was a war being fought at that very moment that they were singing their fool heads off?

When the mother spoke like this, people often turned away. She had a very special way of saying: shame on your heads. The mother spoke for something she called pacifism, and after that, the other people looked at her like someone they could no longer understand. They shunned her. She was not the person they thought they knew. She had made hot cross buns, and in winter she made soup for the poor. She sang at the top of her lungs. Regardless of what they thought, she continued every Sunday to sit in the front pew with the child, and the war song was never sung again, probably because they did not want to see the mother stand up anymore.

When they were done, the corps of child warriors returned to their shiny wonder world carrying the mark the mother had made on their heads, and although it could not be seen, it was there, and they would have to bear it for a long time. It was not so bad because with all the technologies—the electronic whirring and beeping and instant messaging they were occupied with on the ride home—the children did not have to notice it so much.

A while back, when the Girl Scouts had come to town in a bus, the child had learned how to send smoke signals. Inefficient as it was, so far from the suburban warriors' ways of doing things as it was, the child loved this way of sending messages. Falling asleep that night, the child was glad not to have the mark of the mother on her head. The wind blew and the fire burned and the smoke rose high up over the

Valley. Are you there? was the message she sent. Would you like to be friends? And she waited for a response.

There is a deer wading in the pond, she wrote in smoke. I enjoy beading, do you?

Like this, the child is not so lonely.

At night in dreams, the suburban warriors return, texting and emailing as they come. The show begins. Gracefully, with upgraded combat methods, they toss enriched uranium and plutonium atoms back and forth to one another in a kind of slow motion.

There is much applause.

20

SEE HOW THE flies begin to gather around the still-mobile Bunny Boy, detecting the sweetness of his decline, eventual expiration, and demise. But this is still some years off, the mother assures the child, and she scoops up the cat, who had wandered onto the Aging Stage. For now Bunny Boy's end has not arrived, it is just something the mother sees before her like a photograph; she does not know why.

The mother hated photographs, especially the class photos the child brought home from school. The child had heard the mother say that a little school picture to her was like a little death. The French philosopher had lectured about the intense immobility of the photograph, and for once, the mother's protestations about the child's school pictures had fallen on sympathetic, albeit dead French philosopher ears.

Nevertheless, the child would like to order little wallet-sized photos to trade with her friends, and perhaps an 8×10 or at the very least a 5×7 to send to Uncle Lars and Uncle Ingmar, and Uncle Sven and Aunt Inga, and to Uncle Anders, who had never met the child even once, and of course to the Grandmother from the North Pole.

She doubts they will see the claustrophobic jail the mother speaks of when she speaks of a photo. If the mother ever gets a friend again, the child thinks they might try to make a photo exchange. She might put the picture of the friend in the tiny window space in the wallet meant for that, and she might look at the photograph and feel happy. After that, she might look at the little school photo of the child in the next wallet window, and smile too.

AT BACK TO School Night, the mother sits in the classroom as a variety of science experiments are staged by the children. Rows of mothers sit silently and watch, applauding at the appropriate intervals.

One of the Horsey Mothers stands up and peers into the bottle where a tiny funnel has been conjured, and in the swirl of the water she remembers something she had not remembered before. On the flatlands, when she was small and her aunt was big, they would stand in the funnel's path until the very last moment. Then her aunt, laughing wildly, would guide the child to the underground shelter.

The next time the teacher shook the bottle, the girl and her aunt were still small inside the funnel, but before the little girl knew it, they were in her uncle August's basement where there were live minks and dead minks, and the little girl was afraid. Her aunt was laughing with her uncle August and they were drinking elixirs, as her aunt called them, out of miniature crystal glasses. If you looked closer, you could also see chinchillas in cages at Uncle August's, and beavers, and muskrats. And along with live minks, chinchillas, beavers, and muskrats in cages and the dead minks hanging from the rafters, there were jars lined up along the walls filled with a rose-colored liquid. What the liquid was was anyone's guess.

GLAZED SOLDIERS PASS with jars of rose liquid looking for the Burning Field, and the mother puts her hand on their shoulders, soldier after soldier after soldier, and turns them around and points them in the right direction.

FOR THREE DAYS the Fathers had labored building the mute man of wood. It was nearly the solstice, and they had finished early, and so they sat around watching the man they had made and they waited. The man stood nearly fifty hands high. It was a magnificent sight, and the Fathers felt pride. Soon the Burners would arrive; word was they had made it as far as the glen. Months before they had set out on their journey here. It was a transfiguration and a purification as well as a penance, of that she was sure.

The Burners had dreamt of the man for many months and suddenly, at last, there he was before them. All praised the fifty-hand man. How mighty, how noble, they said, and then they took out a long-stemmed match. In the moment before he was set aflame, the mute man seemed about to say something, the mother thought. At last he caught fire. He is the most beautiful Burning Man of all, someone could be heard bellowing. Praise him as he goes!

Fire illuminated the Valley, and there was nowhere one could look and not see it. Inside the fire was another fire, and inside that one, another, and so on. The Burning Man held a multitude of fires within, and all recalled their own origins, and the history of the fires they carried inside, and in not such a long time the man, once fifty hands, was reduced to ash.

Part of the Burning Man Creed was to leave no trace behind, and the Burners stayed until the Burning Man was done, and then they buried the ashes. After the ashes were buried, the Cooling Man Committee arrived to calculate the Burning Man's contribution to Global Warming, and they exacted their fee. Meanwhile the Burners waited for a clue as to where the Fathers might build the next mute man of wood and straw. Ash graves mottled the Valley, and the Fathers and the Burners alike lay down side by side and waited for a sign. The mother stepped over the prostrate men who appeared to be asleep.

Earlier that day, the mother and child had gone in search of the lost spring, the place where they would burn the next man, something the mother and child knew in advance, because Wise Jean had seen it in a dream. Liquid water graces our planet. The place was named "the reed shelter protecting the little water-place spring," or Poughkeepsie, by its Indians long ago. There, a clear water spring had been issuing up longer than recorded history. The child took the mother's hand.

Some time from now after the Burners have vanished, leaving without a trace, the mother will envision the last of the Burning Men, and she will carry that silhouette behind her eyes a very long time. How beautiful you are, Burning Man, the mother will whisper. The child knew there was nothing she could do—a part of the mother had already left to meet him, had always been walking to him, the last Burning Man at the end of the world. And the fire.

OTHER EFFIGIES APPEARED along the route. Four men in bird suits called Operation Migration had arrived at the Spiegelpalais. The four birdmen brought four gliders equipped with four silent propellers. It's so nice to see you fellows again, the people of the Valley said. The four men nodded, and smiled through their beaks, but they did not speak.

The men, dressed as birds, were to teach the Whooping Crane babies first how to eat and then how to fly, and eventually how to migrate. Operation Rescue promised all the basics because there were not enough actual adult Whooping Cranes to perform these tasks anymore. The four men in bird suits with the four gliders would be their substitutes. Day after day they wore the bird suits and silently slipped a crane-head puppet on so as to teach the chicks how to peck and forage.

Because there were no adult birds to sing lullabies to the Whooping Crane eggs, the eggs were played recordings of the glider-propeller song, and when they were old enough to migrate, they would follow that sound, with the four silent, suited men that had taught them how to eat and fly leading the way.

There's no hope for the Whooping Crane in the long term, the birdmen say later, lifting their bird masks after their mission is accomplished. There are just no Whooping Crane habitats left to live in anymore.

Still. . . .

In the off-season, Operation Migration has been sighted on a faraway river, where they ferry salmon on barges past a dam's hydroelectric turbines so that the salmon can spawn. Though the salmon suits are not required, Operation Migration likes to wear them anyway.

ONCE A YEAR, on the night of the Autumnal Equinox, the mother gets out the Glove and places it on the Etiquette Bed. Along with the Glove, there is a dome, a snow globe that says Paris, and a gold locket shaped like a heart. All are assembled for the child to see. It is a night unlike any other night, a night without fear or reproach: the anniversary of the night the child was conceived.

On this night, everything is perfect in the world. The hours are equally divided between night and day, dark and light, and most remarkably, that is the kind of child she has become: perfectly balanced, astrologically prefigured. The child feels dizzy and weak in the presence of these things. The heart stops, but then begins to spin again. Everything at this moment is at the mercy of the mother, and the collection of objects, and the night.

IN THE NIGHT, the mother could hear the beautiful night music passing through the left ventricle. After a while, in an attempt to rest, she would put on the television and watch the screen's deep blues which she found beautiful too.

She couldn't seem to absorb the complex sentences being spoken on the television news anymore though. They came at her in such a way that she became disoriented and incapable of comprehending exactly what was being said. After a time, she learned how to slow the words down and listen in more manageable clauses. It was a pretty good trick. At warped-clause speed, it was a little bit easier. It went something like this when the mother listened in her partitioned way:

Late word
that a body
has been recovered
from the water.
A girl
twenty months old
and her mother
who was five months pregnant
remain missing
along with six others.

The mother shut off the TV and ran into the room where the child slept. The child was still wearing her pumpkin stem hat, and in her small hand she clutched her wand of cornstalks. She had been a harvest dancer the day before in the school pageant.

The mother sat on the bed next to the breathing, sleeping child and looked at her a long time, and it seemed to her as if she sat in the very Court of Miracles.

DOES IN HEAT were leaping hither and thither, and the glen was filled with merriment. Estrus was upon them. In the feverish, leaping world they seemed impervious—nothing could harm them, flush as they were with life and love. Testosterone was high and days were short. The desire to replicate was all, and the splendor of the desire filled up the mother until she thought she might burst. The energy of the days and nights made the world glisten. Who can weather this? the mother wondered.

How she loved the swellings of the season. Foreheads and antlers pressed onto small trees left a scent from the preorbital glands in the forehead or the mouth. The velvet that was being shed from antlers attached itself to the night. In the night, these nocturnal longings come to the mother with full force. Bucks danced by with cornstalks and stars caught in their antlers. Finally the antlers shed, and the mother, walking through the glen, picked them up.

EACH YEAR AT the time of the rut, the mother was reminded that the child would not be with her forever. The rut served as a reminder that soon indeed the child would be gone. The transformation was already in motion: one child would soon exit, and another would take her place. Soon her body would break into night and song. For now the child was still held in the Fawn Enclosure, but she could not be held there forever.

Fire ants are a problem for the fawns, the child will report, and if the fawns make it past the fire ants and the predators, they still must continually find food and cover. During the Rut, does abandon their young and run around as if lost. This leaves only the child to care for the fawns, and she collects fire ants in a jar.

Troubles indeed abound. In the headiness and distraction of the season, the hunters move in to stalk their delirious prey, taking utmost advantage of the situation and paying no mind to the gleaming spectacle before them.

With the child safely tucked away, the mother in a black dress moves toward the hunters now. They are excited—and weird beyond belief. They break out their rattle bags meant to emulate sparring bucks looking for a match, and indeed bucks are often drawn to the sound, raring to compete. If the mother were a shooter, she would certainly consider shooting now. No bucks have responded to the rattling and grunting yet, but as in most things, patience is a virtue. The hunter in her sights throws in some snorts and wheezes and high-pitched grunts for good measure. During the rut, the hunters sometimes wear false eyelashes and don other glamour indicators and make doe eyes in the attempt to attract a buck.

If the mother were not a shooter before this, certainly what the hunter does next would be the tipping point. The hunter is now making doe bleats. Most useful in the hunter's repertoire is the doe bleat. For a deer, the doe's bleat is the origin of song, the origin of well-being, the most important sound of all. A doe's bleat is the first real sound any deer hears. When the doe or buck rushes to the bleat, they are really rushing toward their mothers again.

Also in the repertoire, there is a maternal grunt the hunters know will call fawns, were it not for the child, holding them back, out in the Fawning Habitat.

How foolish and giddy the men are. Today the mother is not surprised at their mass disappearance from the planet. She takes their rattles and tells them it is time now to put away childish things.

Oh, if only the mother had the fortitude to shoot a hunter in his lover's bed when he is at his most vulnerable and distracted during the rut. She pictures a pile of camouflage clothes, drenched in blood, on the floor. How easy it would be to stop them, these men marked by shameful rattling or grunting or making Mother Sounds. Better to lure them into ecstatic union, and at that heightened moment shoot them, she thought; it would not be hard; she could eliminate them from the Valley and there would be nothing anymore to fear.

Let them leap and fall and disappear, leap and fall and disappear.

BABY SKELETONS HAVE three hundred parts. They have more cartilage than bone. So when you are carrying a baby, you are really carrying a package of cartilage or gristle. Over time, most of this cartilage turns to bone in a process called ossification.

Later, when the baby became a child and was doing some long bone growth in a field, she looked up: Uncle Ingmar! In Italy there were cookies shaped like bones called Ossi di Morto. Uncle Ingmar had put one in the child's mouth once. Each long bone had its own growth center. There was something frightening in this. She had a lot to do before the growth plates closed. Day turned to night and fall became winter. She looked to the sky where the wolf resided, waiting to escort her across the velvet divide. Soon she would be grown. Stars and dark brambles formed a crown above her head, and the wolf bent down and nuzzled her.

THE CHILDREN FRIGHTENED the mother every day and every night of the year, so she was better prepared than some for the marauding legions that came to her door on All Hallows Eve.

The Celts believed all laws of space and time were suspended on Halloween, allowing the spirits world to intermingle with the world of the living. At this time, the spirits would come in search of living bodies to possess, but the still-living did not care to be possessed and so would dress up in all manner of ghoulish costume and noisily parade around being destructive and rowdy so as to scare away the spirits looking for bodies. In the ninth century, early Christians walked from village to village begging for soul cakes—square pieces of bread with currants. The more soul cakes you got, the more prayers were promised to be said on behalf of the dead, hovering relatives, so as to speed their passage to heaven.

Not even her friend Jack could have survived the catastrophe, the mother thinks. Not even Jack. But because of his nefarious schemes, Ponzi and otherwise, and his contributions to the Great Malaise, Jack had been denied access into Heaven. Having outsmarted the very devil itself in the end, Jack was also denied access into Hell, and so Jack roamed. The devil gave him a single ember to light his way across the darkness. The candle was placed in a hollow turnip to keep it glowing longer. This was Jack's lantern.

A pumpkin is as good as a turnip when carrying a light through the infinite dark. They stand now at the mother's door, the little urchins holding, like Jack, turnips and pumpkins lit by embers, and carrying loot bags. Apparently the spirits will wait for as long as it takes to find a body to enter.

The mother thought she had remembered something—something the spirits had brought up in her, on this night of roaming souls— but now with the dawn she had begun to forget again. The next day, November came with its beautiful erased sky. She felt an uncommon gratitude, for she had lived to see November again. She was taken aback by the thought. Fallen leaves crackled under her feet. Death pulled at her, and in the glen, many plant species had vanished. Oblivion was above her head and all around, but it had not entered her yet.

vision

THE CHILD SAID that her eyes were hurting her from looking at everything so hard all the time, so the mother took her to the eye doctor, and the child's eyes were projected onto a screen. At first they were almond-shaped and looked like a cat's eyes, obsidian, glittering, but after a few moments, the cat's eyes vanished and what was behind the eyes was revealed. First the mother saw the retina, and then past the retina, and then to the veins which branched in every direction and then beyond that.

Suddenly the mother was a child again in her backyard in winter at night holding the hand of her own mother, the Grandmother from the North Pole. Who could have imagined that her own child's eye was lined with the exact trees of her childhood? How strange is the very world we inhabit and call home.

Standing now, on the orb of the child's eye, the full moon shone brightly and she looked more closely at those bare branches. There were the trees, each one of them: two maples, four birch, then an ash, then another maple, an oak. The mother put her hand to the screen— yes, as a girl she had memorized those trees, and in an instant she was young again and all the brothers were there and baby Inga. Snow covered the ground and the stars were beginning to come out.

The child, off the screen now, tells the eye doctor that more and more, the mother's eyes turn watery and soft, and the doctor says that it is a natural occurrence at a certain age. One thing naturally begins to blur into the next.

The North Pole Grandmother took her small daughter's hand and pointed to the Big Dipper and then to the Little Dipper. We orbit the sun, and the moon in turn orbits us. She loved the winter sky: Orion, the North Star, and Cassiopeia's Chair, and the branches of the trees.

She remembered standing there, looking at the sky the night the Grandmother from the North Pole, who was young and supple, told the mother, that even though she was just a girl, she already held an infinitesimal speck of her own child inside her.

The mother blinked and the Grandmother from the North Pole blinked, and the trees seemed dipped in liquid silver.

THEY HAD TO pass Nine Partners, and Tick Tock Way, and Deer Run, and travel under the Seven Stars Underpass before they got to him—the Boy in the Glen. The boy played a glinting horn and the child thought the boy played exceedingly well. The boy played, and the child danced, and they did not notice that the fox was in the snowy field behind them looking for the chicken. They existed in a magical circle beyond harm. There is something so charmed about a boy in a glen playing a horn while the red fox passes and the child dances.

After a while, it grew dark and the children filled the horn with oil, lit it, and made their way back. When they were together they were protected and had immunity from all the fruitless works of darkness. Making their way to the cottage in the glen, even the boy's father,

touched by the charms of the children and the night, was made powerful and knowing, and without the least hesitation, snatched the chicken
at the last minute from the jaws of the fox.

In the distance their alluring music could be heard: a panpipe,
bells. Give us the courage to enter the song, the mother thought, looking at the path from which the children would soon materialize.

A CROWN OF winterberry adorned the concrete rabbit's head. Beside
it was an identical rabbit made entirely of snow.

Someone had brought the rabbit a Divinity Basket. Someone else
had brought a pair of Hare-Sticks, an auspicious gift, to celebrate the
beginning of winter. The child was delighted to find the Hare-Sticks, each
about five inches long. She placed them end-to-end so that they looked
like a single wand. She then wrapped them in sprigs of wild thyme, club
moss, and mountain sage dug from beneath the early snow. She waved
the festive hare wands above her head. Winter had finally come.

AT THE WINTER Solstice service, the snow- and fire-lights flickered,
and the lost shadows of animals looked monstrous before her on the
cave wall. The mother remembered now making a rabbit of snow. A
rabbit of snow and ice in winter is more precious than any other kind
of rabbit—that is obvious—its long ears shadowed against the firewall.
In the flicker, there was a glimpse of something ancient and in motion,
and she felt herself to be a part of something elusive and more beautiful
than she could understand. Now that winter had arrived, the mother
longed to see the wolf again, though in the Valley it was forbidden to
even utter the word wolf during the twelve darkest days.

She thought of the bats in the nearby caverns hibernating. Before
you knew it, it would be spring, and she would see them again, though

she knew that it did not really matter what guise the bat came in. Whether the bat came as a bird, or an angel, or a wolf, or a rabbit made of snow, it scarcely mattered—she would always recognize it.

EVERY YEAR UNCLE Ingmar arrived with the snow, and this year was no exception. He had come from Minnesota and, as usual, would stay for what seemed a very long time, and the mother, as usual, put him up at the local inn. There is no room for you here, Uncle Ingmar, the mother said. While Uncle Ingmar was jolly and gregarious, the mother was non-negotiable and austere. Side by side it would seem impossible that the two were in any way related.

To the child, Uncle Ingmar was all sweetness and folly and light. The only time he ever exhibited his other side was when he first saw the Grandmother from the North Pole's grandfather clock in the mother's kitchen. Why should the mother have it? Was he not, by birth, entitled to the clock?

Don't stay up late at night with Uncle Ingmar, the mother said, and the child nodded. The obedience of the child frightened the mother, but it also consoled her to know that the she would not stay up with the man who is her brother and covets the clock. The mother thinks of love's unnerving proximity to hate.

If it were up to Uncle Ingmar, they would stay up half the night drinking vodka and hot chocolate and writing poems about the magnificent Swedish clock with its curvaceous body and starry crown.

As it was, Uncle Ingmar and the child had already composed one. They read it aloud:

There was a fancy Swedish clock
It had no tick it had no tock

The brother loved the sister a lot
The sister loved the Swedish clock
And what is foul, looks somehow fair
And what is fair is not tock tock tock.

The mother grimaced looking at the two of them at the early dinner, lit by candles: these were the dark days.

She looked suddenly to the ceiling and remembered during one of Uncle Ingmar's extended visits at Christmas the child, just a baby at the time, pointing at the hanging circle of holly and candles aflame. It was before she could speak. And Uncle Ingmar there with the silver basin of water. The child never forgot the burning wreath.

UNCLE INGMAR WOULD talk about the "Hour of the Wolf" as he assembled his shadow theater. A flashlight and cutouts. A magic lantern. And there in the night, the wolf towered on the child's wall.

Where is your mother? Uncle Ingmar has the wolf ask. And the shadow girl whispers in Uncle Ingmar's girl's voice: she's asleep in the snow under a stone.

THE GRANDMOTHER FROM the North Pole was acquiring extra vision in her left eye. It came from years and years of looking at snow and white light, the Grandmother surmised. To her ancestors it had happened, and now it was happening to her, and maybe one day to the child, it would happen again. The doctor agreed that people of Nordic Origin seemed at a certain age predisposed to this darkly illuminated sight, which was sometimes confused with blindness.

The child could not imagine what the sparkling eyes of the Grandmother saw now as the snowflakes fell into their cereal bowls, but before very long, the grandmother said simply, I see white roses. Sometimes, though not often, she said, you see a thing as it really is.

After a few moments the Grandmother looked up and said, Dark matter really exists, but so does Luminous matter. And above the grandmother and child, the flying reindeer passed.

THE MOTHER WOKE early to bake the Epiphany Cake. As always, it was to be plain with a little bit of spice to commemorate the Magi's gifts to the Christ child, and inside a little trinket or treasure was to be placed.

The mother plucked a fancy almond from the cupboard to place in the batter. She assumed the trinket was meant to be the Christ child. Whoever found it would be designated Queen of the Evening and be allowed to preside over the Night's most exquisite mysteries. The mother and child thought that this sounded wonderful, to be Queen of the Mysterious Evening.

The mother made the drink called Lamb's Wool, and she unwrapped the chalk from its purple vestment. The mother knew that, as usual, the child would find the treasure and she thought, yes, that is as it should be, and as usual, the child would get to write in chalk on the door as a welcome C M B, which stood for Caspar, Melchior, and Balthazar, who were the kings.

The mother now regretted that she hadn't at the last minute, drawn a little face on the almond, or if not a face then at least a smile. There would be golden paper crowns, and candles. The Queen of the Mysterious Evening would wear a robe and carry a glittering staff and genuflect under the cold night sky.

All of a sudden, out of nowhere, the mother was overtaken by a desire so pressing she leapt from her chair. I should love to see the

Snowy Owl, she said aloud, and she ran to the window which already framed the darkness though it was still afternoon. Its white feathers filled her sight. The dormouse took refuge. She thought of the single star slung above the house.

Meanwhile, the silent almond slept deep in the cake, and waited.

IN THIS COLD circle of stones, in the infinite darkness, a grieving mother walks barefoot through the snow. There are roses between her toes and she carries a lantern. It's Mary, poor thing, the Virgin, holding her unending vigil. She's waiting for her son to return.

The mother wishes that the Virgin might stop, and put down her lantern, and rest somewhere awhile—anywhere but here, any night but tonight.

THE WORLD IN its present form was passing away. So said Saint Paul to the Corinthians, and the mother had to agree.

The child and the Grandmother float by, clicking and whirring all aglow in the light of three laptops, five enormous fluorescent force fields, a stack of illuminated discs, headphones, iPod shuffles, glitter wands, shining pendants, voice mails, remnants of music and time, fragments of the world's information trailing them.

A GALAXY IS a massive interstellar phenomenon with gasses and dust and stars and dark matter. One trillion stars might orbit a common center. The child thought of star clusters, star clouds, stellar oceans, and interstellar clouds. The word galaxy is from the Greek word that means milky. The child liked the idea of a storm of milk or a storm of stars.

It is said that Zeus placed his infant son Hercules, born of a mortal woman, on the sleeping goddess Hera's breast so that the baby would drink her divine milk and become immortal. When Hera awoke and realized she was nursing an unknown baby, she pushed the baby away, and a jet of milk sprayed the night sky and became the Milky Way.

THE CHILD CLOSED her eyes and pictured the galaxy's curving, dusty arm. There are probably 100 billion galaxies in the observable universe. They drift through the elliptical cosmos. The child thinks of the Grandmother, fixes her in the moment so that she can never forget her. I feel in my body that you are due, the child says on the phone, trying to coax the Grandmother to them. And with that, the Grandmother from the North Pole fills the sky. She is 100,000 light-years in diameter, 1,000 light-years thick. She contains three hundred billion stars.

THE CHILD'S AUNT remembered the curving staircase and the winding corridors of the house in which she was born. The ventricle, like a shell, floods with seawater. The aunt enters a pre-human slumber. How beautiful is the heart!

NEURAL ACTIVITY SWEEPS across the fetal retinas as if the nervous system is rehearsing for vision by running test patterns across them. Rehearsing for life. You've got to hand it to babies, the Grandmother says with wonder.

There are death rehearsals as well, the Grandmother from the North Pole says, as the eye accustoms itself to the darkening, and the blur.

SOME COMETS HAVE long thin orbits. They may spend centuries away from the sun, frozen solid. When they at last come back, they come as strangers and in a new form. They have no memory of where they have come from, though they have been there for centuries, and they have no idea what is before them, or that it will last millennia. There is a pull and that is all.

SHE LOOKS OUT onto the white field and the word Sneemanden comes to her, and she sees in the distance a man made of snow with his back to her, wearing a sad hat. She has gone back to school, the mother reminds herself. It is the reasonable explanation. At three o'clock she will reappear.

THE BOY, UNCLE Ingmar says, is no longer held together by screws; he is held together by newly knitted bone. The long winter nights had been filled with bone knitting, and now the bone knitting was complete. When he takes out the screws, the doctor will give them to the boy in a jar, Uncle Ingmar says. When the boy returns home with his jar, he will dig a hole and he will place the jar in the snow.

Even though the bones had knitted themselves back together, still the winter had not passed.

QUIETLY, THE MOTHER paddles out to the Isle of the Dead while the child sleeps. There's a little man there she sometimes visits in the night, and he tells her of the vaulted world.

What does he have to do with her? the mother wonders. And who are these people, weeping at the periphery?

She is a little lost among the intense traffic of souls, though it is true that she is not so lonely as usual. The souls create their own night with the quality of their dark light. Each night the mother dreams of the man put back into his flat photographic drawer in his mausoleum on William

Street. At these times she feels not quite alive and not quite dead. When the mother tells the child the story of the man made of vapor and the pull of the drawer, the child protests and says that she does not like to think of the mother like that, though she suspects she is in part responsible for this twilight state the mother inhabits. The mother smiles and reassures her that nothing could be further from the truth.

The mother is in flames. Calmly she turns to the man in his vault and he soothes her. She opens the flat tray he is put away in every night. In his drawer, in the deep freeze, the mother cools down and is at peace. You've got to admit it's lovely in the subzero numbers here on the darkest street in the world, she says, on the most narrow of streets in the world, did she mention that before? Dwarfed by enormous skyscrapers, pillars of black glass, domes—who has seen such darkness? A figure blindfolded holds a scale. There's a large bull in the square. Men and women in their daylight suits, even at night, carrying torches. All moving in vain toward the atrium.

All those who toiled in those Towers are vaporous in the flat drawers now. A drawer opens, and she slips in smooth and quiet and flat. The night a porous, perforated surface.

SNOW FALLS AND the roots call to the mother and the sleeping small-clawed animals in their burrows and tunnels and the winter vegetables that lie peacefully untouched under the earth. When she walks on the earth's crust, she grows drowsy now feeling their sleep. Magnified, so many sleeping creatures multiplied, she can barely lift a foot now. What is wrong? the child says, and lies on the ground on her back, and helps the mother lift her feet one boot at a time.

The child has read that beneath the city of Paris there is another city. There you can find a home for abandoned children. I should like to see where the animals sleep in winter, says the child, watching her mother's eyes slowly begin to close.

THE VIRGIN INVITES the child, lambless, into the sheepfold. The child tells her of the drink the mother made called Lamb's Wool.

A sheepfold holds the sheep who are light and in high winds can blow around or even be taken away by a strong enough gust. Also the sheepfold prevents the sheep from unwittingly walking into the river. When Lamby comes back, she will be sure he is put in a place like this.

The child, who is not that light anymore, wanders the sheepfold and waits. Come to me, the Virgin says. The Virgin wraps the child in a blanket of fleece and pets her hair until she is asleep.

22

the mothering place

THERE WAS ANOTHER mother with another child not far from here, except the child had grown up and gone away as children naturally do. This got the mother to thinking how many times, in this very spot, the mother-and-child scenario had replicated itself through time. She thought of the reproduction of motherhood and the reproduction of childhood, and she found herself caught in the reverberating world—the world of multiplications and resonances and profiles.

Children a long time after they have left are known to return to the Mothering Place, and when they arrive, some remnant of childhood is always still there, waiting for them. Sometimes there is still an alive mother and sometimes there is not.

One child, now a grown man, has just returned from the war. Nevertheless, he limps home to the place of his birth, and his mother is there still waiting. In the forest, she points to a stain on the forest floor. When the neighbors kill a deer, they always call and tell her where they did the field dressing, and she goes in the middle of the night and grabs the heart. The mother is not entirely sure whether her son is living or dead—or somewhere in transit, like the steaming body of the deer.

The next time your life feels bereft of meaning, go to the Mothering Place if you can, and greet that mother, and she will open her cupped hands and show you the heart.

AT THE EDGE of the Mothering Place the gamelan can be heard—it's the Boy in the Glen and his friends come to play their song. Xylophones, drums, gongs, a bamboo flute, and strings being plucked.

THE TROOPS, YOUNG already, grow younger and younger until they are small boys preparing for the first day of school, but while their bodies have shrunk and they have grown backwards into childhood, their uniforms are still regulation size and their helmets are enormous, obscuring their view (maybe it is better that way) but also decapitating them. The boys lift the helmets up and laugh.

THE MOTHER TOLD Uncle Ingmar after the child was asleep, that although it was obvious, she could not get her mind around the idea that the boy in the coffin would not be growing anymore. She had glimpsed him in her sleep and had immediately begun to problem solve, as all good nurses will. She thought the coffin might need an extra hinge as an accommodation just in case, like when the guests suddenly appear at the door out of nowhere and you quickly put a leaf in the dining room table. There was no telling what might happen under the earth. She would hate to imagine. The ancients understood this. She thought it peculiar that the growth plates would stop just like that. With an adult, who had finished his growing, it would be different.

THE SOLDIERS SWOON on the fever field and they call into the future for their betrothed and for their progeny and they weep. The soldiers swoon and call for their mothers. They are between souls—neither children nor men—and in the in-between state they perish.

NOW IT WAS clear. She realized that what she had once thought was a coyote staring at her in the driveway was actually the Egyptian god Anubis, the Jackal, escort to the Afterlife, the god who protected the dead on their path to the Underworld. Even in profile there it was staring back at her now from inside the child's history book. When she at last looked up, she saw four coyote-ushers there to greet her.

CECIL PETER THE one-armed handyman skittered down the icy path carrying a dead rat by the tail. Maggots feasting on a cadaver sound like Rice Crispies popping, Cecil Peter said rather cheerfully in passing. The mother never knew what Peter Cecil might say next. It was frightening knowing that someone the mother needed as much as she needed Cecil Peter was also someone who was going to invariably terrify her again and again in ways she could not even begin to imagine. She bows her head and waits.

THE NEXT TIME a bat entered the house she would be better prepared, she reasoned. She imagined catching the bat in a bag and saying calmly and with a certain authority, yes the bat is in a bag on the porch. She knew the bat, in a bag or not, would always function as a catalyst. Something always shifted after a bat. She hoped next time, if there must be a next time, she would better understand what its appearance signified, so as better to be able to capitalize on the change its appearance foretold.

If the bat returned in winter she would know to bury it in snow. This would ensure its brain, frozen, would be properly encased and preserved for testing.

She would capture it and put it in a hat or a bag, and bury it in the snow and uncover it, when the time came, with her foot. She would paw the snow like a reindeer or a horse. She would not be afraid.

She would never allow herself to be that afraid again.

FLITTERMOUSE. FLITTERMOUSE, WHAT are you doing in the child's house? The shadow bat swooped. The mother was dreaming. She got up and looked out onto the white world and then fell back into sleep. The bats were hibernating, but the shadows multiplied.

UNCLE INGMAR, UNCLE Ingmar what are you doing in the child's house in the deepest of wee hours?

Shh, he whispers, I'm here to steal the mother's clock.

IN THE QUIET and distance of winter, while the snow still blanketed the earth, the mother had agreed to join the local farm cooperative, where for a fee each week, beginning in the spring, there would be a delivery of the Valley's bounty. What could be better than that? the mother wondered. All that nature afforded, available to them.

And she sank back into the calm and white of winter, but when she fell asleep, the Spring was there to meet her:

The Valley is indeed teeming with vegetation. Every week more and more fruits and vegetables arrive, the Valley's pride. Every day the mother dutifully cooks the bounty, but impossibly, the more she cooks, the more vegetables appear. How can she ever keep up with the growing world, wild and alive? she wonders. Now the mother walks on the spongy vegetable floor. Now the walls are lined with rotting cabbage heads, and the child refers to them as skulls. She ponders her problem for a while, and then in the terrible hollow of the room, she begins to weep. Who can keep up? Not she. She welcomes in the white worm, the green worm, the maggots.

I hope there will be a solution soon, the child whispers to her, before more white worms and more green worms and beetles or much worse comes. And the mother nods and sits all day in the center of the house and forces herself to eat, spooning in mouthful after mouthful of the blackening vegetables. Every variety of bug and slug call to the mother now, and she looks around and smiles because at least the child has gotten free. At least the child has escaped for another day.

The child recognized in the mother the charm of withdrawal this terrible nest presented, the dark lull of the vegetable world, mute but breathing in the room. It was dark and quiet and a little mossy in there. How easy it would be to bolt the door and sink into a stupor, into the stench and the heat and the strange echo made by the sponge-blackened decay.

Muffled, swaddled by layers of vegetative matter, the child feared the mother might find her permanent rest there, and she feared the empty cave of her mother's voice in such a room, and the way of all flesh and the specter of decay, which so overwhelmed the space. When the child entered the decay of the room, she entered as a child, but when she left, she felt she was not a child any longer.

And even though when the mother woke herself it was still winter, and the world was white and not a single vegetable had yet arrived, she shuddered. She walked to the child's room and smoothed her hair and pushed a few tendrils away from her face. That night, sitting there on the child's bed, she vowed come spring that she would do whatever it took to keep the child safe.

When the child wakes it is still winter, but the mother is outside constructing a vegetable stand next to the Concrete Rabbit. At this stand, the mother explains, they will give all of nature's bounty to the poor. Before one vegetable or fruit darkens their door, it shall be given away, and God will look with favor on their offering.

Blessed are the poor, for they are among God's most beloved creations. Giving under any circumstances is joyful; feeding the multitudes under any circumstances is a pleasure. Blessed indeed are the hungry; they shall be fed.

At season's end if there was anything left over, the mother, who could not bear the idea of waste, would allow the remaining vegetables into the house where she will store them in screw-top jars. When a person was mummified, their internal organs were placed in canopic jars and guarded by gods. The stomach was put in a jackal jar. The lungs in a baboon jar, and in a falcon jar, the intestines.

Perhaps the outcome, as foretold in a dream, would have been different had she known that certain fruits and vegetables emit an odorless, colorless gas that speeds up the ripening process and leads everything to premature decay. Perhaps, if she had known she should not put the spinach so close to the apples, or the tomatoes so near the cauliflower, things would have turned out differently.

No matter; the mother's solution in the end worked perfectly: the hungry were fed and the mother was spared her madness, and the child, her burden of sorrow—a while longer.

23

FOR A WEEK, nothing had been heard back from the elders who had gone on the spaceship to Mars. They had all won the honor in a lottery. The mission was to be fueled only by solar power, but with winter and the distance they would be travelling away from the sun, they understood that they would inevitably succumb.

It's snowing here, they had recently reported, and they watched the robotic arm unfurl to collect a sample of ice. They had all sent their video farewells because, as they said, their battery packs were getting low. With the verdict clear and so soon upon them, the mother imagined their voices might be filled with flickering and uncertainty and static, but in fact they came in loud and clear with their last thoughts and impressions and reminiscences.

> *. . . beautiful like nothing else . . .*
> *. . . I remember the drowned boy . . .*
> *. . . the three-legged race . . .*
> *. . . the Game of Graces . . .*
> *. . . the Spiegelpalais . . .*
> *. . . not to be believed . . .*
> *. . . Marco Polo . . .*
> *. . . the retina . . .*

Still, in the end, it was a quiet exit: the spacecraft put itself into low-energy safe mode. Daily, it revived itself for a few moments, but the solar panels could only generate enough power for the sojourners to fall into a lovely snippet pattern, fragments like *burning* and *rabbit* were heard, and then nothing more.

Soon, when the sunlight disappeared entirely, temperatures fell to −300 degrees, and carbon monoxide gas encased them. One final fully articulated and beautiful sentence was heard:

There is something . . . exhilarating about . . . the inevitable, the eloquent last man said, *and the call . . . to interminable sleep . . . and the snow.*

WHEN THE CHILD opens the door on the dark winter night, the house is lit from within, and she looks at the clock, and she nods her head.

Come in, she whispers, we've been waiting for you. What big teeth you have!

THEY WERE WALKING by the water when a jet plane materialized before them. It descended serenely and landed on the glinting silver river only yards away from where they stood. Though often when the mother saw an airplane she would flinch, this time she was not frightened at all. More than anything it resembled an enormous gray goose with silvery wings floating in the hypnotic blue-gray river.

There is a plane in the river, the mother said to the child, and the child, mesmerized, nodded her head and said, maybe Lamby is in there. Before long, a hatch opened, and one hundred or more small people stepped carefully out onto the wings. The mother and child took from their pockets their small inflatable boats and blew them up, with help from a few passersby. They paddled out to the little passengers, who had begun to shiver, as it was still winter.

SHE LOVES THE snowy, sealed-up world. The way they'll never make it to the cash machine or the dance lesson. The remote world. The way the American President in black evening coat can appear from around any corner, with his melancholy musings about whether God will preserve or destroy the Union. Profound darkness inhabits him. She has seen him before on one bent knee at the Mothering Place. He tips his top hat now and bows to the mother and child in the white world, as they pass.

THE MOTHER STRUGGLED to wake herself but she could not. That night from the 101st floor, she fell. When the resurrection men came, she was waiting. She had forgotten about the resurrection men by then, and they frightened her . . .

THE TIME OF the mysterious dyings had come. Bellwether creatures were falling from the sky. First it was the frogs, widespread over the continent of Africa, then it was the bees, and now it was being reported that there was, overnight, a sudden precipitous decline in the bat population. As many as had come once, in a torrent from the tree suddenly, quickly now were dying, and with their dying, a terrible foreboding settled in. The mother had grown accustomed to their presence. Not a day had passed when she had not thought of them, sensed them near. She'd drawn them close in her mind, the objects of her deepest dread and attachment, summoning them to her and gathering them in.

Bats perish, and no one knows why, the announcement read.

I'll be your nursling for the end, she whispered. They should have been hibernating in the caverns on the other side of the river. Now she knew that every bat she saw, flying in the winter in the daylight, was a dead bat flying. The obscure objects of her fear, now covered in a white fungus, were flailing in the snow. They were falling, failing in the Bat Hibernaculum. So read the reports from the Vortex Man.

She could not help but notice now that the bats, broken against the snow, exactly looked like her black umbrella—the one she used to protect the child and herself from the summoning God and all the other beckoning forces, bats included, and she wondered why it had taken her until now to see the thing. She considered that perhaps the bat that had come to them, chittering in Pentecostal fervor from the felled tree, had been in fact an angel: something to fear, yes, inspiring great terror, yes; but something also shot through with essential goodness. It had come to help her, to escort her, presaging change, offering the way.

One hundred million years ago, flowers appeared on the earth. Once the air was so loaded with bees it seemed to shimmer. And apple trees. An apple has ten ovules, each of which can produce a seed. In order to produce a seed, at least six ovules must be pollinated. And with that, the apple falls asleep.

She closes her eyes and dreams. The world without us will be a world gone finally back to bees and bats again.

WHEN A SWARM of bees suddenly quits the hive, the Toothless Wonder says, it is a sign that death is hovering near the house. Ask anyone, he says.

And the bats, the mother asks?

THE COLLAPSIBLE MOTHER and the child moved through the Collapsible World, and it comforted them to know that other people, not only they, were at the mercy of the great and terrible collapsing things. It heartened them to know they were not alone.

No one seemingly gave the concept of the Collapsible Mother a serious thought. No one could fathom the notion of a mother who collapsed the way other things collapsed. The notion was just not conceivable. A Collapsible Mother was not a mother who collapsed like many other things in the Collapsible World, but a mother who was flexible: folding and unfolding, accommodating and changing—that is what mothers did after all—like a paper fan, only sturdy, or a space probe, only warm. Mother: a soft-bodied insect, flexible, with a superhuman curiosity that is intelligence, intuition, passion, and charm, and graced with the gifts of critical thinking, deductive reasoning—both practical and grounded—and clairvoyance, immortal and dwelling always in approachable light. This meant you could approach the Collapsible Mother with any quandary and she would come up with a solution to the problem, be it large or small.

Even bats, she read in the newspaper, were collapsing, and though it should not, it made her inordinately sad. The world was amiss. Agents of extraordinary misfortune might appear at any time with their inscrutable tidings, or carry any of them away at any moment against their wills. Anything at all was possible. The child thought of Lamby. And the mother thought of the 4,000 dead soldiers.

She felt unnerved. War was everywhere and it was always wrong, that is what the mother said. All wars were equally barbarous and equally unnecessary. There was a divide, and they sat quietly and looked at it on the horizon, and you fell on one side of the divide or the other. For someone so flexible and pliant, the mother, when it came to the divide, would not give or bend. The mother then, more times than not, felt not flexible, but inflexible, not immortal, but dying.

The Collapsible Mother stayed aligned, and upright, flexible and generous and open-minded, and the child eyeing her felt proud and she loved her. Some called it the Tragic Sublime, others the Heroics of the Everyday. You were always hearing about the heroes on TV, and the heroes on TV always said the same thing: they were not heroes; they were just like other people. Four thousand soldiers from here, and who knew how many soldiers from there, and worst of all, how many thousands of ordinary people, children included, were now dead. All the world collapsing.

When the child was a baby, the mother would carry around one of those collapsible strollers that fit into the trunk of the black car. This came back to her now when she thought of the mystery of the multitudinous bats collapsing like little broken black umbrellas, dying in daylight when they should have been hibernating, falling and folding up on the bright white snow.

In the bright sun, in the snow, dressed in their white coats, radiant in the blood of the missing lamb, it's too bright to see. Covered with a fungus, the wings close up.

SHE RECALLS HIS melancholy years in the Cold Lab through the fog. There in the deep freeze, pressed next to the abandoned embryos, the Grandfather from the North Pole once spent long hours studying the complex properties of snow. If you put a bowl of snow in the refrigerator and come back in an hour, the snow will have changed significantly. Snow, the Grandfather from the North Pole would say, is almost always in motion. And there's nothing more beautiful than that.

The weak layers of snow are faceted, smooth, unbonded to one another, and so more likely to give way. Had the Grandfather stayed in his Cold Lab in his thermal lab coat with his multiplying theories concerning the metamorphosis of snow, he might have lived for something like forever—such was the makeup of his gene pool—but alas, avalanches were his passion. Besides, the Cold Lab was too sad, he said. The parents say they would like their embryos frozen for an eternity. They call them like this their snowflake children, and the Grandfather, passing them—*how silent*—always felt glum. Such a strange and terrible orphanage I've wandered here, he wrote in his log, right before he walked out the door, never to return.

In the mother's mind, he's always there, in the center of the glittering world. He's so beloved—but he's hard to see. In a small shack, he waits while his assistant sets off little two-pound explosions so that the snow buries him—notebook in hand.

Some say the most critical thing in surviving an avalanche is to create a pocket of air in front of your face so you can breathe while you wait for rescue. I would swim though, the Grandfather wrote. I would get prone in the snow and stay on top and skim the whitest surface. Too late, a balloon system for better avalanche-surviving was devised: a ripcord that would make balloons inflate and keep you afloat, just like he said, on top of the snow.

Imagine being bombarded by crystals! the Grandmother from the North Pole cries. When he was finally found, he was encased in glitter and wearing an amulet which held some of the world's most ancient ice—half a million years old, it is said, and cored from a field three miles deep. What a sight! Around his neck an amulet, and in his hand a love note: the Grandfather from the North Pole, drowned in beauty—frozen, bright.

passage

THE LITTLE POPE, very old, holds a glass dome, and under it is a very tiny green tree. The Vatican, he explains, is the only sovereign state in the world that is carbon-neutral. The ancient buildings have been outfitted with solar panels, and someone, he says, has donated enough trees in a Hungarian forest to nullify all carbons emitted from the Holy See. The Pope, who oversees the Global Church, says that he is known now as the Green Pope. It is humanity's responsibility to care for the planet. Time is short.

As of late, we have invented seven new sins, the Pope informs his audience. Number four is Polluting the Environment.

A little dim energy-saving lightbulb comes on as evening arrives. I am a steward to God's creation. I shall protect the children, both born and unborn, from exposure to environmental poisons, especially the poor. And all of those who are most vulnerable. And the cats, born and unborn. The Pope loves cats. He has had, he says, a lifelong love of cats. He often chats to them in German at length, and they follow him around, fascinated by his gibberish. The Pope is lovable in his fondness for felines. The Pope says that cats are forbidden where he lives in the

Apostolic Palace, and that it has been one of the biggest adjustments of all. You can see the Pope some days walking around the carbon-neutral grounds with a small ball of twine in case a cat should happen by. He meets up with them in the garden, feeds them, bandages their wounds.

The mother hands the Pope a notebook listing one thousand boys and girls who have been injured in the Boston archdiocese alone. An Inquisition found that the Pope before he was Pope had obstructed justice in the case of the priests who had committed the gravest of all the sins on earth. Before he was Benedict, he was Joseph, and when he was Joseph, he ordered bishops should be protected by the Pontifical Secret. The sexual abuse of children is somehow allowed to be hidden by the Pontifical Secret in something called the Obstruction. To reveal the Pontifical Secret is to risk excommunication. Until the child-victim reached eighteen years plus ten more years, the gravely sinning priests are protected by the Secret. So if you are a child of nine, for instance, the offending priest gets an extra nine years until the child reaches eighteen, plus ten more, for a total of nineteen years in all before he has to worry. By then the nine-year-old is twenty-eight. Cases such as these are of a delicate and grievous sort.

The Pope, of course, does not have children in the way that mothers have children. The mother wonders whether under the category of Secrets there might be a Secret Neutering Process for those in the church who harm children, and for those who protect them. Neutering is not really so bad given the magnitude of the trespass. There is a Biblical logic to the reasoning. The prim Pope blushes. The mother gently takes his hand and says that this way, the problem of the pri-vates might be resolved once and for all. Bunny Boy, she tells him, her cat, seems to have made his peace with it.

☙

THE POPE APPEARS again on the tarmac of Andrews Air Force Base and is met by the War Crimes President. They are accompanied by the millions of children they have put in harm's way, both grown and ungrown, both alive and dead, and also the many who are somewhere between the two: not really dead, not really alive anymore, but in a perpetual half-state, thanks to the Supreme Power of the Men.

Is a slow death better, or a fast one? A complete death, or a partial one?

The children are gathered a few miles deep and many, many thousands of feet high, standing one atop another ad infinitum. From a bird's-eye view it's all pretty awful. The Pope and the President on the tarmac walk hand in hand. How puny they are from this vantage point. The Pope, a holy man, has shuffled known perpetrators into fresh dioceses and has put the interests of the Church above the interests of children. The President meanwhile, unprovoked, is the instigator of unimaginable violence and suffering. The red carpet is seepy and spongy with blood. The two Fathers gingerly tiptoe across it while the children trudge behind. The children's skins, peeled back by firebombs and the lips of doughy priests, bleed easily. Who will protect them? the mother wonders. The Pope has instructed the Faithful to pray *in perpetuity* to cleanse the Church of Predators. The children wonder who, if not he, with staff and crown and lamb and beneficent smile, will be on their side?

The child also wonders while questions are being asked, whether the Pope has seen her lamb, perchance.

The Vatican has said that every parish should designate a group of people to pray in a kind of relay for the Church to rid itself of scandal.

Prayer will take place in one parish for twenty-four hours and then move on to another so that there might be continuous prayer. In the fourteenth century, to rid the world of the Black Death, the Church instituted a similar policy of Perpetual Prayer.

From the very depths of darkness the men shake hands—over the bodies of the maimed and dying or not quite dead, or the definitely dead children. The two Fathers are in a friendship trance. Even though they are quite tiny on the TV screen, and in real life they are in Washington DC, which is quite a ways away, the mother puts up her black umbrella anyway for protection. She has been made custodian on earth of this very child, and she will not let her down. Not on her watch will a raft of unbearably lonely priests take her away under the guise of the First Scrutiny or the Sanctification or Special Intentions. Not on her watch will the President remove the children in a coma on a stretcher to a place off camera where they will be left to die, counted with deepest regret as collateral damage. The soul alights strangely, and the souls of children flutter at the Andrews Air Force Base. Sometimes we sense the devil where the devil does not belong—under the Pontiff's hat, or hiding wedged in between the lines of the Constitution, that remarkably shiny document, the sleeping Congress nodding off. There might be glimpses of the devil in a wink or a pat or an embrace. A clever devil has been known to hide in a glass of golden ale, or an anthem or a cliché or a prayer—things we are almost but not quite numb to, the devil hides there.

There is always the threat of invasion to guard against. Every single child who has ever lived is aware of this. Those both dead and alive. And all those sentenced to Limbo: they are beautiful, but they are neither here nor there.

The question might be, why let a fetus through if in only a few years, this is what you are going to do? The Pope does not know. The Pope is happy to confess to all he does not understand under the category the Mystery of Evil. He has also been known to attribute it to the Dark Night of the Soul, but never mind, let us meditate on the miracle of cats.

Bunny Boy, who in a certain sense is crimeless, has lived happily enough with the Neutering Process.

The War Crimes President has insisted that an enhanced interrogation technique called waterboarding is not torture and so . . . He fidgets now wondering what the mother, who has always been a problem solver, has in store.

The Pope holds a small Frozen Charlotte and a cat and a glass dome. Under the glass dome is a little model of Vatican City. The little dome glints in the sun.

You've got to hard-wire certain rituals into a child early; otherwise they might not take. You've got to take advantage of the Genuflect Reflex while you've got it, as it is only so long before the Genuflect Reflex dissolves into cake.

Mother Teresa is now known to have doubted everything. For one year she had God visions, but then she never saw or felt God's presence again. Only that God was a desert. She wanted God with all the power of her soul—and yet between them, there was only a terrible separation.

To eliminate the gray wolf, those going westward in the Great Western Expansion introduced mange into the wolf population. For forty days they waited for the mange to take and then set out on their way. A wave of suffering preceded them, and a wave of suffering was left in their wake. The suffering made a sound pitched just above the hearing range of the adults, but all the girls could hear it, and it made their trips in the covered wagons excruciating. Many of the girls in this weakened condition became susceptible to cholera and other catastrophic illnesses. Perhaps it was a kindness to die, they thought to themselves, by the side of the road rather than endure the intolerable screeching in their ears.

The adults forged on, having buried their girls by the side of the road, and were praised for their courage and stamina in the face of the last images of their daughters holding their ears. They continued with even greater resolve. Their girls will not have died in vain. Native plants, native animals, and finally native people were in the way of the great westward progress to Hollywood. The wolves lost fur in patches all over their bodies. Mangy wolves, without fur, are susceptible to freezing to death in the winter or catching fire in the summer. Like fire, however, and young girls, the gray wolf can never really be extinguished. Like fire, you cannot snuff out a girl or a wolf. But no matter, the pioneers did not allow this to deter them. The mother and the child closed the book. The history lesson for the day lay heavy in them. What could she do, the child wondered, for those children who were already dead over a hundred years?

Much of the west, toward which they strived with such fervor and at such cost, is a desert. Cities are built on sand in drought. Rivers are dammed and debilitated. Every time the child opened her history book, something else like this was popping up at her. Their fevers rose to 105. The girls were covered in flat, rose-colored spots.

ᕽ

THEY RISE UP again now, the girls, as if out of that same place—though over a century and a half has passed. Women and children emerge from the mist on the horizon line still in pioneer dress, still emptying the bit bucket. Look, the child says, calling for the mother. Come quickly! The mother and child stand mesmerized. There before them are the girls in home-sewn, ankle-length dresses, with their hair pinned up in braids, tilling small gardens, pumping water, and doing chores in the shadow of an eighty-foot gleaming limestone temple. Self-sufficiency is paramount, because the Apocalypse is near.

Mothers and daughters work together on the Yearning for Zion Polygamist Ranch. What is the use, the mother wonders, of taking such good care of a girl—making her clothes by hand; feeding her only the freshest and most wholesome of foods: whole grains, fruits, and vegetables; giving her fresh air; keeping her far from the cities and the fumes and the bad influences; making sure she is happy and fit—if you are only going to hand her over to the fifty-year-old Fathers in the end? What is the use if you are just going to offer her up joyfully to become a child-sister-wife?

The women in gingham and bonnets look up curiously; they do not remember this part. What is the use of surviving on the plains if your own mother is going to hand you over before you are grown? The child brides cannot read or write or state the date of their births, the TV is saying. In the outside world avert your eyes, they are instructed. In the outside world avoid the color red, for that color is reserved for Jesus Christ who will return to the earth wearing red robes one day. The mother shuts off the TV. Enough, she says.

In the Great Girl Giveaway, the Indian girl, Little Bird, was taken by an opposing tribe where she was turned into a slave and named Sacajawea, and that tribe, when the time came, was all too happy to sell her to a Canadian fur trader three times her age, as a wife.

Enough, the mother says, but at night the girls follow them into sleep. On the Polygamist Ranch the men take girl children as brides, and so the girls know it is only a matter of time. Where are the mothers when they are needed? One of the girls dreams of introducing mange into the Father Population. When the fathers come near, too sunburned and with patchy fur, they howl in the dirt. There is a resourcefulness to girls in trouble, the child thinks to herself.

The child says that she has seen the girls staring into the soup pots in a daze, dreaming, like all girls, of their futures. Once the soup is evaporated, they will meet their husbands, so it becomes the child's job to provide a constant source of soup for the girls so that the pot will never be gone. The mother marvels at the miracle of the child: her poise, her good sense, her intelligence, her resourcefulness, her beauty.

WHEN UNCLE INGMAR comes with his giant steps, the sea level will drop. Don't forget, the mother whispers to the child, to fill the pot.

THE CHILD NUDGES the mother and points. On the horizon a tiny flame. She sees fire in the distance. At last, after the proper time of mourning, the Torch is revived. There it is, she is sure of it, glinting near the Muir Woods, in the City of Forests.

THE THREE SCHOOLGIRLS hold evergreen sprigs. The mother is grateful that all along the children have made themselves visible to her, that they are whole, and that they have not, in all the chaos, lost their backpacks.

THE WHO HAS Hair Where Conversations had begun. Except on her head, as of yet, the child had none. In a few years after all the hair had sprouted, the child would look at her mother strangely. With the hair in private places there would be a need for other privacies, and this would increase over time until finally the child would be gone. At the same time the Boy in the Glen was having the Why, When, and How Deep or High Are Boys' Voices Conversation at home with his father.

For now the child was attached to the wall because the mother had grown tired of paying the bill for the walk-around phone. Soon the child will be older, and the child will still be attached to the wall and she will feel as if she cannot move around and speak in confidence.

Once, the mother will say, when she was a child and living in a house with the North Pole Grandmother and Ingmar, Lars, Anders, Sven, and baby Inga, everyone was attached to the wall, and if you wanted to talk in confidence, you had to invent a private language. There was a secret yodel she was fond of when she was a growing child on the wall trying to leave her mother. A keening sound had come out of her as she tried to leave. On these days she would stand high up on a mountain yodeling, waving, gasping for breath.

THE SNOW WAS slowly melting, which meant that things that could not be seen before would soon be seen in the Valley again. The mother and child looked out at the Valley they loved, but also hated a little. Out the car window: two goats, free vegetables, a pink toilet, the signs that said Mabbetville and Pulvers Corners.

Sometimes the child wondered what it would be like to live in any other place.

MANY OF THE People of the Valley wanted a white person to live in the White House. There was a simplicity to it that appealed to them. They were not interested in having a person of any other color or stripe sullying things up.

The People of the Valley knew enough to know what they liked, and there was a simplicity to that as well. They also knew what they feared—and all around them was darkness.

About four million years ago, the wolf, the coyote, and the golden jackal diverged from one another. All three have seventy-eight chromosomes. This allows them to hybridize freely and produce fertile offspring. First-crossed wolf/dog hybrids are popular in the US, but the dog retains many wolf-like traits. This the mother remembers from her Wolf Studies long ago.

A coydog is the hybrid offspring of a male coyote and a female dog.

The dogyote is the result of breeding a male domestic dog with a female coyote.

Coyotes also breed with wolves, resulting in coywolves. Other breeds to have hybridized with foxes are huskies and hounds: this animal is known as a dox. The neighbor has a wonderful dox is not an unheard-of thing to hear in parts of the Valley.

Let us not forget that the wolf and the jackal can interbreed and produce fertile hybrid offspring. What is a dingo, the mother does not know, but she knows what a coy-dingo must be. If you cross a coyote with a dog, you get the ferocity of the coyote with the friendliness and fearlessness of a dog—an unfortunate mix. What if you tried to pet it?

It is thought that the Ancient Egyptians crossbred domestic dogs with jackals, producing a jackal-dog that resembled the god Anubis.

If the blacks stay black and the whites stay white, it still remains possible to think clearly. There is something to be said for clarity, there is something to be said for understanding the lines. If the Jews were meant to breed with the Gentiles, God would have written it down through the prophets, the People of the Valley like to say. What if you cross a jackal with a child?

On a death barge a mongrel in robes might float by. What if without permission, the dog-child wore a crown and began to decree?

If you interbreed the races you are in for trouble, the People of the Valley are saying. Murky children rise up out of their dreams and walk the not-so-distant hills. You are left with the question when you bump into them picking flowers of what exactly they are. If you misguidedly vote one of these mixed-flower people, these freaks, into public office, you will only add to the National Nightmare.

But like it or not, fluidity and connections and dualities define the world now. Like it or not, forging hybrid identities is where it's at. It does not help that the Morbidity Table indicates the kind of White People who live in the Valley right now will be dying off sooner rather than not.

The question in the Valley more and more becomes how to disable permanently the mongrel so he will not be able to run, but only hobble.

There is a lot to consider when pondering mongrels and men. The child should hurry and graft horse-running legs onto the mongrel candidate's body. She should hurry and graft enormous white eagle wings to his back; a surgical expertise born of necessity will move into her hands. Among the species there is an aptitude for survival one can only call admirable. Winged, horse-legged, felled candidate, how are you feeling? Fine, he says. I feel great. The child and the mother and the candidate's aptitude for bouncing back are unmatched.

If you cross a mother with a bat, then what have you got? Something shining and night-loving with a sonar intelligence of the first order.

Some things once brought into being can never be killed. Some things brought into light refuse to retreat back into the darkness. Not only that, but they obtain a lightness unlike any other thing in the world. There is a luminosity not to be believed.

If you cross the mother on the Equinox with the Night and introduce a Glove, a miracle will occur.

A BLUE MULTITUDE of children huddle around the mother. They've just come in from the blueberry patch. See them now as they doze off with their full blue buckets—Lars, Bibi, Ingmar, Anders, Sven. Baby Inga is not yet born.

INGMAR TUGS AT his mother's blue dress and whispers, it is rumored that the Cold Lab is making its way to the Spiegelpalais.

Yes, she smiles. There are great hopes that the Grandfather from the North Pole at last will be on display.

FATHER TED HAD disappeared, and so someone ran to prop up the one-hundred-year-old Father Finch to say the Sunday Mass. The mother loved Father Finch best, for he seemed always furious, and he spoke with a slight stutter, and there was something in his fury that steeled her to his side. When he arrived at last, he started immediately telling the congregants that there was a word in Hebrew, and that the word meant when you save one person, you save the world. Plainly he spoke of the suffering of the children, and the mother imagined God's infinite indifference in all matters big and small. Pity, Father Finch said, the children for whose suffering we are directly responsible. The child, sitting next to the mother in the front pew, could not understand how this could be.

When he was not giving the sermon, Father Finch was prone to stutter, particularly at the letter B. The latter part of the Mass was especially difficult for him with all the body and blood and breaking bread. At these times, a loud baritone voice would come out of the mother's chest, and she would bellow *bread*, or *blood*, and it gave Father Finch the momentum to go on. The child stared at the mother as if she could not believe the mother was capable of producing such a sound.

The God Father Finch spoke of directed the leper to plunge himself seven times in the river, and with that, the leper's flesh became the flesh of a child, and he was clean of his leprosy. Next, the God cast seven demons from the Magdalene. The mother put up her umbrella. There was no telling what the God might do next.

DOWN THE ROAD, the artist groped in the dark for her brushes and shouted to those who passed by, on this Fifth Sunday in Ordinary Time, that she had been blinded in the Spiegelpalais. She said not to go in there: all had transpired or would transpire, and all that was promised was nothing but a mirage.

FROM THE FOG the soldiers came now, singing their crooked songs. First a few and then a few more and then a cast of thousands. They are just over this last dune—Grave Alice and Laughing Allegra and Margarete with the Auburn Hair—you're nearly there.

SHE PINNED THE Obligation Doily to her head. Once it was forbidden to walk into a church with the head uncovered. In those days, hatmakers' shops flourished in the Valley. The ladies went to great lengths seeking out hats that might please Him. If not a beautiful hat or an intricate lace Obligation Doily, then what, the mother wondered, was the offering He was waiting for?

THE MOTHER THOUGHT while the child slept she might go out and confront the God, head on. Go outside and stand on the mountain before the Lord, the faltering bat whispered; the Lord will be passing by. A strong and heavy wind was rending the mountains and crushing rocks before her—but the Lord was not in the wind. After the wind there was an earthquake—but the Lord was not in the earthquake. After the earthquake there was a fire. After the fire there was a tiny phishing sound. When she heard this, she put her face in her cloak and went and stood at the entrance of the cave.

THE VIRGIN STANDS with her lantern at the mouth of the cave and gestures for the mother to come forward.

Yes, the mother says, but I'm not ready yet. I need a little more time. The Virgin smiles and puts down her lantern and rests awhile.

SOMETIMES, WHEN THEY were gray traces on a page, and the hand loomed and hovered and pressed down on them, when they were glyphs across the divide from one another, she despaired. In those times she was aware of the ampersand—the thin squiggled figure that both joined and separated them. The notion that someone had created them filled her with sadness; she did not know quite why. While the inventor slept, she slipped from under the great hand and went out untethered into the silence.

The mother wishes for the place where they are not already decided, not already made, the place they are autonomous, unmediated, free. She looks out a small window in the text. The hand asleep atop the manuscript. In the pre-dawn, she makes her way back home from the cave to the child and she runs into the members of the parish making their way to the sunrise service. She does not look up, but they see her anyway. When they greet her on the path carrying a torch, she sidesteps them. They are on their way to morning Mass, but she has had enough of the Creators, all of them, even the child, asleep, dreaming her, venturing out into the forest, seeking her once more, dragging the little ampersand.

HE HAD PULLED a fishbone from the throat of a choking boy, he had talked a wolf into releasing a pig for a starving old woman, he had visions of the risen Christ everywhere he looked—for his trouble, his skin was shredded and he was beheaded and named the patron saint of animals. And once a year, the mother and child were blessed with candles at the throat in his honor.

IN THE CAVES of Allah, the soldiers, sheltered, grateful to be out of the monstrous heat, crouch and talk a kind of baby talk: Tora Bora,

Lahore, and then just gibberish. Before the youngest among them closes his eyes, he says, look! By the light of the last match: a lion, a deer, a running man drawn 24,000 years earlier. How filled with joy they are at this last moment, and how unexpectedly—at the very end.

THE CHILD WAS learning French in school and studying ancient Egypt. After Egypt would be the Greeks. And next year there would be Latin. The ancient world was alive and well.

The child thought she might like to try to embalm one of the bunnies and put it in a mummy suit. Now that the snow was melting, certain things seemed clearer. That was not a coyote they saw in the driveway—she opened her book and showed her mother—that was the god Anubis.

The mother remembers now Anubis, one dark night, caught in the car's headlights, stared at her as she pulled into the drive. She was afraid, and she and the child waited, until it passed.

26

T HE FIRST WOMAN to be inducted into the National Society of Thatchers had come to the Valley and proceeded to thatch roofs for the stone houses that were being built. She was a small woman, the people thought, to be balancing such heavy bundles of straw on her shoulder and wielding that legget while going up and down to and from her perch on a biddle. She was always smiling, for she loved the green hazel smell and the rustle of the reed and straw and the connection she felt with all the other thatchers who had ever lived.

What a peculiar sight, the few remaining men in the Valley remarked.

THE MOTHER THOUGHT that when thinking about the lamb or the vanishing men or the bees and the bats, it was best to keep the larger picture in mind and to take the long view. In the furnace of the stars much had happened, and in everyday carbon molecules, there was stardust from the time the asteroids crashed on the planet millions of years ago. Best to think of all five of the earth's Great Extinctions, or at the very least, the extinction paleontologists call the Great Dying. Two hundred and fifty million years ago, 90 percent of all living species perished.

Someone is finding an unusual chemical signal in an ancient layer of an Italian city. Irradium. So much has happened, and is happening, under the earth and in the oceans and above the earth and all around. The mother takes the child's hand, and they make their descent. What are space and time to them?

At the K-T Boundary they pause.

At the Boundary between the Cretaceous and Tertiary periods they pause. They marvel at the tortoise. When the asteroid came, it killed everything within hundreds of miles. The animals that weren't incinerated or gassed by fumes either froze or starved to death soon after when the dust stirred up by the impact blotted out the sun for more than a year.

They stand in a trance at the P-T Boundary. The place where the Permian and the Triassic meet. When thinking about extinction, it is best to have some context. History, the mother believes, even at its worst, always consoles. Today, mastodons and mammoths and giant sloths have no living counterpart remaining on earth, though some plants and animals that disappear, stay gone for millions of years and then return.

FOSSILS EXTRACTED FROM the fine-grained mudstone and limestone rocks near the Green River in Wyoming were said to be forty-seven million years old. She made a note to herself to place the Grandmother there, when the time comes.

A WOMAN WHO built stone walls had moved to the Valley. There she was, shifting, sorting, and shaping rocks. How does she manage it? the people remarked. She gathered rocks for the face of the wall, rocks for the heart of the wall, sand, and some stoppers that break up the pattern and create character. She loved doing this ancient work outside to birdsong, she said, as she watched the seasons day by day unfold. On her coffee breaks, she chatted with the passersby.

What an edifying sight, the few remaining men remarked to one another.

THE MOTHER WAS dreaming. If the heart of the deceased outweighs the feather, then the person has a heart made heavy by evil deeds. In that event, Ammit, the god with the croc head and hippo legs, will devour the heart, condemning the subject to oblivion for an eternity.

The Grandmother from the North Pole is certain that the heart of the President, soon to be the former president and a significant contributor to the vanishing world, would be gobbled up, though for the thousands and thousands of dead, this is little consolation.

The Grandmother adjusts her Doghead and walks with the child to the pageant, dragging the President's heart. Anubis weighs the heart while the Ibis-Headed Thoth, the god of wisdom, records the verdict.

The child, having taken off her Ibis head, reveals malachite eyes.

WHEN THE GREAT Wind came and the electricity went out, and the tree fell on the house and bats poured from the tree and entered the house while the child bathed, the transformation had already begun. What the mother had neglected to say was that the bat had brought clairvoyance, and that she saw in an instant what she had not been able to see before: all that had happened and now all that was to come.

FROM HER PERCH atop the world, she sees a blue horse in the distance. It was a troubling vista, and it exhausted her. She thought of all the things that might appear out of nowhere, unbidden. Seen from afar, but utterly out of reach—its great forelegs rising into the air. It was not approachable; there was no way you could ever get to it, so that when travellers passed it as their plane accelerated, they caught a glimpse of an ominous blue blur as they rose, the last thing they would see. The boy with the toy jet reached for it nonetheless.

The September sky was so blue it hurt her to look at it. Something of the shape of the horse, flickering, fleeting, unable to be grasped entirely, remained in her for a moment and then was gone.

THE MOTHER DID not know why everything had to change—she just knew that it did. Things were changing even though they seemed not to be, and they would continue to change now at a faster and faster rate.

SHE HAD MADE the sparkling snow rabbit a crown of winterberry, which the catbird came to sup on. She put an orange in its paw and thought of the day the Baltimore Orioles would return. That migratory corridor of birds the mother and child were lucky enough to live along. The French called those birds *les passereaux*. Everything is passing, Saint Paul said.

EVERYTHING WAS CHANGING: the child, the Grandmother. Everything was melting. The child hoped more than anything that before too much longer they could play their Santa game again. She hoped that her grandmother would still remember it. The Book of Wonder, the child thought, would reveal what the reindeer did in the off season, or the stitch Mrs. Claus used to sew the large brown wooden buttons to Santa's jacket, and what games the elves excelled at during the Winter

Olympics. She looked at her twinkling grandmother. Her village at the top of the world seemed to come forward in the mist as the stories unfolded and then to recede again, back into white.

Do you remember when you were a baby and I took you to the top of the lighthouse in Maine? the Grandmother asks. No, the child shakes her head. I don't remember that.

You were very small.

A BODY AT rest is still accelerating, the Grandmother from the North Pole tells the child. Isn't that amazing? And she whooshes by on her dogsled. Wait up! the child calls. The child remembered how the mother had shaped the snow into a sparkling rabbit, hoping to call the Grandmother back to her side. Just a minute.

EVERYTHING WAS SPEEDING up now. Soon the child herself would be growing at Girls' Peak Growth Velocity. They would have to hold on tighter than they had ever held on to anything before. Only the Virgin with her Infinite Patience was in no hurry.

SLOW DOWN, THE Grandmother says, when the child goes too quickly. Press Enter, the child says, and then she puts her hand over the hand that holds the cursor, and everything slows.

THE PEAK GROWTH is the combination of three mini-peaks. The first peak involves the lower limbs, the second involves the trunk, and the third involves the thorax. The first phase involving the limbs is called the ascending phase, which corresponds to the acceleration in the velocity of growth in girls.

Chronological age is of no significance; everything depends on bone age. Girls' Peak Growth velocity happens when girls are eleven in bone age. It is normal to feel the acceleration of bone growth during puberty. A not uncommon question among certain sorts might be, what do you think your bone age is?

Also, different bones in a child age at different rates. A child may be said to be composed of bones in a Bone Age Mosaic.

The Risser Sign is still zero and the Triradiate Cartilage is still open at the onset of puberty. When they found the femur in the shallow grave, they had suspected it was the missing preadolescent, because the bone had not yet fused. The mothers gravitate to the scene.

After the closure of the Triradiate Cartilage, there is still a considerable amount of growing remaining. The descending phase of puberty is signified by significant growth of the thorax.

IN THE TIME everything was accelerating, everything was moving so quickly and there seemed to be no conceivable way of stopping it, the Slow Lab entered the Spiegelpalais. The Grandmother was moving at hummingbird speed, but at the Spiegelpalais, the Slow Clock was being assembled. It was run by beads. One bead dropped every five minutes, and time seemed almost to stop.

THE NORTH POLE Grandmother had bright white hair and light, light sparkling eyes. Wait up, the child called to her, and the Grandmother smiled, skittling along the ice. She was going full speed ahead with great deliberateness—she knew the way. What the child feared was that right out there before her, her grandmother would become lost. Everything is changing, the child thought, but she was not ready yet. She cast a glacial spell on their lives and fell for a minute headlong now into the ravishing, precious luxury of slowed-up time. She stopped the Grandmother's skittle across the ice, the Great Amnesia, the Peak Growth Velocity, the folding up of the mother.

THE SLOW LAB had moved into the Valley to quell the vertiginous passing of time. The World Institute of Slowness would hold a Symposium soon. The Slow Lab was run on the tenets of the Slow Food Movement— local, organic, responsible—it emphasized slowness in the creation and consumption of food. Now this idea was being applied to every aspect of life. There were even websites—SlowPlanet.com, LifeinSlowMotion .org—for all things slow: slow travel, slow shopping, slow life—a Credo of Slow.

AS THE GRANDMOTHER neared eighty-three, the mother took her in her arms and refused to let go. In Italy there were Slow Cities, she told her, and they might get on a boat.

WHITE PHOSPHOROUS OBSCURED the view for a moment. From the fog could be seen the figments of mothers. Fire came from the bodies of our children, they said, and they wept. My daughter melted away. The burn reached to the muscle and bone, the Doctor without Borders lamented. It is a war crime to use such a thing as white smoke on a civilian population, the mothers murmured, walking through white.

THE MEN LEARNED to walk in slow motion while they slept. It was as if they were in a kind of coma. Only the notion of Grave Alice, and Laughing Allegra, and Edith with Golden Hair propelled them forward at all—the girls at the end of the war. But they moved more and more slowly, and no one knew anymore if they would ever get back.

CAREFULLY IN HIS sleep, the Vortex Man lifts the eighty-year-old
Yangtze Giant Soft-Shelled Turtle, the only female known to exist,
and he places her on his back. Slowly, he carries her six hundred miles
to the zoo in Suzho to meet the one-hundred-year-old male—the last
known of its species. Good going, the Grandmother from the North
Pole whispers, watching from afar, as the Vortex Man slowly moves
across the continent of Asia, the turtle strapped to his back.

MORE AND MORE now, the mother called Bunny Boy *Bog Belly*, as
he seemed to carry the bog with him wherever he went. Each evening
he would materialize from the mist. In the day now, no one knew
where he went exactly, but he always came home in the evening, and
he always carried the bog on his fur. When the mother reached out to
him, he passed her, seeming not to see her, too fixated on the bog, even
at night, at home, at the foot of her bed. It was the strangeness and
slowness of cats that sustained her now.

WHERE HAVE YOU been, Mr. Min?
    Slowly he pulls bat after white bat out of his hat at the Spiegelpalais.

WHEN THE LAMB returns, it will be resplendent in a teal blue City
Opera T-shirt, and its wool will gleam, and so will its eyes. When the
lamb returns, he will be asked: where have you been? He will be asked:
why have you been absent so long? And then the question that must be
answered in order to continue: how, little lamb, will we know you will
not be leaving us again?
    The lamb will smile, but, as he is stuffed, he will say nothing in
return.

MID-STEP, THE VORTEX Man puts down the turtle, and moves no more.

You have engendered in us the desire for knowledge; you have awakened in us a desire we did not know we had, the travellers say at the gates of the Spiegelpalais. You cannot fall silent now. You have instilled in us an insatiable longing. You have provided balm. Answer the twelve questions you have posed, before you go. Reveal your face, just one time. Show us the way. Point us in the right direction. You offer boons. You work mighty deeds, we've heard. You have the gifts of healing; you speak in tongues. Speak to us.

All is Illusory, the Vortex Man said and got up and passed through the midst of them and was gone.

WHEN THE SOLDIERS realized they were walking in the exact opposite direction of Grave Alice and Laughing Allegra and Edith with the Golden Hair, their hearts filled with sand and their beings were drawn into the earth and it was as if they were being buried alive. The bat had advocated flight, but they could not stay aloft; they just kept sinking further and further into the earth.

FORCE OF TIME, Ultimate Reality, Having Form and Yet Formless, the Divine Paradox, the Divine Smokescreen, Ruler of the Five Elements, and the Object of our Meditation. How can we stand here, how can we bear your Absence now? The End of Illusion. The Redeemer of the Universe, Sender of Bats, practicing austerity and renunciation. Time shall devour all, ineffable and inconceivable. He presides over the mysteries of both life and death.

At the place of the Disillusion of All Things, the people wept.

All Hail the Vortex Man, the People of the Valley said, and were afraid. All Hail the Vortex Man!

She thought of a blazing fire and a gloomy darkness and a storm and a trumpet blast, and the countless angels in festal gathering. All gathered at the sensational head of the Vortex Man, along with the assembly of the firstborn and the spirits of the just made perfect, and the Hare, mediator of a new covenant and the sprinkled blood. A gleaming gun at the center, it seemed, was the cause of all the commotion.

SHE HAD NOT known that at the time Lamby had disappeared, miles away, the Vortex Man with great violence had taken his life, and she now thought that perhaps this enigmatic force whom she had loved had pulled the little lamb with him into the massive vortex of his despair.

HE HAD SURVIVED for millennia, inhuman, apart, source of wisdom and perfection, but there was a dark aspect to survival, and it pained her to think of what his existence had become. First his mind had faltered, he who had so many thoughts and had posed so many questions, and the Vortex Doctors opened his head to look, but he was never the same after that.

She knows when the body is opened and flattened and exposed to the other world, it fears invasion from every side forever more.

She knows that when cells in the brain become filled with the Stilled Wind, they release teardrop-shaped pearls called enzymes into the blood. The part of the brain affected by the Stilled Wind cannot grow back or be repaired, it is said.

How unknowable is the world of the Vortex Man! His head streaming blood, his pearly eyes closed; the whole world can feel it, the mother thinks, in a kind of ecstasy. In the manner that the mother has friends, the Vortex Man had been her friend. And she tried to absorb the shock of his absence.

IT WAS THE gun in the broken glass case that had produced all the commotion: a single bullet to the head. But when she thinks of the Vortex Man she thinks there is something to be said for the end of questions, or the end of heartache, or the end of suffering, or rest.

transformation

THE CAT CARRIED the bog on his fur. The universe was expanding into darkness. The Vortex Man was dead; everyone said it. Somewhere, the sleeping Aunt Inga lies; she cannot be revived.

The child's birth had coincided with the discovery of Dark Energy and had heralded the end of certainty, and Absolute Knowledge one more time was suspended. They had exchanged their postulates of linear laws for curved space. The universe will expand eternally. And when the last stars die out in ten trillion years, the universe will grow dark. Something is speeding up the expansion of the universe despite the Slow Lab, and despite every effort of the mother.

Attempts at an explanation for the accelerating universe included many hypothetical models: Dark Energy, Phantom Energy, Cosmological Constant, Quintessence. As the universe expands, the density of Dark Matter declines more quickly than the density of Dark Energy, and eventually, Dark Energy dominates. An expanding universe means that density drops. She considered the implications. If acceleration continues indefinitely, the ultimate result will be that galaxies outside the local supercluster will move beyond the cosmic horizon; they will no longer be visible because their line-of-sight velocity becomes greater than the speed of light. The Earth, Milky Way, and the Virgo Supercluster will remain virtually undisturbed while the rest of the universe will recede.

Now, THE YOUNGEST Master Saddler in all of Wales came to give a demonstration at the Spiegelpalais. On a table she placed the tools of her trade: awls, an array of needles, threads, creasers, knives, stitch-markers, mashers, flocking, and filling. Next she unpacked a large bale of sheep's wool and leather, all from traditional English tanneries, and placed them in a stack. The Valley's Saddler did not know why this Saddler from Wales had come, and he felt a certain sadness. Still, he was fascinated to see how she could cut and dress and stain the leather all alone, and how she worked with both hands to create strong interlocking stitches.

A cavalry of men rode up. How interesting, the Valley's dimming infantry remarked.

Now A FIERCE wind began to blow. The mother felt besieged. Seven levels of sky and seven levels of earth pressed down on her. Where was the Vortex Man?

She was growing pyramidal. She increased her base, the distance between her feet widening so that she might withstand more, become a sturdier structure for the assaults that seemed not to stop coming now. She turned in all directions at once, for she could not predict from which directions the next sorrow would come.

She had turned herself into a pyramid: firm, and dark—the color of iron, anchored to the ground and with heft. She was squat, hardened, with a thick carapace as protection against the assaults, which were many—and the assaults had made her more obdurate. She wondered why it had to be this way. She wondered why the men had to disappear, some with great deliberateness and violence, others seemingly against their will, or on a whim.

She thought of the Sleeping Man, and she thought of the American Tenor, and she thought of the Hanging Man, and the Blue Man, and the boy with the spots, and also of her friend who turned into a harp, and she thought of the others who had walked back to their offices, briefcases in hand, because they had been instructed to do so, high atop the burning world, and who burned and turned vaporous. And she thought of the war, and all who had perished and continued to perish. Each of these men called her now, and said, it is time to come; it is over. She turned her back on all of them.

And she thought of the boys who ran in the apple orchards, years ago, and lived among the apple trees and reached through blue sky toward the blossoms, or the brightest fruit, and grew little by little, day by day, until they were grown and began losing their teeth, tooth by tooth by tooth, all the teeth in their heads, and then not long after, they were dead. It seemed a particular affliction in the Valley—the Apple Orchard Deaths.

She wondered if there was some limit to heartbreak, or a way to become immune to it, as she grew larger and heavier and wider. In silence, people gathered and pointed to the horizon, that sorrowing landscape where the pyramid stood—immense, gray, heavy—a foreboding shape, next to the Spiegelpalais.

THE NIGHTMARE INVOLVED the atrium, a corridor, rising heat, a kind of inferno, the baby motionless inside her capsule.

AND THROUGH THE desert the beheaded soldiers walked in ghastly procession. And in ancient Fallujah, babies were being born with three heads, or an eye or a nose in the middle of the fontanelle. We should never have dispensed the fogs, the soldier said.

SHE FEARED SHEETS, struts, and pinnacles of bone. She feared the life of bone, relentless, in motion, alive the way nothing else is quite alive. An ocean of bone moved toward the mother. She went to the child's room and looked at her as she was growing in her sleep. She lifted each limb, knowing from the sleep spindles the child was emitting that at this moment, nothing could wake her. In the dream, the child grew enormous. The mother marveled at her appendages.

THE MOTHER TELLS the child that a part of the child's body remains in the mother long after the child is born. She says right now, she carries some of the child's tissue in her clavicle. Eventually the child will dissolve inside the mother, but not for a long time. It takes many years for a child to dissolve into a mother. The child thinks about this for a long time. Is it only us? the child asks.

Every mother carries a bit of her own child in her body. It's Science, the mother says.

This means, the child says gravely, that when the Girl with the Matted Hair's mother died, part of the girl had been buried alive.

The mother nods her head. What is also true, and it is the marvelous thing about mothers and children, is that the part of a child that stays inside the mother helps to heal the mother, rushes to assist the mother whenever she needs help; it's a fact, the mother says.

What about her friend then? What about Lula? The child insists on calling the Girl with the Matted Hair by her birth name. What about Lula's mother? Why couldn't Lula help her mother?

Here is a story for you, the mother says, and she has a grave expression, the face of a teacher or the face of a nurse—a face the child loves.

Are you listening? the mother says, and the child nods.

A woman dies of a terrible disease. After her death, a specimen from the small intestine—the part of the woman's body that failed, disintegrated, and eventually caused her death—is examined at the autopsy. What the examiner finds is that trillions of cells from both her daughter and her son had rushed to that very spot to try to save her. It was all there afterwards when they examined the tissue. If there is a more beautiful story, she said, I do not know of it.

It is even more beautiful than the God who lived in the man or the way he flew up out of his dead body on the third day, the child says. The mother nods. Yes, even more beautiful than that. And the child, suddenly minute, is enthralled, breathless at the mother's perfection. There is nothing she would not do to save her.

THE CHILD GASPS. The mother has the head of a lion, the body of a goat, and the tail of a serpent. She is more wondrous, more beautiful than anything else on this earth. She is a terrifying thing, a thing for a moment immortal: not human, lion-fronted, a goat in the middle, and a snake from behind, and inside, the remnants of a tiny child—a child who at a moment's notice might rush to the brain or the liver or the heart. I will keep you healthy, the child vows—for who otherwise will instruct me? Who will provide for me? Who will take care of me, more exquisitely than you? Who will keep us here, alive, on this side of the divide, if not you?

The lion-headed mother folds up. The Chimera closes like an umbrella. Yes, of course, she says. I will.

THE CODES BETWEEN mother and infant are so profound that artists and writers have often felt the need to replicate them in literature and art their whole lives. The mother wonders where her own mother is at that moment. She feels a pull and opens the window to see if she can detect her presence.

She looks to the heavens.

A small number of fetal cells stray across the placenta—a rash of stars in the bloodstream. A fluorescing protein derived from jellyfish makes the cells glow bright green. The mother closes her eyes. Outside the frogs and fireflies make the night alive.

IF A MOTHER is in a car accident, her child will move toward the wreckage, arriving quickly at the ruin, while her body is medivaced and packed in ice. The child's cells migrate to the wounds, becoming six times more concentrated in the area of damage. SOS signals from the mother are always heard.

The child survives for decades in the mother's skin, in the liver, in the bloodstream. No harm can come to her, the child says. Serenely, the child crosses the blood-brain barrier as if on a barge in summer. If the thyroid is damaged, the child turns into thyroid cells; if the liver is damaged, the child turns into liver cells; if the heart is damaged, the child turns into heart cells; if the brain is damaged, the child turns into brain cells. How amorphous and fluid, how ready to take any shape is the child!

And the next day, the mother gets up from the accident as good as new.

SHE'S VERY SMALL, and she hasn't been seen for some time. For a while she had been sighted darting in and out of the bushes, small and sleek. She had become, the mother thought, like something hunted. But lately the Girl with the Matted Hair seemed to have disappeared completely. This made the child sad, as she missed her friend, unpleasant at times as the friend could be.

THE CHILD PICTURED the Girl and her mother together. She hovered at the nape of her mother's neck like a small marsupial. Something with a pouch, something with a marsupium. It was a beautiful sight.

Though neither the mother nor the child can actually see her, the Girl with the Matted Hair has retreated deep into the woods where she was beginning her first preparations for the Hamster Ball.

THE ICE WAS changing to water, the young to old. The Poles were dissolving. Infinitesimal bits of the child's body carried by the mother slowly began to melt, and the North Pole Grandmother could only feel the barest trace of her own children anymore. Still it was wonderful, wasn't it—lichen was collecting on the antlers of Santa's reindeer. Wild night swirled all around them and the collisions of dark stars. Life was an adventure—whenever she was with the Grandmother she felt that.

When the Grandmother was a girl, she told the child, she liked to ice fish, and each year right before the Mistletoe Feast, they would fish for a fortnight. Sometimes the child called the Grandmother from the North Pole my Snowmere, and she would hug her, and she would say to her, remember that enormous snowman several stories high that we once saw together? Even in summer, Snowmere, she said to the Grandmother from the North Pole, you will never melt, and she hugged her shrinking grandmother hard.

THE MOTHER THINKS of the Grandmother from the North Pole, and she knows that inside the child resides the mother too, for the mother has never walked on this earth without the Grandmother from the North Pole; she has never walked with only her one body, but always with multiple bodies. She knows even now she still carries the Grandmother from the North Pole inside her. Otherwise, how to account for the blue lips, or the antlers, or the seal whiskers, or the night?

soul

THE EXTERMINATOR HAD come to size up the situation. There were multiple problems, he said, quietly, descending the attic stairs. And this was not counting the wasps and the white hornets, the mice and chipmunks, the flying squirrels, or the solemn congregation of moths. Okay, the mother whispered. She had heard the great collision of flying foxes above her head thudding to the floor. There was that, yes. She knew that there were sick cows known as Downers making their way across the floor above her head. She already could tell they were not well by the way they lapsed and tripped across the ceiling, their odd syncoptic step. Yes, she knew about that. The exterminator shook his head.

It had been a wet springtime and now it was nearly summer. She heard a warped waltz coming from the rafters. Soon it would be prom night again, and the teenagers in the car in the dark in the rain would careen through the night. By dawn they too would join the others in the attic.

Inert objects were quietly being transformed into talismans of obtuse meaning and beauty. A car fender gleamed. Liquid glass and

steel beams from the fallen towers were being fused into safety walls
and fallout shelters, obdurate and durable. A pocket watch, a tat-
too, a love letter, a birth certificate, a passport were all playing their
parts. The everyday dreamers were reviving and reanimating the
scene. Meanwhile, as they sat cataloging the inhabitants, an ominous
announcement was made over the loudspeakers. A quarantine had
been placed on the Valley. No one was to leave the attic.

The influenza had arrived.

Outside, birds dropped from the sky.

COMPELLED INTO THE dark forest after midnight, the mother, in a
brown suede coat, went out in search of a buck in order to mate. In
her mind it had seemed that she had ventured far into the night driven
by desire, deep into the heart of the forest, though in reality, but a few
moments had passed before she was shot dead through the heart.

That night long ago, the hunters ran to find their prize, but when
they realized their mistake, they were sore afraid—what was a woman
with a brown suede coat and hoofs doing out in the forest during the
rut? they wondered, and horrified, they covered her body with leaves
and fled.

Meanwhile, the deliriously hallucinating mother sees the enormous buck in the wood and she calls to it with lust's strange call. The
planet is suspended in darkness, and there is violence and mystery at
the heart of existence. Sexual congress provides wild, new life—a life
impervious to bullets or harm—and the mother gets up at last, and
brushing off the dry leaves and moss and twigs, she makes her way
home where the child, sitting at the window, waits.

The men who had covered her steaming body with leaves had fled
the scene utterly, but their fleeing stayed in them, and many times they

returned to the place where nothing was left but a light brown suede coat. There were no other earthly remains—not hair, not bones, not hoofs, and for the rest of eternity, the woman stalked the men and haunted them.

SHE OPENS HER arms as if for the first time. The artist, the magician, the cat have any number of lives, the mother sings, and so do I! Sparkle is surrounding us, she says. And glitter, and bits of paper—that is what I find so astonishing.

THE SPIEGELPALAIS IS flooded with bluish greenish light. Today they read if it were possible to see the universe from afar, it would appear pale green, somewhere between turquoise and aquamarine. What a beautiful thought that is, and they feel unaccountably serene. She drifts without fear. Someone has come to console them. The light of blue stars combines with the light of red stars, to produce aquamarine. We float in a vast—but vast cannot begin to describe it—infinity of bluish green.

THE MOTHER HAS turned into a boat and is travelling in a northerly direction downstream against the prevailing north wind. She is carrying the Grandmother from the North Pole, the child who is a baby, a package and a bower of roses. A beautiful conduit, a vessel, but nothing more. On the journey, the mother must transfer a package she has carried her whole life but has been forbidden to open. The package is off-limits to the mother—it is just something she must bear. This gift from the Grandmother is to be passed to the child through the mother's body. Afloat, astounded, the infant opens the glowing box. She holds the gorgeous glowing braid of the genetic code, reserved just for her, in wonder. The Grandmother and child step onto the shore hand in hand, cradling the gift.

The mother, rose-laden, having done what she has come to do, drifts off. The smell of roses is overwhelming. German scientists say that the scent of roses perceived during REM sleep leads to the most astonishing of all dreams.

JUST LIKE ALL children, the child would leave before too much longer. The electronic world, shining and mysterious with its bleeps and trills, beckoned.

The mother would pack a little bundle for the child to carry there. In the sack she would put a pinecone, an acorn, a branch of berries, beeswax, an evergreen sprig.

WHEN THE GRANDMOTHER from the North Pole gets back into the boat for a moment and lies down under a blanket of roses and closes her eyes and rests awhile and smiles, she is really paying homage to the mother; she is really saying that she thinks it's okay—the person her daughter has become.

IT WAS REALLY all right: the mother was lost, but to what no one knew—to her daydreams, or visions, or whatever it was, as the child too would one day be lost to the glyphs floating past on the blue screen. The Grandmother from the North Pole beckons her daughter to join them in the next room on that cool electronic field, but the mother, sparkling in her own right, demurs, and gently closes the door.

For the mother, there is no obvious way out of the labyrinth.

PERPETUAL READINGS WERE being held in the hopes of setting off a Memory Chord. On the second day of the readings there seemed to be some eye flickering that signaled recognition. Photographs had been placed on an altar, and the elders stared at them. Once I could see birds, but now simply the presence of birds is enough, one of the elders, the bird-watcher, had once said.

All stood on a veranda and looked out onto an indefinite field. In the near distance, a figure could be seen sitting under a fig tree.

How beautiful is the aging process, the Grandmother from the North Pole thinks.

WHEN THE GRANDMOTHER from the North Pole becomes suddenly woozy and falls to the floor, the mother far off in the Valley rises automatically from her bed and lifts the window sash where snow has begun to fall. She looks for her where the medians of longitude converge.

The mother's hair stands on end. She is something winged now as she leaves the window. She is iridescent.

THE CHILD PULLS at the mother's sleeve. They had fallen asleep in front of the giant screen. Except for the mother and child, the theater has been vacated. She points to the dark stage as if something is about to happen. And suddenly before them. *Mother, look!*

THE EARTHQUAKE IN GinGin Province killed over ten thousand children. Mothers rushed to the sites. Most of the schools were too flimsy to hold children in the event of a catastrophe. The wreckage is filled with the bodies of children. On top of the findable children's bodies, small branches of pine, evergreen sprigs have been left. Many of the children's backpacks remain even now, and books are everywhere.

Too many of the dead are children in a country where families are allowed to have one child, and one child only. Some parents are digging with their hands for their only children, but many of the only children are now dead, and even if permission were granted, some of the parents are too old to have another.

THE SCHOOLS WERE among the most flimsy buildings in GinGin. The GinGin mother is not flimsy, but she is at the mercy of the Flimsy World she has placed her child in. Schools are a keystone in any community. Schools are relied upon in a society to fulfill one of the most important missions of all. The schools should have been greatly bolstered and fortified.

The bodies there had turned to vapor, and the city was enveloped by ghosts. If the GinGin government acquiesces for a time and allows people to conceive another child to replace the one under the rubble, this time the people of GinGin Province vow they will build a better child. Instead of waiting for the schools to be upgraded, they will take matters into their own hands. The people are determined that next time they will build a fortified child, a child with an astounding rebar structure and reinforcing rods. A guard against disasters and further tragedy.

The government, for once in accordance with the parents, thinks that instead of retrofitting the buildings, it would be better to come up with a way of retrofitting the children, seeing as they are such precious resources to their parents. In the future, the goal of the government as well will be to build a better child. An indestructible child. A child with a more solid armature—an earthquake-resistant child. Concrete slabs might replace the thighs, and they might be reinforced with steel rods and supporting braces. Iron rods in concrete could boost the resilience of the child's central columns. As an early warning system, their blood would be designed to detect the motion of magma, the bubbling and broiling from a distance moving toward them. Children then might walk with ease through the Trembling World, and there would be no long banners with dead children's names written in their parents' blood. A child fifty stories tall might be the norm. A child like no child anyone has ever seen before.

BUT FOR STRUCTURES and children to withstand an earthquake, the ground itself must hold together, and so along with building a better child, it will be necessary to build a better earth. When loose or wet soil shakes, parts of the soil rotate, and the soil then acts like a liquid or a gelatin.

A foundation firmly connected to solid rock, deep in the ground, is required. Beams and columns of child must be strapped together on the rocks with metal, and the floors and tops of the child must be securely fastened to the walls. Then the child must be sprayed with liquid concrete and reinforced with steel brackets. The brain must be bolted to the skull.

A certain amount of swaying and flexing must be built in. The future is a swaying motion. A tall girl who does not flex and sway might crack or collapse.

THE SOUTH TOWER was the second tower to be hit, but it was the first to fall. She watched it buckle and sway and warp. Firefighters who reached the crash zone before the building broke up described seeing two pockets of fire. This is what she knows: that buildings should be able to withstand disaster, that mothers once standing should continue to stand, that children should never perish. A plume of smoke appears behind the mother's head.

OUTSIDE THE SCHOOLHOUSE amidst the rubble, a mother from GinGin Province was weeping. I hope God will give my daughter a chance to survive. I can lose anything in this world—except my daughter.

THE SCHOLAR CHONG Heng invented the first earthquake detector in the year 132. On a bronze vase, eight dragonheads and toads were arranged to work like a pendulum, and when the earth shook, a brass bell would pass from the mouths of the dragons to the mouths of the toads.

A mother sits next to the rubble of what once was her child's school and waits. She refuses to move. Weeks pass, months.

In addition to the fortification of the children, the mothers' hearts must be replaced next time with stainless steel hearts.

THE SOUL DOES not adhere to the bones of the deceased but flies up and is free, this the mother believes. The Egyptians thought the soul was placed in an eternal chamber, and a sheep was sent to guard it.

THE PRODIGY PLAYS a black cello made of carbon. In fact, all the instruments are carbon for the occasion, as carbon fares better in frigid temperatures and there is now the question of the unseasonable cold to consider. There are no flowers here today, only carbon and cold. A carbon cello has a flooding, deeper sound than a cello of wood.

GIRLS ARE GATHERED together and held for one more afternoon in the light of the schoolyard. The next time you see them, they will have disappeared, and young women will have taken their place. The girls ride their horses, talk their talk, giggle, sing loo-loo and la la la. This is the day when childhood becomes irretrievable, though no one will realize it until some time after. Though we could not have predicted the moment in advance—all had changed, as if in an instant.

Without a doubt, the bat had presaged change. Still we linger, keep them in sunshine skipping here awhile longer in this afternoon, though it is getting darker and cooler already now. We dally—relishing the moment that, unbeknownst to us, has already passed. How else to account for the sudden sadness, the melancholy as evening comes on? They are bathed in last light, and then they are gone.

AS CHILDHOOD COMES to an end, the Girl with the Matted Hair's mother has already been dead for over ten years, and there is something unforgivable about that.

Her resurrection concoction left forgotten now in the far corner of the schoolyard. Her recipes—drain the blood of the toad, pet five sleeping sheep—tucked into the stone wall.

29

CAREFULLY THEY WALKED into the Spiegelpalais. Even from the periphery they could feel the great sleep pulling at them, and they were afraid. The atrium's walls were lined this day with fifteen metallic medicine cabinets filled with medication. Thirty sheep slept floating in thirty formaldehyde tanks arranged in rows, and they half resembled schoolchildren nodding at their desks. Nodding and humming, this multiplication of sleep made the child yawn. The sheep beckoning were branded in red with stencil. What do they want of us? The child tugged at her mother's arm.

Submerged in a twelve-foot tank slept two sides of beef, a chair, a row of linked sausages, an umbrella, and a birdcage housing a dead dove.

The sheep were branded in red with a stencil. The child, anesthetized, dreamt on the floor of the Spiegelpalais, and the mother had to pick her up and carry her over her shoulder as she did when the child was an infant. More and more, the mother remembered Infant Time. All heads, sleeping and not, slowly turned toward the mother and child. The somnambulant sheep seemed to nod in their direction and gesture with their cloven hoofs. Their eyes were open, but not seeing, glassy and smooth, and the lightest light blue—like the mother's eyes.

THE CHILDREN GATHERED in the firefighting wing where many of
the fire stories had been collected and preserved. Relics from the great
incinerations were housed in glass. In one of the cases the children saw
a scarlet bird, a glove, a briefcase, a burning bush, a rose the size of
a human heart, a father suspended in liquid. No one was sure if the
objects behind glass had done the saving, or were part of the saved. It
did not really matter—the child thought the fire world was beautiful.

WONDER POURED DOWN on their heads. Sometimes the adventure
of being alive felt too great. On these days, something began to fray in
her. Smoke was filling the stairwell.

Oddly, as there would have been time, she might have said *billowing* while she looked out the window, which in turn sounded
like pillow . . . pillowing, as she grew sleepier and sleepier with each
breath.

A PLATOON OF soldiers, enveloped in smoke, drift to the shore. Every
one of them is dead. They have been snuffed out like wicks. They have
nodded off and could be revived no more.

But should living soldiers ever return, should any war ever be
over again, on that day the mother will eat the pasta called campanile—campanile is Italian for bells—and they will dance with a kind
of joy reserved only for the most auspicious of occasions: the Great
Resuscitation, or the return of the bees, or Easter.

LATER, WHEN THEY were back in the house and the fire was lit, the
child would take out a piece of paper and draw an elaborate prismatic
snowflake, and underneath it she would print: The way nobody is perfect and God is. For now, they kept walking. The moon shone and the

coyotes turned into liquid light and spilled into luminous shapes on the night's page, and the light in turn was devoured by great swooping night creatures, not bats—she knew not what—and the world in its wonder and violence entered her and she did not flinch. The birds appeared, and flying wild cats in the night in primordial splendor and chaos abounded, undeterred by whatever civilization may have tried to tame or diminish.

THE MOTHER YEARNED for the wolf, at once so dapper and so wild, who had escorted her across the threshold so many years ago now. Shiny, bright. She paged it in the night. She did not want it to leave the child behind. She wanted the child to grow up—immersed in world and in time; she wanted the child to thrive.

SHE CANNOT FATHOM the time that has elapsed since the galaxy was formed or the vastness that they are situated in. The oldest star in the galaxy is 13.2 billion years old, and the galaxy itself about 10 billion years old. The next arm of stars can be located about 7,000 light-years away. What is 7,000 light-years to her? She cannot imagine how infinitesimal they are; there is not a word that comes in her language to describe the quality of the smallness or the distance or the wonder or the fear. In the vast black cosmos, the planet floats. She thinks of their planet, beautiful beyond belief, swaddled in blue.

She looks to where the child now stands under the arbor in the Children's Garden. It is the first time she has been allowed to use the sharp clippers to prune the roses. Light floods the entrance to the darkened garden.

Holding the glinting clippers above her head, the child whispers, I feel important, and she reaches up. All time, all space rush to her side. Her life is flooded with beauty and purpose. All the energy of the universe streaming toward that tiny, immeasurable, yet indelible, inde-structible moment, the child illuminated and on tiptoe—it can never be destroyed: *I feel important.* Or taken away.

All had been preparation for this moment—so that the child stand-ing in the Children's Garden under the arch, pruning the roses now with great seriousness and delicacy and care for the first time, might feel the full force and enormity of her one life—claimed for a moment from the vast and rushing void all around her—and the flames, and the heartache. This was their job all along, the mother thought—to make transactions with beauty and enchantment—morning glories and roses covering the arbor.

One day, the mother imagines, without her, the child will stand under the Arc de Triomphe in Paris, and she will reach up as if to touch it, and it will come to her again suddenly, gravely, inexplicably: *I feel important.*

IT WAS IN the Garden of Night Miracles where the moth—now half-moth, half-mother, made its appearance in the moonlight. How beau-tiful the half-mother is—and how alone. The child longs for her, but she cannot find her anywhere, and she is afraid to go outside.

THE MOTHER PUTS out one of the small blue chairs of Childhood, and the tea set, and she waits. Though the little being may not come, the mother thinks if she sits long enough, there is always a chance. The mother has read of the Little Hominid in the local paper. This tiny per-son once occupied the island of Flores, one, maybe two million years ago, and does not fit into any place in the evolution of the species. He's got no place in the early human family. He's a hobbit, an anomaly. Out of place in time and geography, his ancestry an enigma.

Come to me, she whispers, completely inexplicable little person. He's terribly small, but not a pygmy, his skull the size of a grapefruit. Little Hominid who lived isolated, while others made their way to Australia.

Some scientists insist he was a mere human dwarf with genetic or pathologic disorders, but the mother, who was a nurse, rejects this so-called Sick Hobbit Hypothesis. Come to me, Little Hominid, and stay awhile, and I will protect you from the ardent hobbit skeptics. Come to me and we will have some tea and keep each other company. The same mysterious force, discovered the year of the child's birth, that is speeding up the expansion of the universe is also stunting the growth of the objects inside it, the mother reads to the little one.

Little Flore, the mother whispers, and the tiny hominid slowly shuffles out from beneath a Trufulla sprig.

Such were the days when the child was away, and the mother was left to her own devices.

ALL THE MOTHER wants some days is to go back there, but she does not know how. Sometimes she cannot see or think about anything else, not even the child, whom she loves with every fiber of her being.

Though she is drawn there, she is drawn against her will. Layers of ghosts enfold her, gauzy as a Halloween tale. The mother is compelled back, but she can't get back far enough, and so she must stand forever on this windy hill overlooking the blueberries, neither here nor there, next to the vibrant, streaming world.

THE CHILD SKIPS home from her choral practice. The big black bat flew back! The mother ran to see. The big black bat flew back!

Where? Where? the mother said, running to the umbrella stand.

It's our Enunciation Exercise, the child said dreamily. For chorus! Say it with me. The big black bat . . .

But in fact not a single bat came back to the Valley the following spring. The mother could not explain why, but it made her inconsolably sad. The solitude now was mounting. They waited for a new sign, but no sign came.

SHE THOUGHT OF the prairie vole. When isolated, a prairie vole had increased levels of oxytocin, its heart rate went up, and the size of its heart increased over a four-week period as it tried to stave off isolation. Little prairie vole, the mother called, and it crawled out shyly from beneath a prairie leaf.

SOME DAYS THE mother is a very dim light in a jar. At times like these, all the child can do is press her brilliant eye up against the glass, lumbering, impossibly large, her warm hand encircling it. Glass was a miracle—that is what the mother always said, and at once the child thought of the flowering of fire and water and sand and the work of human hands, and this jar—the glassblower's vessel. What was she signaling with her flicker? Perhaps the mother had come to say good-bye. Perhaps it was not possible to die all at once. What if she had made a bargain? Perhaps a deal had been struck, and she had been allowed nine years with the child. But there were now only a few days left until her tenth birthday. Soon Aunt Eloise would be by with the beehive cake once more and the next year of the child's life would begin.

THE CHILD WONDERS sometimes where all the guardian angels have gone.

No one, the child says that night, will come and steal you while I'm sleeping, right?

No one will hurt you with a sword.

No one will put you in a fire.

No one will run you over in a car.

You won't get lost in the woods. Tell me you will find the way out. You can always find the way out.

DARK ENERGY SUGGESTS one day everything will be black. This calmed the mother. The commotion would be over at last. The universe was expanding beyond all human understanding; the child tugged at her sleeve.

CECIL PETER HAD said to hang human hair from the bushes and sills to repel the animal kingdom, and the mother had dutifully done what he had said. Perhaps she had followed that advice too well, for now she longed for the animals; their teeth, their fur, their claws, their talons. Not this. Overnight they seem to have disappeared. She was sealed off, losing sensation. Collecting locks as they fell from the executioner's chair, she had put them on the sill. Now she went from room to room and removed them, the tresses of the child, and the tresses of the war dead, and she wept. She would donate those tresses now to the Virgin for her Dormition Wig.

EASTER CAME EARLIER than it ever had in any of their lifetimes, and ever would in their lifetimes again. Never would it be celebrated as it was this year, in the winter, and in the dark. At the sunrise service it was twenty-four degrees by the Fahrenheit thermometer, and the motley congregation built a bonfire next to the Virgin, motionless in her grotto. The mother wrapped the child's head in a woolen shawl, and all remarked that she looked exactly like the Magdalene.

Without the gaiety of flowers or springtime, they could better feel the austerity and gravity of the situation. They traipsed around the frozen fire and someone maneuvered the boy with no legs in his wheelchair over rock to the altar. The women had gone to the tomb.

Why are you weeping? The words could be heard through the darkness.

We do not know where the Christ's body has gone! The tomb is empty, someone in the dark pronounced, and the women sighed, and someone urged the child toward the fire, and the mother pulled her back from it. There was a legless boy, and a rasping death head, and the weepers, and the Toothless Wonder. But the child knew that the disappeared Christ would soon enough appear to the people again as he had promised, and the sun would begin to rise. Everyone was frozen, despite the promise of the sun. No one was warmed, the temperature had not changed, and the fire was dying. When Jesus finally appeared it was to the women, and their heads were covered.

On a bare branch the mother saw a single bird's silhouette.

Do not touch me, He says, for I am not of this world—*or the other*. Everyone gasped! The child's arm remained extended. They were being battered by beauty.

At once, unaccountably, there were a thousand stars pouring from the sky like diamonds. The moon had been full and the sky dark when they arrived and a bonfire burned, but as the sun slowly rose, the moon sunk, and the sky, a dome above them, seemed divided for an instant, one half of the dome dark, one half light, until light began to spill and bleed into the darkness, and all at last was brightness, a translucent blue, and the full moon falling behind the child's head—a perfect halo. They broke the bread and took the cup, and the mother thought of the Burning Man she had seen in the fall and the quiet ashes in the ground.

Austere as it was, and as unnerving, the boy with no legs felt there had never been a better Easter service—and the mother had to agree.

ON GOOD FRIDAY the child's fish, Miss Tippy, had died and was outside in a plastic bag awaiting burial in the Children's Garden. What could be better, the child thought, than Miss Tippy on the third day, floating and gold above their heads?

THE MOTHER REMEMBERED when the child was small and her head was as round as a planet and she would fit perfectly in the mother's lap. The child's feet came to the mother's knees and it seemed to her the most miraculous of designs.

The Slung Hip Configuration, too, seemed a perfect fit even though in the time that the child and mother made that perfect Slung Hip Configuration, the mother seemed to be always lying prone and crying. The mother could not be saved by the beauty of design, but her tears kept the child alive. They were flammable, and so protected them from the evil that everywhere surrounded them.

Inside a circle of flame she kept the little baby safe, but to this day when the mother sees a baby, she runs in the opposite direction because she does not want to ever feel that way again.

WHEN THE MOTHER looked back, the bird was gone. She longed suddenly for the day of Phish and Phosh and the Ovenbird. The covered nest. The beauty of the Father. The Easter story had moved her as if she had never heard it before. She thought despite its grievous short-comings, any religion that could conjure such a beautiful story was certainly worth something. When Christ rode into Jerusalem, he rode on a donkey, which meant he came in peace. If you rode on a horse you would have come to conquer and in war.

The mother was filled with sorrows. Four thousand soldiers this March were dead—and five years had passed.

WHEN THE BABY sat on her lap with her little legs reaching the mother's knees, the mother's mouth would fit perfectly at the back of her skull and the mother would take the opportunity to cushion the baby's round head with kisses.

The baby's head, cushioned with kisses, became impervious to the cruel and petty ways of some of the children who seemed to roam the earth, belligerent as if already in training for war.

Even now the child felt her head to be kiss encrusted, and wherever she walked in the unkissed world, she was protected.

time

THE MOTHER IS leaving behind a gesture of her time here. The way she moved through space. A gesture of utmost care and protection, a repetitive one, her hand moving through the child's hair (that streaming and gleam) and what comes from it, this engagement with time and this one human life. The mother's hand running through the smooth of the daughter's dark hair. Is it not like silk as the darkness pours down, pours and pours, and the mother's gesture reverberates through time and space, leaving no visible trace, but leaving a trace nonetheless. These were the records left beneath the official records. Undocumented, incapable of being caught by a camera or any other means. Beneath the story of the mother on a tablet, or a book, or a grave, is the gesture. The fingers starting at the forehead move through her hair, gently raking it back, and then in a circular motion, curling it around the right ear.

How mesmerizing is this single, simple act of love and concern and protection. There's a feeling that no harm can come, though harm is everywhere around them. How mysterious they are, and how light, as if they were made only of wind and of dust. How buoyant. The way this singular but not uncommon gesture, left to the child, will live on. As the child runs her own hand through her own child's hair one day, a shadow mother accompanies her. The smaller gesture asleep in the memory of the child, dormant, but waiting. The child's hair, that gorgeous cascade of darkness, shrouding her face, and then the hand coming seemingly out of nowhere to comfort, to help, to arrange—and the tenderness of the mother, which is more, some days, than the child can bear. And that is what the child recoils from, when she recoils—from the tenderness. Sloughing off the mother, for how otherwise is a child supposed to grow and live?

Long after, the child will regret that shielding—what did she think she was protecting herself from? Long after, sitting by the river, the child will still wonder whether the mother died with the recoiling that day in her mind's eye, as she tried to push the hair gently away from the child's face, and the child veering slightly away—No, she had pulled away, as if from a demon. This makes the dead mother smile. Children always believed themselves to be the center of each and every instant of their particular adult's life. The mother closes her eyes. A velvet curtain closes before her.

And even now, the mother cannot be sentimental. She had watched the child vanish over and over into another phase of being, and it had hardened her, and it taught her never to get too attached to any person, especially a child. Attachments were not what the world suggested. The world tended toward change and suggested it was the changing, the metamorphosis, that was important. It was one of the most useful and most difficult things she had ever learned while on earth. From here she floated and watched the child grow and grow and change, and change again, vanishing so many times until she, the child herself, had become an old woman like the Grandmother from the North Pole, who is eternal.

SHE CONCENTRATED ON the moth—its pale green wings against the screen. She put her hand to it. In winter, she would remember that simple gesture—her desire, the silence.

THE MOTHER THINKS it is sad that after she is dead, the child, who will be a grown woman, will have no way of knowing that this day ever occurred. No one will remember this afternoon—the child so young, the moment so ordinary, so easily forgotten. She will have no recollection of it whatsoever. That they made a collage, that they made paste from flour and water and sometimes they spread it with a paintbrush. They buried little figures inside their Playdough cakes. Grumpy or Sleepy. We make our appearance here. Forgetfulness closes up over us from both ends of the life cycle. In a hundred years the mother and child will be forgotten. The mother called in her orders to the Rose Bakery, and the child filled them. I would like a wedding cake with blue roses, and five loaves of heart-shaped breads, and three dozen hot cross buns.

No one will remember this afternoon—the child so young, the moment so ordinary, so easily forgotten.

AND ON ANOTHER afternoon: when the mother and child played Vet, there was often a problem with Bunny Boy's purr box, and they had to wrap him in scarves. Bunny Boy, a reluctant patient, wriggling out of his clothes, remained unamused. There is nothing wrong with my purr box, he said.

SLOWLY THE MOTHER and child emerge from the amorphous world of marble, though it is so difficult, and the mother appears half immersed in it, until the last minute, and were it not for the child urging her out, she would sink back into the silence and gorgeousness, and be subsumed. One cannot help but think of the great artist liberating the figures imprisoned in the stone. Come to me, the child beckons to her mother, who is half in earth and half emerged, and for an agonizing moment, the mother is petrified there. The mother has a mind of stone, but the child with her touch calls the mother forth, releasing her from oblivion's pull.

AND WHEN THE mother gets tangled or trussed in the Cat's Cradle, the child sets the strings smooth again.

OUTSIDE THE SPIEGELPALAIS, a little impromptu play was being staged. Bits of dialog were carried out on the breeze. Nothing was heard in its entirety, and yet nothing was missed. The play came together remarkably: complete, whole in its fragments. There was a smattering of applause. Though no one could agree on its content.

It's a history of the Valley; it's a story of the river; it's a pageant; it's actually rather more a pastiche, the last remaining professor in the Valley said; but whatever it was, all seemed unruffled, and all seemed pleased, and there was a lilting quality to the day. It was all there this time right before them, spoken above the breeze. No one seemed worried that it was not entirely accessible.

Where the Spiegelpalais had come from, something that had once troubled them, long ago had fallen away, and they could not remember anymore a time when the Spiegelpalais had not been here.

Once they might have wished the play to be something more solid, more continuous, less troubling, more legible, and that there might be something they could take away from the experience and put neatly somewhere, some insight, some truth. Once they might have hoped for a meaning—that it had all actually meant something. So often the assumption had been that there was a message, waiting to be excavated, decoded. Once they had yearned for a truth that might be absolute, but all that had passed—they could not explain how. The Spiegelpalais had worked its strange magic.

When the play was over, the mother felt sure she knew something she had not known before. There was something of a recognition; there was no way beyond that to articulate what she felt or knew except that the play had made certain longings emphatic and would allow, she suspected, for other feelings on other evenings to come to the fore. The Palatines who had come to the Valley named everything for the Rhine, which they missed with all their hearts. It's a history of our desires. Memories of the breathing and billowy world.

And what we thought was central turns out to be peripheral. And what we thought was solid dissolves. Gone, the emphatic orb of afternoon. Dusk had arrived.

SOMEHOW SHE KNEW infinite grace was available to them. The key to happiness was in trying to understand how to receive it. The Rite of Ascending should be the right of every human alive, she reasoned. She herself was a soul waiting for purification. The bat had said as much. The bat had come and set into animation what had been still and lay dormant in them. The bat had made all the rest possible and available to them, of this the mother seemed somehow certain.

The tree had split in two, and from it had emanated an extraordinary light, like the light now in the pit where the towers had once been. The thousands of distressed souls that had blackened the day now gave way to an extraordinary void, flooded with light. It was the only place in the city that opened up like a suture—a vast cavern, but also a plain.

How strange is the present, with all that past streaming in, and all that future seeping through. It was something exhilarating, the present—open, fluid, malleable—and it both pleased and frightened her. Moments of the past invading the present from one direction, and from the other direction, the future. All was in coexistence—there was really no way around it.

THE BAT, AS a last gift, had made it possible to see the velvet backdrop so that one could glean information from the twilight, and from the night. Like the bat drinking the night, the mother drinks the night, as it comes on now. Like the mother and the bat, the wolf laps up the night as well and waits for the child. The mother smiles. The night magnifies and makes possible what seemed unimaginable in the day. She goes to the Mothering Place and prays.

ON CERTAIN NIGHTS while the mother slept, an antler would sprout from the center of her forehead. The antler was soft to the touch and covered with moss, and all night the mother roamed through forest and starlight to places she had never been before. In the morning when the mother awoke and discovered the antler, she panicked, as she did not want to frighten the child, and she would, as quickly as she could, saw it off and slip it into the night table drawer. After that, many nights would often pass without incident, until the mother came slowly to forget about the antler almost entirely, and that is when another antler would appear.

And it would go on like that: sleep and dream, sleep and dream and saw, sleep, and dream, sleep and dream and saw, and sleep . . .

The mother and child laughed and time passed, and after a while, the mother somehow grew more capable of keeping the antler in check inside her lavish green night-roaming dream. Now and then a nub would appear, but nothing more. And in the night table drawer only, a little stardust and antler dust remained.

From time to time now, the child would put the wrist of her hand to her forehead and then wave her fingers in the semblance of an antler, and the mother would look at her and smile sweetly.

One night while the mother slept, the child huddled next to her on the bed and watched as the antler slowly began to grow from her mother's forehead. The child had never touched anything like it before. It was something like a tree branch but not exactly—it was at once more solid and more hollow, a horn of sorts, covered with an indescribably soft moss, and it had the most extraordinary hue.

At the end of the night but before the mother awoke, the child removed the antler. Gently she slipped her finger under the mossy soft base, and it felt as if she were releasing the air from beneath the pad of a suction cup. She removed it with ease, and without the least violence.

Then the child wandered out the door and into the dawn. Maybe she will happen on the bobwhite. To build their homes, bobwhites find an impression on the ground, line the impression with grasses, and weave an arch over the cup in a tussock of grass. Carrying the antler, the child walked out into the morning and gathered reeds and dawn grasses and cattails, which she wove together into a kind of glimmering harness, and she placed her mother's antler in it. She then went to her mother's room, and though the mother was still sleeping, in sleep she seemed to bow her head toward the child as if she might nuzzle, and the child in one simple motion attached the antler back to the mother's head and climbed into bed next to her.

THE GREEN CHAPEL was a triumph of the intangible, and it was the place toward which the mother and child now walked. It was a masterpiece of luminescence, and they marveled at how the walls seemed to disappear, leaving only windows that looked out onto the flickering green world. In the distance, at last, the mother sees the transparency to complete the one in her, a shape to meet her shape. Together, the mother and child will fold themselves up into the gleaming. From a distance, the galaxy was a greeny blue. They were filled with a serene feeling. Soon they would become the next thing.

S HE DREAMS OF a lake. It's very blue and deep. It's fed by springs. The mother kept the child tethered to her by a silk strand of the most remarkable resiliency. The silk was durable and flexible, and it stretched to accommodate the farthest places the child would ever want to go. The mother reeled out the tether now, and the child swam far.

The mother thinks she would like gently, gently to suggest to the child that it might be possible to sever the thread.

You have all your teeth now, she says.

SHE REMEMBERS THE way the South Tower seemed to buckle and bend, then blur and be gone. Perhaps it was true that where she stood on the 110th floor mesmerized, looking out onto the world, she stayed, when she might have descended the stairs. The nightmare involved the right atrium, a corridor, rising heat, a kind of inferno, a baby motionless inside her capsule. Smoke.

At the pond, they had harnessed the fog. In the night they had placed an almond inside a cake and waited. They had visited the Boy in the Glen and the child had danced. Had it all been a dream? Anything was possible, she supposed. But for the smoke—so dense, so dark— they might have jumped into that blue lake of sky and survived. It's very deep. And no bats skim the surface. She looked to the child for a sign.

MAYBE THERE IS time to separate in advance, the mother to her fiery, already transacted fate, and the child to her own blue lake of sky, free to live out an entire life, unburned. Every child, the mother murmurs, deserves to grow up.

Perhaps it would be possible for the child to chew the tether now and jettison herself away—

Don't be absurd! the Vortex Man bellows. And he is back, just like that, in full, lavish form.

But I thought you were dead, the mother says.

Don't be absurd!

ON THE NORTH Pole of Mars, liquid water is being searched for tonight. Beneath the polar ice, well into the permafrost underground, deposits of water are believed to lie. From this distance, it certainly does seem as if those smooth, bluish areas on the crater floor could be ponds.

I can't wait to get there, the Grandmother from the North Pole says. She thinks about the planet's obliquity—the angle at which its Poles tilt toward the sun. Liquid water, she smiles, and she opens her mouth like a baby bird awaiting a droplet. I can almost taste it.

Still the crust is thicker and colder than previously thought, says the child. And the liquid water, if it exists at all, is a lot deeper below the surface than once thought.

You might as well stay here, the child says, a while longer.

IN A TRANCE she makes her way to the Flagship. She skittles across the frozen tundra to the vault where the world's seeds are being laid to store. There, beneath the shining ice, seeds and sprouts from every plant on earth will slumber, protected until the end of time. No earth-quake or nuclear catastrophe or funnel or any other heartache or sorrow, including the heartaches and sorrows yet to be invented, will harm this bank of seeds and nascent growing things. After the end of the world, there is another world.

I know, the Grandmother whispers, that we are losing biodiversity every day . . . She is talking in a sweet and swaddling voice to the little dreaming seedlings.

The Grandmother from the North Pole has been consumed by a lifelong mission that is only now revealed to the child. All her life she has scoured the earth collecting seeds from every plant in the world to be stored in the great vault beneath the snow, singing to them as she goes. One by one, she cradles and then drops them into liquid nitrogen where they are preserved in frozen, suspended animation. The seed crib strapped to her back.

Legions of grandmothers carrying sacks of seeds from every position on the globe can now be seen. They nod and wave to one another as they pass.

Having traversed once more the entire world, the Grandmother from the North Pole arrives again at the Global Seed Vault, only six hundred miles from her home at the North Pole. She waits for admittance. No one person knows all the codes. At last the door opens, and she unstraps the seed crib from her back. With this the Grandmother's head grows pointy, and she bores through the hard, smooth ice and deposits the seeds inside the earth. Over and over she does this in silence, until she is finished. The crib is light now, and she will stop home for a moment before resuming her toil.

Once the Egyptians saw her pass on a papyrus raft. Once the people in GinGin asked her what she was looking for. Once when her children wandered down for breakfast, she was not there. Things begin to make more sense to the child. Open your eyes, she says, tugging at her grandmother's sleeve, and she puts her hand to the Grandmother's glassy forehead.

The seeds will sleep in the climate control far beneath the permafreeze for something like an eternity. With each deposit now, the Grandmother lingers longer and longer under the earth. She is more and more exhausted now. Luckily, the child has finally gotten a picture phone. Luckily, the picture phone has been vastly improved so it can still reach the Grandmother who is now surrounded by a fog of dry ice, five hundred feet beneath the surface.

She smiles for the child and waves, even though she is so tired. Luckily the child can recognize her even when she has assumed the shape of a barge, or a lozenge, or a seedpod, or a toboggan. Luckily, the child can picture her even when the picture phone clouds and the reception is bad and the fog of ice does not lift. When the Grandmother, surrounded by seeds, falls asleep, no one can blame her. Eventually an automated voice will say to please hold. The child doesn't mind. The child can hold on for a long time.

SUDDENLY THE ATRIUM is flooded with sea light and we are helpless before it—at the mercy of it—its perfection, its splendor.

Come out. It's safe now, she whispers to the Girl with the Matted Hair, you don't have to hide any longer.

THE GIRL WITH the Matted Hair stands naked before the gilded mirror. This is the evening she has been waiting a lifetime for—the night of the Hamster Ball.

She tiptoes over to the ancient pine tree armoire where she begins to select her adornments. Never has any choice seemed so grave before. Never has so much been at stake. She selects her undergarments first, made of silk from the most precious silkworms in Persia. She steps into them and already she has begun to transform. Next she takes out the sea otter skirt, heavy with salt, then a corset of crane, and the wolverine bodice.

In the drawing room, her white-maned father in elegant foxtails waits, checking his golden pocket watch every few minutes. At last, he walks down the dark hall and knocks on the Girl's door. She reaches for the swan wing cape, puts on her cloven-footed shoes, grabs her pony purse, and opens the door.

Father!

She has never seen her father look like this—so elegant, so handsome, so at ease. He offers his arm, and she takes it, and he escorts her to the next station of the evening. One more minute, the Girl whispers, and she puts on, at last, the final crucial garment—her gleaming ermine head. How resplendent the Girl with the Matted Hair is now! She takes her father's arm.

The mother understood that after having a mother, the next best thing to have is a Sacred Animal Totem, and she has to admit that the Girl with the Matted Hair has chosen beautifully. Slowly, she walks in her ceremonial garb down the palace path and into the ballroom. She feels a little topply; thank goodness her father is there.

The band begins to play. Dall Sheep take the floor along with Snow Geese. In the rafters there are owls. It is a charmed night. A night of extravagance and consequence, and she knows not what to expect, but for once, among the beautiful creatures of the night, the world seems entirely open to her.

She nods to the snow bear and the Arctic Cat on the dance floor, and the Red Fox, and the Egret, and the herd of Caribou, and suddenly her dance card is filled. No one comments on, though everyone notices, the conspicuous absence of bats. It is nighttime, after all, and the vessel for bats.

Shining from the corner are fragments of Rabbit, and Whooping Crane fledglings, and also in the gleam, one can see a soldier licking its hind leg. Sorrow is iridescent and the whole room is glistening. Human troops in turtle shells make their way to the fore. Their mothers accompany them wearing kidskin dresses—the softest dresses in the world—more soft than anything anyone has ever touched.

The Armadillo escorts some children across a floor festooned with exploding things. Above them flies the Gray Goose. The Grandmother appears and rubs her lucky rabbit's foot, courtesy of the cat. Maybe the Girl with the Matted Hair will never see day again—she could live like this forever, she thinks, with the night creatures, protected. Love floods the room. A Reindeer nuzzles her; lichen silently grows on its hoofs.

The Bat is a gentle creature, it is true, and everyone casually scans the rafters. Inside the body of a mother, a small creature is lepping.

In the great swells of music, the Girl might be carried anywhere next. The Mantis, Archivist of Lost Mothers, takes the Girl's hand and leads her to a clearing in the music.

In the clearing, the Grandmother from the North Pole in sealskin now stands. She bows deeply and says to the Girl in the Ermine Head that she has, as recently as yesterday, seen her mother. The girl peers at the Grandmother through her shining, ferocious Ermine eyes. It is a night of fear and awe, but also a night of unspeakable splendor, and it unfolds quickly now. First the Grandmother gives the Girl a living sled dog to hold. When the child is settled, the Grandmother continues. Your mother, she says, calmly and directly, is an Arctic Tern, who flies from Pole to Pole and back again, traveling the entire globe every year, twice. She sees now on her flights all there is to see. The Girl thinks her mother must be very tired by now. On the contrary, the Grandmother smiles. The Grandmother from the North Pole touches the Girl's shoulder blades and feels the first inkling of wings. She has been watching you all this time.

With this news, a very deep sleep-like state overcomes the Girl, and her heartbeat slows to almost nothing. Because it is winter, her ermine head is thick and white.

Mother, she says, and she reaches her hand up toward the tern, who had materialized, and sure enough, the tern comes to her. How easy it all is. Though she is afraid, she knows, if invited, she would not hesitate to fly away with her. But before the Girl can give it another thought, the mother has swooped down and taken her child high, high up into the sky. From on high, she scans the floor for her white-maned father, who is little more than a speck. There he is in the distance, fox-trotting, nonetheless. His horse hoofs gleam in the moonlight.

How very much I love you, the feathered mother says through her beak. And how very lucky I have been to see you twice in every year!

Later when the Girl takes off the ermine head, her hair is not matted anymore.

And they fly like that for some time until the mother grows large and white like a stork, and carries the Girl for a moment longer, then opens her beak, and allows her to drop.

wings

T HE JACKAL HAD returned. But it was okay, the mother said—
it had not come for them this time. The activity that had once
attended them had ceased. Perhaps they were no longer in transit.
Perhaps they had now crossed the line, the line of accessibility; perhaps they were closed off now, the mother thought, sealed off—it was
difficult to take in, but it was now how she felt. They had already been
come for. Anubis had been the usher, the go-between, and had taken
many shapes: coyote, jackal, bat. Silently he had walked between the
shadows of life and death and lurked in the dark places. Perhaps they
had crossed over, but if so, when, when had that happened?

Still, she could not help but think it—perhaps they were no longer
in the in-between state.

IT WAS THE fluttering sound behind the walls of the house, or outside
on a pure clear summer night—the flapping of unseen wings—that had
once made it so hard to go on. Or the wing-beat that seemed to come
from within her, and which she had always dreaded—that inward
movement, that imperceptible fluttering. She wondered whether it

was wrong to move without fear now, because anything could happen then.

ALL SHE COULD do was notice. Now the step into fearlessness was as easy as crossing the rabbit path. It was that absence of fear that would make it impossible to understand exactly what the bat exacted.

Sensate life was falling away. The mother could not help but notice and feel a tremendous gratitude. She was not far now.

TAKE THE CHILD, the mother whispers to the wolf, as you once took me. Ferry her across the divide now back into life. Initiate her into the world of grown up charms. How beautiful you are and how handsome; look at the stars in your fur!

The wolf's eyes glistened sadly.

Help me. I've not much time.

THE BAT WAS an angel. The bat was a messenger. The bat, it is true, has an enormous capacity for poignancy—a marvelous creature—it has a true aptitude for geometry. All in all, it is a miraculous being.

The wind came up and they walked looking straight ahead and at no time from side to side. Behold, the bat says, and it begins its Annunciation. The mother is desperately trying to decipher what it says at this moment from the shape its mouth takes. And then, just like that and no one knows why, least of all the mother, she gives up trying and lets the bat sink back into its jibber and lets the revelation slip away.

Whatever metaphors the bat dragged and carried with it, it could no longer touch her. Whatever associations there might have once been slip from her as if off utterly smooth black wings.

EVERYTHING WAS HAPPENING so quickly and seemed now to be speeding up. The mother did not know why everything had to change; she just knew that it did. Things were changing even when they seemed not to be.

THE MOTHER PICTURES a wondrous girl. One day she will awake and the child, gigantic, beautiful beyond belief, will stand before her, a girl capable of anything, towering impossibly in just a few years' time, surpassing even the height of the Spiegelpalais.

Pupa is from the Latin for puppet, and from puppet, or young girl, comes an animated doll-like puppet creature. Pupa is the life stage of some insects undergoing transformation. The Romans also noted that when you looked into the center of the eye, you saw a small doll-like image of yourself reflected, and this was called the pupil. Look, the child said, shining a light into the Grandmother's eyes.

THE CHILD HAD a plan. She would place the Grandmother in salt for forty days. Then she would soak her in molten resin and preserve her in perfumed oils. Then she would wrap her in linen. After that, she would put her in her kayak and climb in beside her.

THE GRANDFATHER FROM the North Pole says that the ice is a dynamic, living entity. The Grandmother says *mush*, and eight huskies obey. Frosty Boy leads the pack. Visibility is so low you can't see from flag to flag. Whiteout conditions, someone manages to call, above the snow!

From the gleaming depths, the Grandfather from the North Pole sits bolt upright and bellows in an arresting baritone:

Who has made me rise
unwillingly and slow,
from beds of everlasting snow?

He looks to his daughter. It's beautiful here, Bibi.

But what about the child, Father?

He shakes his head.

What about the child, she repeats.

You already know Bibi. You already know it was always too late.

And with that he lay back down, and once more froze again to death.

HERE FROSTY BOY, the mother whispers, and her voice echoes in the room. She looks at her father, sunken back into splendor.

THE NATIONAL SNOW and Ice Data Center's ice expert says that the cap of floating sea ice on the Arctic Ocean is shrinking at an unprecedented rate. This year's ice retreat is unmatched by anything in the previous century.

Even though the Grandmother from the North Pole is a strong swimmer, the mother was grateful that when the ice waters come to be the size of six Californias, the Grandmother from the North Pole would no longer be alive.

THE TIME IS running out. The world in its present form is passing away. What Saint Paul had said was as true now as it was then.

She was neither here nor there, and like the infants stranded in Limbo, she felt such discomfort, and it seemed to propel her—but whether up or down, whether back or forth, and whether she was asleep or awake, she did not know.

Even in sleep, the body was accelerating because the earth was in rotation. Even the coffins spun under the ground, with the spinning of the earth. All she knew was that the child was there again, at her side. And she smiled.

IT'S FRANCE, SOMEONE shouted, and the child jumped up and down with glee and pulled at her mother's sleeve. France had come to the Spiegelpalais: A four-dolphined fountain was brought in, a glass pyramid, a grotto, and gargoyles. Fragments of the river Seine arrived—it glistened in the mirrored walls and kept the great American river company. The Little Sparrow sang.

BY MOONLIGHT THE mother works tirelessly. If she had made a bargain and had, as a result, been allotted so many years so as to watch her child be born and grow, she could not remember. All she knew was that she could feel the Great Fading, and along with the fade, the desire to make the child a safe place.

See how hard the mother is trying to fend off a catastrophe that has already happened. See how desperately she is trying to save them—and see in this last effort how beautiful they have become.

THE CHILD POINTED to the burning sky in fear.

Look! she cried.

The mother and she stood high, high atop the towers, which were in flames. From there it was clear to the child that the mother, who appeared very pregnant, could never have survived. It was almost ten years ago now that the towers had fallen, taking the three thousand souls. The child gasped, for she knew what it meant for them.

ON HER BACK she felt a searing heat. Maybe she was on fire. Instinctively she rolled on the floor to smolder the flames. Still she was not burning. There was no fire yet, only heat, and more and more smoke. People broke windows. The mother told herself to breathe. Maybe if she had a wet towel and could place it over her face.

One by one they were falling asleep.

She was falling into the smoke-filled Valley of Sleep. But for the baby, she might have succumbed. On her hands and knees she crawled over the sleepers in an effort to get closer to the window.

SHE WONDERED WHERE the Spiegelpalais had come from—why it had materialized, and why, in the end, it had gone away. One day it was just there, and she could not remember, after a time, having ever lived without it. It seemed always to have been in her presence. And just as it had appeared from nowhere, and out of nothing, so it had now disappeared, and she could no longer be sure that it had ever existed at all. All that remained was the longing for something: large, circular, luminous, very beautiful—but what? She wept, for soon she knew even the memory of the Spiegelpalais would vanish.

SEE THE INTENSE immobility of the mother. The mother had been put into a twilight state. She saw that the bat swooped around her head in shallow circles, but there was nothing she could do about it. The circumference of a circle in Romania is determined by the diameter of the arc made by those heat- and halo-seeking creatures. Saint Stanislav, patron saint of Poland, throws a discus or a Frisbee to them, lifts his hand as if in protection, and gives a benediction. The mother, in a twilight state, feels something like fear. She has no idea what part she is being asked to play. But it is a part, now hers, that she will not relinquish.

WITH SOME DREAD and some excitement, she stepped into the capsule. More than anything, she wanted to be a winged thing. She lowered her head and assumed the pose she had seen in the great science books of the Fathers. She tucked her head down to her chest. Slowly her eyes blackened and grew liquid. Her legs were pressed together, and her feet were crossed one over the other as is often depicted in the crucifixion.

She was wrapping herself in filaments, threads, gossamer, papery thin skins. Brown leaf-like strands were attaching themselves to her back. All was quiet. In a stillness, which seemed to signify a coming into being, and also the sloughing off of being, she was enclosing herself slowly in a firm case.

When the child came upon the mother, she was already wrapped in her mesh dress. Wrapped like a little mummy princess in papyrus and rags. Her gold-leafed head was elongated, her inky eyes had blackened, her appendages were immovable. She was gold-encrusted, sun-soaked, sessile, remote. Her pupa hung motionless and mute. Seeing her mother like this, the child, for the first time, begins to cry.

There is the mother like a mirage at the end of the Sphinx Road, and though the child walks toward her—the mother comes no closer. Now she was spinning more and more threads.

Moth pupae are usually dark in color and formed in underground cells, loose in the soil, their pupae contained in protective silk called a cocoon. Cocoons may be tough or soft, opaque or translucent, solid or webby, of various colors or of multiple layers. Insects that pupate in a cocoon must escape it.

PUPAE ARE IMMOBILE and have few defenses. Some species are capable of making sounds or vibrations to scare off potential preda-tors, or sometimes just for communication. The child waited outside. She hoped her mother was the sort of species that made sounds.

She remembered now the mother singing, Tomorrow will be my dancing day, and it pained her to think of it. Her mother wrapped tightly in thousands of overlapping filaments.

NOT TO WORRY—if the world ends at this moment, the child said, God keeps track of where all the bodies are, the ones in the ocean, the ones scattered as ashes hither and thither, the ones entombed in silk and gold filaments, silent.

THE CHILD SITS quietly next to the little mother holding the shin-ing pod in her hand. The mother seemed to be working very hard. The mother had assured her she would be back. The child smiled. She thought that she could see at last the place where her mother's wings had finally begun to form.

Extreme darkness pours down on them, but they are not afraid anymore.

IN THE WOOD, a girl child is breathing like a beast. The mother is careful to stay very still. She recognizes the girl from a long time ago, but wonders how it is that this girl has not changed. She has remained exactly the same. The girl can hear her mother's voice call-ing to her. She becomes a brindle color and light and gallops. It is the

Grandmother from the North Pole who calls, but the Grandmother is young, and her yellow hair gleams. It was a mysterious life. Every night the girl thinks of the infinite forest that lay just beyond her door: immense, dense with totems and stars. She soothes herself by pulling the darkness and the cool around her like a cloak. The girl gets out of bed and goes to find her Bird Atlas, and her book of animal tracks. She cannot wait for morning to come.

AFTER THE MOTHER had her hair shorn for the war effort, the back of her neck could be seen for the first time since childhood, and it was only then that the child noticed that she had a stork bite at the nape, as infants often have, to mark the place they had been carried before they were dropped to earth. Mysteriously, the mother's stork bite would appear and then fade, and after a while, it would disappear altogether only to come back at another time, bright red again. It was as if she were continually being born and carried and dropped to earth, over and over. Each time she landed, she was brand new and she possessed no hindsight and no foresight; she remembered and had learned nothing—but also, the world was always new, never seen before, and she never aged.

THERE IS A fire at the center of the earth. From the fire, a child's voice, so pure, so true, makes itself heard. It is marked by the peculiar suffering of children. It is refined, perfected—innocence and experience held in such sublime balance, and possessing wisdom, ancient and new. She could hear the child from upstairs calling her name—stranger than music, more plangent than bells, sweet in a way we have forgotten entirely. A child is reciting numbers. A child is making up a song. A Happy Dance, a Fippy Song, a Fippy Dance.

SHE WAS ENCLOSED in a firm case. She remained in her pod stationary for ten days, and each day the pod would darken. About a day before the emergence of the creature, the chrysalis would become transparent.

THERE IS SOMETHING so luminous and clear passing through the child, and so momentous. She can hardly express the grandeur she feels. She thought of the pictures of the glass pyramid in front of the Louvre and how it matched the one she carried inside her now. If there is anything the child wants to see for real before she dies, it is that glass pyramid. She closes her eyes and she sees that shape in three dimensions travelling through space.

Right before the mother emerges again, the chrysalis becomes transparent. The child thought of Blanche Neige gleaming from her glass casket. She imagined her mother would at last be perfected and her soul purified, and at that moment their transparencies might speak. What is too sublime for you, seek not; into things beyond your strength, search not, the false prophet had said. The child's body is transparent. Blanche Neige gleaming from her glass casket is at rest—everything is shining and bright.

SHE THOUGHT OF the Luna Moth, very late at night, spinning silk, wrapped in a walnut leaf, and the slow formation of pale green wings.

THERE IS A world not yet visible but there, before us. Welcoming, not hostile. And translucent. It is a matter now of attention—of perceiving the opening in the veil through which they might slip. The Virgin appears and welcomes her through, under a mantle of blue.

AT THE LAST moment, the mother had an odd visitation. It was not exactly a visitation; it was more an intimation, but it came back with such intensity that it threatened to change the course of all that now lay fixed securely before her.

She could feel herself and the child, who was a baby—the two of them, in the drafty, dangerous house, lying on the floor on a carpet she had purchased because that is what one did when you had an infant come to live with you. You made the surfaces softer. She read there were rubber edges you could put on the sharp corners as well, but she hadn't gotten around to it yet. This is what she saw, and what she felt now in her body as she emerged. Perhaps she had tried to fly away from the catastrophe, and the flames, as would have been the only solution. She was a large winged Luna Moth. Black smoke billowing against the sky, arms outstretched, she was pregnant after all; she was sure of it. No, she did not die, she says to herself.

NOW SHE WAS falling. And still she sees before her: the mother and the infant are lying on the carpet together. The phone rings in the next room, and the mother puts her hand behind the baby's head to support it before picking her up and gathering the little one to her breast. And for an instant she feels completely happy, and it is as if she knows, for once, exactly what to do with this world. On the phone it is the Grandmother from the North Pole who is whispering as she bestows something like a blessing on the new mother and the new child and the new world. Everything is so beautiful, and so new.

FOR AN INSTANT they stood without moving, the mother and her child, who was now almost ten years of age. They were both whole and they laughed and they ran in the grass. And they did not tire, and they saw a deer in a clearing, and its antlers were covered in velvet. They should have known who the deer was, and what it wanted of them, there in the dark wood, with its incomparable poise, and its terror—but their eyes were prevented from recognizing it. It did not matter. It was enough to be adorned in the charms of twilight. It was enough to be alive.

acknowledgments

F OR THOSE WHO make their appearance in these pages, my
gratitude:

Louise, Louis, Henry, Lisa, Paul, Liam, Emma, Genevieve, Hazel
Ann, Jim, Larissa, Cathy, Jan, Jean, Peter, Krista, Michael, Emma S.,
Sally, Peter S., Martin, Ellen, Jill, Eli, Lorraine, Kenny, David, Dugan,
Bunny, Nico, Reteeka, Eleanor, Kathy, Andrea, Father Ted, Father
Chepatis, Father Flynn, Hardscrabble Jim, Mr. Min, Coco, Paris, Puff,
Winter Bear.

And for all those along the way who have offered their heart or
their hand:

Aishah, Alexandra, Anita, Annabella, Linda, Liz, Melanie, Therese,
Jan, Lora, Jack, Georges, Barbara, Jean, Peter, Angela, Alison, Mary-
Beth, Duke, Ben, Laura, Romulus, Catherine, Harry, Melissa, Cathy,
Regina, Alicia, Sue, Thalia, Toad, Jill, Brad, Lance, Deborah, Ronnie,
Ilene, Kelly, Micaiah.